Stories of the Golden West: Book Six

Stories of the Golden West: Book Six

A Western Trio

Edited by Jon Tuska

SAGEBRUSH
Large Print Westerns

First published in Great Britain by ISIS Publishing Ltd.
First published in the United States by Five Star

Published in Large Print 2008 by ISIS Publishing Ltd.,
7 Centremead, Osney Mead, Oxford OX2 0ES
United Kingdom
by arrangement with
Golden West Literary Agency

British Library Cataloguing in Publication Data

Stories of the Golden West: Book six.
– Large print ed. –
(Sagebrush western series)
1. Western stories
2. Large type books
I. Tuska, Jon II. Thirsty acres III. Hell for sale
IV. Proud rider
813'.087408 [FS]

ISBN 978–0–7531–8011–2 (hb)

Printed and bound in Great Britain by
T. J. International Ltd., Padstow, Cornwall

Table of Contents

Foreword

A short novel is a story too short to be a novel — 40,000 words or less — and too long to be a short story. It was a literary form that once was encouraged and flourished when there were numerous fiction magazines published weekly, monthly, or quarterly in the United States, and it is a form at which numerous American writers excelled. The present collection consists of a trio of Western short novels by different authors. Each short novel is able to stand on its own and to perform its function of introducing a reader to characters and situations that are deeply involving, and at the same time each is a story that can be read with pleasure at a single sitting but with the satisfying complexity of this more expansive literary form.

The greatest lesson the pioneers learned from the Indians is with us still: that it is each man's and each woman's *inalienable* right to find his own path in life, to follow his own vision, to achieve his own destiny — even should one fail in the process. There is no principle so singularly revolutionary as this one in human intellectual history before the American frontier experience, and it grew from the very soil of this land and the peoples who came to live on it. It is this principle that has always been the very cornerstone of the Western story. Perhaps for this reason critics have been wont to dismiss it as subversive and inconsequential because this principle reduces their voices to only a few among many. Surely it is why the Western story has been consistently banned by totalitarian governments and is sneered at by the purveyors of political correctness. Such a principle undermines the very foundations of totalitarianism and collectivism because it cannot be accommodated by the political correctness of those who would seek to exert power over others and replace all options with a single, all-encompassing, monolithic pattern for living.

There is no other kind of American literary endeavor that has so repeatedly posed the eternal questions — how do I wish to live?, in what do I believe?, what do I want from life?, what have I to give to life? — as has the Western story. There is no other kind of literary enterprise since Greek drama that has so invariably posed ethical and moral questions about life as a fundamental of its narrative structure, that has taken a stand and said: this is wrong; this is right. Individual authors, as individual filmmakers, may present us with notions with which we do not agree, but in so doing they have made us think again about things that the herd has always been only too anxious to view as settled and outside the realm of questioning.

The West of the Western story is a region where generations of people from every continent on earth and for ages immeasurable have sought a second chance for a better life. The people forged by the clash of cultures in the American West produced a kind of human being very different from any the world had ever known before. How else could it be for a nation emerging from so many nations? And so stories set in the American West have never lost that sense of hope. It wasn't the graves at Shiloh, the white crosses at Verdun, the vacant beaches at Normandy, or the lines on the faces of their great men and women that made the Americans a great people. It was something more intangible than that. It was their great willingness of the heart.

What alone brings you back to a piece of music, a song, a painting, a poem, or a story is the mood that it creates in you when you have experienced it. The mood you experience in reading a Western story is that a better life *is* possible if we have the grit to endure the ordeal of attaining it, that it requires courage to hope, the very greatest courage any human being can ever have. And it is hope that distinguishes the Western story from every other kind of fiction. Only when courage and hope are gone will these stories cease to be relevant to all of us.

Thirsty Acres

by L. P. Holmes

L. P. Holmes was born in a snowed-in log cabin in the heart of the Rockies near Breckenridge, Colorado. He moved with his family when very young to northern California and it was here that his father and older brothers built the ranch house where Holmes grew up and where, in later life, he would live again. He published his first story — "The Passing of the Ghost" — in *Action Stories* (9/25). He was paid ½¢ a word and received a check for $40. "Yeah . . . forty bucks," he said later. "Don't laugh. In those far-off days . . . a pair of young parents with a three-year-old son could buy a lot of groceries on forty bucks." He always claimed that he was born with an urge to write and went on to contribute nearly 600 stories of varying lengths to the magazine market as well as to write over fifty Western novels. For many years of his life, Holmes would write in the mornings and spend his afternoons calling on a group of friends in town, among them the blind Western author, Charles H. Snow, who Lew Holmes always called "Judge" Snow (because he was Napa's Justice of the Peace in 1920-1924) and who frequently makes an appearance in later novels as a local justice in Holmes's imaginary Western communities.

His first hard cover novel was *Roaring Range* (Greenberg, 1935). It has the swift pacing he learned from writing for the pulps but also some less attractive elements: characters inadequately drawn, sometimes just named in order to be killed, and a vague sketchiness even about the hero. When his son was sent to the Pacific theater by the Navy during World War II, Holmes for a time became involved in shipbuilding. However, even with this job, he continued to write, and unless his pulp fiction from this period is read the transformation that occurred with publication of the novel, *Flame of Sunset* (Curl, 1947), will come as something of a shock. This novel concerns riverboats on the Sacramento. "Hides on the River" in *Western Story* (11/46) is clearly a precursor of the later novel (albeit the riverboats in the short story are on the Colorado). What followed was a series of novels that deserve a high place in any basic library of traditional Western fiction. Holmes's Golden Age extended from 1947 to 1957. In that decade came such polished and engaging novels as an excellent railroad-building story, *Desert Rails* (Simon and Schuster, 1949), a no less fine freighting story, *Apache Desert* (Doubleday, 1952), and an unusual story of a lawman, *Delta Deputy* (Doubleday, 1953), and the type of story at which he was truly adept: the ranch romance. This is the basic plotline of *Water, Grass, and Gunsmoke* (Doubleday, 1949), *Black Sage* (Doubleday, 1950), *Summer Range* (Doubleday, 1951), *Dead Man's Saddle* (Doubleday,

1951), *High Starlight* (Doubleday, 1952), and *Somewhere They Die* (Little, Brown, 1955).

Some aspects of Holmes's Western fiction even during his Golden Age were already hackneyed in the traditional Western, having been used and reused by Ernest Haycox and several Haycox imitators: the theme of the two heroines (one of whom the hero must choose), the "destiny" theme in which the confrontation between the hero and the villain is fated, and the terrific fistfights that Holmes narrated with the kind of intensity to be found in Luke Short. However, equally basic to Holmes's fiction are his own individual themes: the loyalty that unites one man to another, the pride one must take in work and a job well done, and the innate generosity of most of the people who live in the West. There are generally progressions in the novels and shorter stories of the Golden Age, changes through which the characters must pass, and the need of some people to learn things the hard way. Holmes's heroes are seldom alone, but bound to others by imperishable ties of friendship and to the communities in which they live. Indeed, whether Holmes is writing about actual places, which he did about half the time, or imaginary ones, he could make his Western communities so desirable and populate them with such interesting and well-developed secondary characters that often a reader would prefer to live there.

August Lenniger was Lew Holmes's agent throughout his finest years. Due to a disagreement (Lenniger didn't read a Holmes manuscript before he sent it out to a publisher), Holmes switched agents and began producing potboilers as original paperbacks for Ace Books and hard cover novels for Avalon Books that were never issued in paperback. He published his final novel, *The Distant Vengeance* (Warner, 1987), in his ninety-second year.

"Thirsty Acres" was sent to the Lenniger Agency on December 31, 1937 and was sold to Fanny Ellsworth, the editor of *Ranch Romances*, on March 14, 1938. It was published under the author's title in *Ranch Romances* (1st September Number: 9/2/38) and was later reprinted as "Thirsty Acres" by L. P. Holmes in *Triple Western* (6/51). At his best Holmes's style, his striking images, and his craftsmanship leave a lasting impression.

CHAPTER
ONE

Sheriff Bill Waller, wrinkled and grizzled, his leathery skin burned almost black from wind and sun, wiped rivulets of sweat from his gaunt, dust-caked jaws and spoke in a regretful drawl. "You're his big brother, Clay. You got to head him off and straighten him out."

Clay Garrison paused in his restless pacing back and forth across the living room of the old Garrison ranch house. "You say Buck was seen riding the lava pockets with Kirby and Ringo, Bill?"

Waller nodded. "It ain't the first report of that kind I've had on Buck. So far I've tried to laugh 'em off and just put it down as a few pranks by a restless kid looking for excitement. But the time for laughing has just about run out. Looking back, Clay, I ain't got a single regret for anything I ever had to do while carrying this star. But that record would be all shot if I ever had to buckle on a gun and go out after one of old Buck Garrison's boys."

"You had a talk with him yet, Bill?"

The sheriff shook his head. "Me tackling him on that kind of a proposition would only make him bow his neck a little more, Clay. I figured I'd better let you work on your own brother first."

Clay Garrison stopped before a window and stared out with narrowed, burning eyes, hands tightly clenched. "It's this everlasting heat and dust," he said hoarsely. "If we don't get a rain pretty quick, I'm liable to do something violent myself. This cursed drought has got everybody fighting their heads. There's something about it that sets a man's teeth on edge, rubs his nerves raw, makes him savage and reckless, maybe, and anxious for excitement. But Buck's not really bad, Bill."

"If I thought he was, Clay, I wouldn't be out here. Instead, I'd knock his ears down and give him what for."

"Thanks, Bill. You always have been a swell friend to the Garrisons. I'll talk to Buck . . . plenty."

"Fair enough, Clay," said Waller heartily. "I'll leave him to you. How's the water holding out?"

"The Buttonwillow quit running two weeks back. Just pools left now. Some are going stagnant. Probably by digging we can make the water last another month or two. It's the range that's about gone. Cattle are growing weaker every day . . . Bill, why can't we get some rain?"

Bill Waller walked to the door, stood there a moment. "Back when you were a button, Clay," he finally said, "we had a spell like this, only worse. Lot of the ranchers folded up. But your dad and Rock Orde and Ben Cullop hung on. And finally that drought broke, just like this one will. And then who hung on came out of it bigger and stronger than ever. So tighten your belt, Clay, and stick with it."

6

Clay Garrison managed a twisted smile. "I'll stick until something breaks, one way or another."

"That's the talk. Well, I got to be traveling. *Adiós*."

Clay walked out on the porch and watched Bill Waller jog away on his staid old roan. From where he stood, Clay could look over just about all of the Buttonwillow range. At the moment it was a torrid, heat-blasted land. To Clay's feverish eyes the corrals and feed sheds of the Sleeping G Ranch looked like shrunken skeletons. In the heat mirage the corral posts seemed to weave and float. And it seemed to Clay that he could almost hear the shakes on the sheds crackle and split in the sultry, blistering sun.

Farther out, the range ran away in long, sweeping rolls of mirage-cursed distance. Ordinarily that range would have been an eye-cooling green or a rich tawniness. Now it had a sort of lifeless, gray look, like dead ashes. Away out to the south, jutting into the hard, copper sky, lifted the gaunt shoulders of the Poncho Mountains. To the west spread the low, table-topped mass of black lava known as the Lost Hills. Away over east the range broke off into the yellow haze of the Dry Lakes Desert. And to the north was old Bear Foot Peak, lifting a scarred crown 8,000 feet into the air.

Up on top of Bear Foot, Clay mused, it would at least be cool. There would be still, rich-scented pine and fir thickets, and cold, sweet mountain water. Yet even the massive flanks of Bear Foot were being drained of water, for it was from this water that Buttonwillow River drew, and the river had quit

7

running. The lone spot of greenery visible at the moment to Clay's moody eyes was the willow and alder thickets along the river and even these were beginning to wilt and droop under the relentless fury of that burning red sun.

A movement by the river caught Clay's eyes, and he watched a slim figure on a pinto horse come angling up toward the ranch house. Momentarily the scowl on Clay's brow was smoothed away. Clay Garrison never looked at Leigh Orde but what he was struck by one dominant note in her appearance. That note was a cool, immaculate purity. It lay in the silken gleam of her auburn hair, in the depths of her clear, gray eyes, in the lithe, swift grace of her. As she swung lightly up the porch steps, Clay smiled his welcome.

"Howdy, Leigh. Girl, how do you manage it? In all this cussed heat and dust, you look like you'd been playing in ice and cool winds."

Leigh Orde laughed, and even her laugh held a cool, tinkly note. "You've got a touch of sun, Clay. I'm roasting, half cooked. Show me to a chair. Whew! Isn't it awful?"

"Pretty bad." Clay nodded. "What does your dad think about it?"

The girl shrugged. "You know Dad. He's a regular bulldog. He says the rain will come one of these days, and then all will be right again. Dad should have been a great general. He could have whipped the world with an army of ten. Last night Ben Cullop was over, moaning about the drought. Dad looked him right in the eye and offered to buy him out, lock, stock, and barrel. Old Ben nearly fell out of his chair. Then he began to grin. 'Rock,' he said, 'you got more innards than any man I ever knew. Reckon I'll stick with it, same as you.' "

The girl laughed again and Clay joined her. The line of her slim, brown throat, he thought, was lovely when she tipped back her head as she laughed.

They were silent a moment and a certain gravity settled upon them. The girl bit a red lip, then spoke a little hesitantly. "Clay, I heard something yesterday. I heard that Buck was hanging out pretty steadily with Spike Kirby and Shell Ringo."

"That's right," said Clay. "Bill Waller was just out to see me about it."

Leigh caught her breath. "Buck hasn't done anything to put Waller after him?"

"Not yet," said Clay grimly. "But if the kid keeps on running around with Kirby and Ringo, he's a cinch to get into trouble. That's what Waller wanted to see me about, to tell me to try and spur a little sense into my wild brother. I'm wondering if I can make a job of it."

There was a note of anxiety in his words that brought the girl's eyes to him. The ruggedness that had been a part of old Buck Garrison was each day becoming more apparent in his elder son. Clay's face, like his big, six-foot body, was raw-boned and angular. Not a handsome man, Clay Garrison, but a strong, steadfast one. A certain bold hawkishness lay in the cut of his features, in the square line of his jaw, the grimly set lips, the jut of his nose, and the steady, penetrating gleam in his deep eyes.

"If anyone can do it, Clay, you can," murmured Leigh. "And you've got to. For if Buck went bad, I'm afraid it would hurt me, pretty dreadfully."

The revealing statement, thought Clay, was indicative of Leigh Orde. Honest, straight from the shoulder. No simpering, no blushing, no beating around the bush. It hardly surprised him. For a long time he had suspected how things were between Leigh and Buck.

"I'll put him over the jumps, Leigh," Clay promised slowly. "I'm afraid Buck is pretty selfish. Natural, maybe. Dad babied him a lot, and, since Dad died, I've sort of done the same. Buck hasn't got a bad strain in him . . . just full of the devil and recklessness, natural for his age. But at heart he's a Garrison. I'd gamble my life on that. I reckon I'll be able to get him to steady down. And if I have to, I can always have a talk with Spike Kirby and Shell Ringo."

This last mild statement did not fool that girl. She knew what such a talk would be like. It wouldn't be his own voice that would speak. It would be the voice of those two big, black guns that swung from Clay Garrison's lean, saddle-toughened flanks, whenever he left the ranch. A queer, inexplicable fear caught at her throat.

"Not that, Clay, not that," she said breathlessly. "If Buck won't listen to you, send him over to see me. Maybe I can make him understand."

Clay knew what she meant. In spite of himself he winced.

"Reckon I'll be able to handle him," he said, his voice a little hoarse.

A big, sweating clay olla stood near the door, a tin dipper hanging on a nail beside it. Leigh went to it and drank thirstily. Then she crossed over to Clay, put a slim hand on one of his iron-hard fists.

"You'll do to take along, Clay Garrison," she said gravely.

"That," said Clay, "goes double, Leigh. Tell your dad that the Sleeping G will hang on until it rains, or until the whole world dries up and blows away."

After she had gone, Clay looked down at his big fist where her hand had rested, and a shadowed wistfulness crept into his eyes. Then he shook himself savagely, got his hat, buckled on his guns, and went down to the cavvy corral where he roped and saddled and headed northwest toward the town of Black Rock.

It wasn't much of a town to begin with, Black Rock, only a squalid, ugly little place, uninspiring and desolate. Just now it seemed to cower like a whipped dog under the blasting lash of a sun gone mad.

Clay Garrison left his pony in a scanty block of shade thrown by an overhang and clanked his way into the Humbug Saloon. Behind the bar Dumpy Kling, the bartender, sweated profusely and slapped a grimy bar towel halfheartedly at a couple of bluebottle flies. The only customer at the moment was swarthy, dapper Frisco Dan Drew, who owned the Humbug. He sat at a card table, dealing a hand of solitaire. He got to his feet as Clay entered.

"Hello, Clay," he said. "Any man brave enough to ride through this sun deserves a drink. Name it. It's on the house."

Clay shook his head. "If you had some beer on ice, I might say yes. But whiskey is dynamite, this kind of weather."

Drew laughed, and there was a queer slurring quality to both his laugh and voice. "We got beer, but it would be a mighty tall lie to say it was cold. I don't blame you. Warm beer is slop, and you're right about the whiskey . . . Looking for somebody?"

"Yeah. Buck. He been around?"

"Not since last night. Anything wrong?"

"Nope. Just want to talk to him about something."

"He'll probably be in again this evening," said Drew. The alarm clock behind the bar said four o'clock.

"Reckon I'll wait for him then," drawled Clay. "Too hot to ride home again now."

He crossed to one of the tables and sat down, shoving his hat to the back of his head and wiping his brow with a dusty shirtsleeve. Drew sat down opposite him.

"How about a few hands of crib? Help pass the time. Four bits a game."

Clay nodded. They cut for deal and Clay won. Silence settled in except for the flutter of the cards and the low-voiced drone of the count.

At half-past five a horse jangled to a stop outside and a man with a shriveled red face came in, Boley Stevens, who owned a small ranch over toward the Lost Hills. There was a whipped, hopeless look about Stevens. He came directly over to the table.

"That offer you made me last week good, Frisco?" he blurted.

Drew looked up. "What's the matter, Boley? Lose your nerve?"

"Call it what you want," said Stevens hoarsely. "Call it any blame' thing. All I know is, I'm done. This blasted set-up has got me licked. Oh, I won't lie to you. That water hole of mine, the one thing I've been gambling on all along . . . well, it's gone bad. Gone arsenic on me. I found twenty head of poisoned cows around it this morning. This cussed heat would poison anything . . . Well, how about it?"

Frisco Drew's black eyes narrowed calculatingly. "I'll take the place, Stevens, but not at the first price I offered. That water hole going bad takes a lot of value off the ranch."

"Any price you think is fair will suit me," said Stevens. "I've had enough. I fought a drought like this before, and I know now that it ain't worth it. Life's too short. I've caved and I don't give a damn who knows it."

Drew stood up. "What do you think, Garrison?" He smiled thinly at Clay. "I'm a good enough businessman to grab a proposition while it's hot."

"Fly to it." Clay shrugged.

CHAPTER
TWO

Drew took Boley Stevens into a back room. Clay walked to the front door of the Humbug, stood looking up and down the street. The sun was low in the west, a fiery, crimson disc, about to set in a scorched sky. Long shadows, queerly black, ran out on the east side of various buildings.

Clay left the saloon and jingled his way down to Pete Flood's Emporium. Flood was wrinkled, weazened, white-haired. As far back as Clay could remember, Pete Flood had run the Emporium. Clay sat on one end of the battered old counter.

"Pete," he said, "what do you know about poison water holes?"

"I've seen a few of 'em," admitted Flood in his nasal twang. "Back when I was a cub about your age, I did some muleskinnin'. Worked on a freightin' job across the Sarco Desert down in Pinolino County. I remember two water holes, the most invitin' things you ever saw. Water looked clear and pure as you please. But one drink of it would kill a man or a mule inside of four hours. Arsenic. Then I've seen bad alkali holes. Water was wet, but thick as syrup. It wouldn't kill you right off, but, if you drank enough of it, it shore would curdle your insides . . . Sa-ay, why you interested?"

"These arsenic water holes, do they stay that way, winter and summer, rain or shine?" asked Clay. "Or only turn that way during a hot spell?"

"They were arsenic, first, last, and all the time," Flood asserted emphatically. "A arsenic spring never changes. It either is or it ain't. I heard folks claim different. I've heard 'em say a good water hole can thin out to fairish water after a real storm, but that don't go for arsenic. How come? Your water going bad?"

"If this everlasting drought don't end pretty quick, I won't have any water holes left, good or bad," parried Clay as he sauntered out.

It wasn't until eight o'clock that night that young Buck Garrison showed up. He came into the Humbug alone, leaned against the bar, and ordered whiskey. Clay got up from his seat in a shadowed corner and walked over to him.

"Hello, Buck," Clay said easily. "Forget you had a bed out at the ranch?"

Buck colored under his heavy tan, tightened his lips, and shrugged. "You been on a still hunt for me?" he demanded defiantly.

"Maybe. You ain't showed up home for a couple of days, you know. I was getting a little worried."

"Forget it," snapped Buck. "I'm old enough to look out for myself."

Clay looked hard at his younger brother. A good-looking young fellow was Buck. His features did

15

not have the rugged, jutting hardness of Clay's, but were rounded, smoother. Like Clay's, his eyes were blue, but lacked that penetrating, silver clearness. And just now Buck's eyes were a trifle bloodshot, as though he had been drinking too much and sleeping too little.

"There's work to be done out at the ranch, Buck," Clay said slowly. "And the way this drought is hanging on, there'll be a lot more."

"Then why ain't you out there, instead of here, bothering me?" Buck rasped pettishly.

For the first time a glint of anger showed in Clay's eyes. "Dad left the ranch to both of us, kid, share and share alike. Your place is out there, working with me and the boys."

"To blazes with the ranch!" snarled Buck. "All it has ever meant is work, work, work . . . without a let-up. I'm looking for an easier way to earn a living. You can have my share of that damned lay-out. I'm through with it . . . Hey, Dumpy, another shot of bourbon."

"Forget it, Dumpy," ordered Clay. "He's had enough."

At that moment two other men came into the saloon — Spike Kirby and Shell Ringo. Neither of the Garrison boys noticed the arrivals, for Buck was staring angrily at Clay, who met the look unwaveringly. Buck put his hands on his hips and squared himself before Clay.

"Let me get this right," he rapped. "You trying to tell me whether I can buy a drink or not?"

"You've had more than is good for you now," Clay answered grimly. "So . . . that's all for tonight. You and me are going home. Come on."

Clay put out a hand, but Buck struck it aside.

"I've had enough of this foolishness!" he cried angrily. "Here's something to chew over. I'm free, white, and twenty-one. I'll drink when I please, where I please, and do as I damn' please."

"You're half drunk or you wouldn't be acting this way," growled Clay. "You're going home with me."

Down the bar a harsh laugh sounded, then a mocking voice.

"Baby can't have the bottle he wants. Bucky, why don't you grow up and tell that big lunk of a brother of yours where to head in at?"

Buck whirled, saw that it was Shell Ringo who had spoken. Scarlet blood flamed in Buck's face. "I been trying to tell him that, Shell. But he's too thick-headed to get the point, I reckon."

"Come on over and have a drink with Spike and me," Ringo invited. "We want company."

Buck walked over and lined up with them.

"Make it a tall one, Dumpy!" he called. "Bourbon."

Clay Garrison stood stockstill, his face in no way indicating his thoughts. Both Kirby and Ringo were watching Clay, grinning mockingly.

Kirby was a compactly built rider, with the bent elbows and hooked wrists that told of powerful arms and shoulders. He had a hatchet face, with pale little eyes. Shell Ringo was tall and lanky, with a twisted mouth and a crooked nose. At one time Ringo had

17

been the cheapest kind of a tinhorn — a shell game man. From that he had drifted into a more dangerous game. And the deftness of hand that had enabled him to handle the shells now made him highly dangerous with a gun.

The mockery of the grins Kirby and Ringo were showing built up a cold, slow fury in Clay Garrison. In even, purposeful strides he walked over to them. Kirby edged a little way out from the bar.

"You weren't thinking of getting rough, were you, Garrison?" he said softly.

"Depends," was Clay's harsh reply. "I'll let you figure that out."

Then he hit Kirby with a flinty right fist that whistled as it traveled in a short, lifting arc. It caught Kirby full on the side of his narrow jaw, lifting him almost off his feet. Kirby's knees sagged, and he fell into a left fist that nearly tore off his head. When Kirby hit the floor, he was as cold as a wedge.

Startled, Shell Ringo cursed, and tried to step back, one hand whipping down toward a holstered gun. But Ringo had forgotten the bar. Halfway through that backward step he banged into the bar and bounced away, staggering and off balance. Clay smiled thinly and knocked Ringo halfway across the room with a smashing punch that was as lethal as a battle-axe. Ringo's gangling length brought up, sprawling, across a card table, which overturned with a crash. And Shell Ringo lay like a dead man.

A cowboy farther along the bar and well past his liquor limit laughed foolishly.

"Somebody . . ." — he hiccupped — "somebody just got hit . . . hard."

"You'd better keep out of this, pard," Clay said, not unkindly.

The cowboy hiccupped again. "My sentiments," he said, and moved farther away.

Clay, after a quick glance at Kirby and Ringo, centered his blazing eyes on Buck. "Come on, kid," he said grimly. "Me and you are going home."

Buck Harrison looked at the men on the floor and then, without a word, walked out into the hot night, Clay stalking at his heels.

From the far end of the bar, Frisco Drew had watched the whole affair with narrowed, expressionless eyes. Now his lips curled slightly as he glanced at Kirby and Ringo.

"Straighten 'em out, Dumpy," he told the bartender. "I'll take over the trade . . ."

Work at the Sleeping G for the present meant spreading the last remnants of grass as far as possible. Clay Garrison sought out the spots of fast-disappearing forage and, with the help of his three cowpunchers and the sulky, disgruntled Buck, drifted one bunch of ribby cattle after another slowly across these precious areas.

Clay had taken his cue from what Rock Orde had told him. "It's hell on the stock," Orde had said. "But there is only one way to fight a drought. Keep your cattle moving. Don't let 'em hang around all the water, or around all the grass that is left. They'll go down and die on you, shore. Nature of the brutes. So you keep 'em moving, Clay. It'll be tough on you and your crew, and on the cattle, but it is the only answer. I fought a worse drought than this that way, and it worked. It'll work again."

And so, with Bib Osborne, Luke Pierce, and Charley Curtis, the Sleeping G crew, Clay endured the blasting punishment of the savage sun stoically, and kept the gaunt, protesting cattle on the move. Buck was silent and moody, cursing now and then to himself. Once he ventured an aside to Charley Curtis.

"Damned if I can see any sense to this sort of thing. The cattle are weak enough without keeping them always on the move. The whole herd will fall down and die any minute. This drought is going to clean the Buttonwillow range, and the quicker a lot of fools realize it, the better for everybody concerned."

Charley Curtis was a wrinkled old cowpuncher, lean and tough and wiry as seasoned rawhide. He never talked a great deal, but when he spoke, it was generally right to the point. Now he looked at Buck with unreadable eyes, cleared his leathery jaws of one cud of tobacco, and gnawed off a fresh chunk.

"A quitter is always easy to lick," he twanged. "Takes a man to lick a tough set-up. Clay's all man. This outfit will come out all right."

Then he spun his horse and rode away, leaving Buck with a burning face. The inference in the old cowpuncher's words was unmistakable.

About mid-morning Sheriff Bill Waller came jogging up. He rode straight up to Clay and stuck out his hand.

"Last night you did a swell job, Clay," he said. "Shake."

Clay smiled. "Ride clear out here just to tell me that, Bill?"

"Mainly," said Bill. He nodded toward Buck. "How's he taking it?"

"A little sullen and sulky, but I think he'll shake out of it."

The sheriff nodded. "Hear about Boley Stevens's best water hole going arsenic, Clay?"

"Yeah. I was in the Humbug when he came in and offered to sell to Drew. Drew bought, didn't he?"

"So I understand. Funny about that water hole."

"Yeah, funny."

Waller gnawed his lip. "So blame' funny," he murmured, "that I'm wonderin' about it. I'm headin' out that way now to have a look at it." Then he grinned. "Nice weather we're having."

"Oh, fine," answered Clay, grinning in return.

It was easier, thought Clay, to keep after a tough job when you had a little talk with a man like Bill Waller. Tough and seasoned and indomitable, that was the sheriff. A man who could grin when the going was toughest. Clay went back to his toil in a more cheerful frame of mind.

The day wore through and ended finally. The blazing sun went down, leaving the range cloaked with a hot, turgid twilight haze. The Sleeping G outfit rode back to headquarters and ate a silent supper. When the cowpunchers returned to the bunkhouse, Buck Garrison began a restless pacing to and fro, Clay watching him guardedly. Clay seemed to arrive at a sudden decision.

"Kinda restless myself," he drawled carelessly. "What say we jog over to Rock Orde's RO Up and Down and see how things are there, kid?"

"Not interested," snapped Buck shortly.

Clay shrugged. "We're going, just the same. Come on."

"Be damned if we are!" yelled Buck in sudden fury. "I'm sick of being led around by the nose like I was a baby. You hear me, I'm sick of it! You keep away from me. I'm going where I please, when I please. I'll pick my own friends. I'm headin' for town . . . now!"

"You're not," growled Clay harshly. "If I've got to lick the devil out of you to make you show some sense, then I reckon I've got to. Here's where you get it!"

CHAPTER
THREE

Clay Garrison started for his brother Buck, but halted abruptly, for Buck had shot a hand inside his shirt and jerked it out again. In it was a gun and the gun bore steadily on Clay's belt buckle.

"You see?" Buck said thickly. "Brother or no brother, you touch me and you get it!"

Clay seemed to tower. "You'd throw a gun on me, your brother?" he said hoarsely. "All right, I'm done. Go on, get out. Go to hell in your own way. But when they tighten a noose around your neck, don't squeal for me. I never did you a dirty trick in my life, yet you pull a gun on me."

There was stark tragedy in Clay's voice that seemed to strike through the defiance of his younger brother. The gun wavered slightly. And then, echoing in from the outer darkness came the racing, rapid pound of approaching hoofs. There was something ominous and threatening in the very speed of that approaching rider. Clay and his brother reacted much the same. Clay stared at the open door, waiting. Buck put the gun from sight, and, had Clay been watching him, he would have seen a slow pallor building up under the tan of face and throat.

Spurs clashed as that rider struck the ground, there was the *click* of boot heels across the porch, and then a sweating, grim-faced figure stepped through the open door. Turk Conroy, one of Rock Orde's riders.

"Clay! Thank Gawd, you're here. Hell's to pay!"

"What is it, Turk?"

"Rock Orde. He's been shot!"

"Shot! Killed, you mean?"

Conroy shook his head. "Not dead yet. But he's bad, awful bad. Shot through the body."

"Who did it . . . and why?"

"Don't know. Nobody knows. Happened somewhere out on the range, when he was alone. He came in on his own bronc', layin' over the horn like a dead man. I'm tellin' you that iron-jawed old catamount rode his own horse home, and was still in the saddle when he was plumb unconscious! Miss Leigh, she sent me after you."

Despite his own trouble with Buck, despite the ominous import of Rock Orde's shooting, something swift and warm shot through Clay Garrison. He knew how Leigh Orde adored her bluff, bulldog father, knew of the rare companionship between father and daughter. He knew what a crushing blow this would be to Leigh, and she, in her grief and shock, had asked — for him!

Clay reached for his hat and guns. "Be right with you, Turk. Somebody gone for Doc Peets?"

"Yeah, Slim Bucknell."

Clay seemed to have forgotten all about Buck. He walked past him to the door as though Buck did not exist. And Buck stood there, staring out through the open door, not moving until he heard the pound of hoofs fading into the night. Then he went out himself, caught and saddled, and headed for town.

In the RO Up and Down ranch house, to which he had come on the run, Dr. Peets hunched his shoulders and spread his hands, palms upward.

"I'd say the chances are about seventy-thirty," he said, "with Rock on the wrong end. His age is against him, yet he's such a rough, tough old juniper you can't write him off. If he makes it through the night, his chances are better. I'm staying right with him."

Clay Garrison, Bill Waller, Ben Cullop, a neighbor rancher, and Jerry Hyatt, the RO Up and Down foreman, tiptoed from the living room of the ranch house and stood in a sober group under the stars, spinning cigarettes.

"You went over Rock's guns, didn't you, Bill?" asked Clay.

"Yeah." Sheriff Waller nodded. "They were clean and hadn't been shot. Whoever got Rock, got him before he could shoot back . . . the damned lobos! I wish I knew where to begin to look."

"You could backtrack Rock's horse, maybe," suggested Cullop hopefully.

"I aim to try, come daylight," growled Waller. "But it's a thin chance. You got any idea, Jerry, where Rock might have been riding?"

The foreman shook his head. "Ever since this drought has been going on, Rock's done a lot of riding.

He's been all over the range, watching the cattle, measuring grass and water. He might have been in any of a dozen places when the shootin' took place."

Somebody came shuffling through the darkness. It was Westy Fall, the ranch cook.

"Clay," he said, "Miss Leigh wants to see you."

She was waiting for him on the porch, slim and straight. Her face was a pale, oval gleam. Clay could sense her banked grief and worry.

"Clay," she said, her voice tight but steady, "I guess you're wondering why I sent for you. But some time ago Dad and I were talking about you, and Dad said that, if I ever needed help, or if anything ever happened to him and I needed someone to lean on, I was to send for you. Dad's own words were . . . 'Clay Garrison is the strongest man along the Buttonwillow River.' And . . . and Clay, I need someone to lean on now."

Her voice quivered and broke, and she tottered toward him blindly, her hands going out in a queer, pitiful little gesture. Tears that she had held back now burst forth. Clay put a big arm about her and she clung to him, her face buried against his brawny shoulder.

Clay did not try and fool himself. She had come to him because she needed his strength, his dependability, much as a sister might have come to a brother. He said nothing, wise enough to let her have her grief over with. He made no attempt to speak until the violence of her sobs definitely lessened and the shaking of her slim shoulders stilled.

"I reckon you can always depend on me, Leigh," he said then, a little huskily.

"But if . . . if he dies, what will I do . . . what will I do?" she wailed softly.

Clay patted her shoulder. "He's not going to die. Men like Rock Orde don't kill that easy. Keep your chin up. Your dad would want you to."

She drew away from him, dabbing at her eyes. "I will," she promised tremulously. "But who, Clay, who would have had reason to do that to Dad?"

Clay shook his head. "Who knows? This drought, this everlasting heat and sun, it unbalances men. It might drive some completely loco. No telling what they might do. Come daylight, Bill Waller and I are going to do a little investigating."

She was still for a time. Then a new thought came to her.

"Buck . . . was he home when Turk brought you the message?"

"Yeah," said Clay grimly. "He was there."

"He didn't offer to come over with you?"

"No, Leigh, he didn't. But I reckon that was because he was plenty mad at me. I jerked him up pretty hard the other night and he hasn't gotten over it yet. But he'll come around. Now, you better go and try and get some rest."

She turned wearily away, and Clay sought out the sheriff. They rode off together.

In the gray dawn, they made an attempt to backtrack Rock Orde's horse, but with no success. Restless cattle, cursed with hunger and thirst, had wiped out the sign during the night.

So they rode back to the ranch, where they learned that Rock Orde was doing as well as could be expected. Then Waller went back to town and Clay to the Sleeping G.

Buck was not around and the cowpunchers were out with the cattle. Clay realized suddenly that he had had no breakfast, so went into the house to fix up a bite. A pair of saddlebags lay on the floor near the door and he absently boosted them out of the way. As they struck in a corner, a little thread of white powder trickled from one of them.

Clay stared. Those saddlebags were Buck's — his initials burned into the yoke strap. Clay went over, dropped on one knee, and opened the bags. Both were heavily dusted on the inside with that fine, white powder.

Clay went suddenly haggard. Automatically he got a smear of that powder on a fingertip, tasted it, then spat. He stood up slowly. He hovered in momentary indecision. Then his jaw tightened and his eyes took on the flare of savage, furious anger. He forgot all about eating. He caught up the saddlebags, went out to his horse, and headed for town.

Clay reined up in front of Sheriff Waller's office, still harsh of face, burning of eye. Bill was in his office and he looked up in amazement as Clay stalked in and slammed the saddlebags down on the table.

"What the . . . ?" began Waller.

"Take a look at those, Bill," gritted Clay. "See if you can recognize 'em."

"They're Buck's."

"Right. Look inside 'em and taste what you find."

Waller followed directions, started from his chair to stare at Clay.

"My Gawd!" he exclaimed hoarsely, "that's arsenic!"

"That's right," said Clay, his shoulders sagging in a sudden, despondent weariness. "And Boley Stevens's best water hole turned arsenic, plumb mysterious."

Bill Waller sank slowly back into his chair. "Clay," he said harshly, "you could have hidden those bags, or destroyed them and said nothing."

"And double-cross as square a man as ever drew breath, which is you?" Clay shook his head slowly. "I'm not so straight-laced that I wouldn't do a lot of things for Buck's sake, but there's a limit to what I can do . . . and he can do. This is it."

Bill Waller filled a battered old pipe, lighted it, and puffed furiously.

"The cussed young fool!" he burst out suddenly. "He ought to be horse whipped."

Clay beat a clenched fist into his open palm. "I can't believe he did it. I can't believe Buck would poison a rancher's water hole at a time when water means so much."

"You brought in the evidence yourself," Waller said dryly. "Knowing your dad and knowing you, Clay, it's hard to believe that Buck would do a thing of that sort. Yet there it is." He tapped the saddlebags with a knotty forefinger.

Clay scowled. "There was some purpose in fighting this drought . . . up till now. Now, what's the use?"

"Listen," said Waller. "For your sake, Clay, I'm going to stretch a point. We'll keep this to ourselves for a while, until we have a talk with Buck. Maybe he can explain this, though I don't know how. If he can't, there's only one out for me."

"I know." Clay nodded. "And I won't hold it against you, Bill."

Waller put the bags in a corner closet, locked it, and, picking up his hat, jammed it on his head.

"Let's go find Buck," he said. "There's one thing we don't want to forget, Clay. If Buck did poison that water hole, it was at the suggestion or order of somebody else, for he'd have no reason under the sun for doin' it, otherwise. So, we have a water hole poisoned. Yesterday some time, Rock Orde was mysteriously shot and wounded seriously. Maybe it just happened that way, but maybe it goes a whole lot deeper than that. Maybe there's something ugly brewin' on this sun-blasted range and we're just stumblin' onto the first effects of it. We play this close to our vests."

They left the office together, headed for Pete Flood's Emporium as their first stop in their search for Buck Garrison. Flood always kept an eye on what was happening in town. And he had seen Buck.

"He's down in the loft of the livery barn, sleeping it off," old Pete told them. "He went on a roarin' drunk last night and Jigger Dugan took him down there and threw a blanket over him. Clay, you better put a plumb strong check rein on that brother of yours, or he'll wind up in a mighty tough spot."

Clay didn't answer, but stalked out of the Emporium and down to the livery barn, Bill Waller striding beside him. Jigger Dugan, the liveryman, a little, bright-eyed Irishman, was soaping a set of harness. He nodded toward a little cubbyhole room in one corner of the stable.

"He's in on my bunk, wit' a head on him like a ball of fire," said Jigger. "I made him douse his head in the waterin' trough and thin I gave him a wee snort of likker. But he's one sick bhoy right now, I'm after tellin' ye."

Still fingering the harness, he eyed them morosely.

CHAPTER
FOUR

Buck Garrison was not a pretty sight, stretched out on Jigger Dugan's bunk. His hair was tousled and full of bits of straw. His eyes were bloodshot, his ordinarily clean-cut young face bloated with whiskey, and grimy with dirt and whiskers. He stared sullenly up at Clay and Bill Waller, and said nothing.

"Feelin' kinda low, eh, Buck?" said the sheriff cheerfully.

Buck grunted, ran a hand over his brow.

Waller laughed. "Yeah, I know. Nothing like it for pure misery. Well, get hold of yourself. You're coming over to my office for a little talk. Come on, I'll give you a hand."

"Go 'way," mumbled Buck. "Leave me alone. I'm sick of being talked to."

"Just the same, you're going to take it." Then Waller's voice cracked like a whip. "Get up off that bunk and come along!"

Buck licked harsh, feverish lips, got slowly and unsteadily to his feet. He wobbled a trifle and Clay took him by the arm. "All right, kid," he said gently. "I'll help you."

Slowly they went up the street and into Waller's office. The sheriff closed and locked the door. Buck sank into a chair, holding his head in his hands, staring at the floor. Waller produced a bottle.

"Another good drag at the hair of the dog will help a lot," he said.

Buck took the drag, coughed, then straightened slightly. "What's the idea?" he mumbled. "Some more preachin'?"

"Maybe," said Waller curtly. "Let's call it cold turkey. Buck, who got you to poison Boley Stevens's water hole?"

Without a word Waller went to the closet, got the saddlebags, and tossed them on the table. "Yours?" he snapped.

The whiskey-bloated young face seemed to tighten, go slowly pale. "Yeah," blurted Buck hoarsely. "Mine."

"They're still smeared with arsenic powder," said the sheriff, indicating the white powder.

"I carried arsenic in them," admitted Buck slowly. "But I didn't poison that water hole."

"You know who did?"

"Yeah."

"Who?"

Buck shook his head. "Not sayin'."

"You mean you won't say?"

"That's right. I won't."

There was a long moment of silence. Buck stirred restlessly in his chair, staring at the saddlebags. A sudden thought seemed to strike him. He straightened with a jerk. "How'd you get hold of those bags?" he demanded of Waller.

Clay spoke quietly. "I brought them in from the ranch."

"You did? You found 'em and brought 'em to Waller? You brought evidence to a sheriff . . . evidence against me . . . your own brother! A regular Holy Joe, eh? Of all the snide hypocrites! Turn against your own flesh and blood. Why, you damned —"

Buck's furious tirade broke off abruptly. Bill Waller had him by the shoulder, yanking him upright, then slamming him across the room until his shoulders banged against an inner wall. And then the sheriff pressed in on him, his blazing eyes cutting into the younger man.

"Shut up!" Waller roared. "Not another word out of you, you snivelin' whelp. For a red cent I'd knock the everlastin' tar out of you. Yeah, Clay brought those bags to me because he's a man. But you wouldn't understand that. You don't know what a man is, because you're so far from being one yourself. You don't know what honesty means, or honor or truth or courage or anything else. You'd turn down the faith and trust of a brother who's been plenty good to you to run around with skunks like Spike Kirby and Shell Ringo. You'd dirty up the name of as fine a man as ever breathed . . . your own father . . . and then yelp like a yellow dog when you got caught. Yeah, for less than a cent I'd whale you within an inch of your life."

Bill Waller was shaking with wrath. His keen eyes blazed, his jaw jutted out like the prow of a battleship.

34

One clenched fist was waving up and down under Buck Garrison's nose. "Yeah," he went on, "you're a weak, snivelin' whelp who don't deserve the Garrison name. I could put you behind bars. I could cinch you with a case that would send you over the road for twenty years. I could make you crawl . . . plenty. But for the memory of your father and for the sake of a brother who is worth twenty of you, I'm goin' to play fast and loose with my oath of office. I'm paroling you over to Clay. You're to go home and work . . . hard. You're not to take a drink or come near town without Clay's permission. You're not to have a blasted thing to do with Kirby or Ringo. In other words, you're to start in being decent. And if you break one little part of that parole, then it's you for a long stretch. I'm hangin' onto those saddlebags. I got a club to swing over your worthless head and I'm goin' to swing it. Now you've heard somethin' and you better believe I mean every word of it."

Bill Waller turned away, walked across the room, and stood with his back to Buck Garrison. The room grew still. Buck stared at the floor. Under the flailing broadside of the sheriff's wrath, he seemed to shrivel. The vast contempt in the sheriff's gesture of turning his back on him sent Buck's face to a flaming, shamed crimson.

Then Bill Waller whirled on him again. "Go clean yourself up, get some breakfast, and be back here with your horse, ready to ride in not over an hour. Get!"

Buck Garrison shuffled to the door, hangdog and shamed. He threw a single furtive glance at Clay, and, to his immense surprise, Clay was smiling at him.

"I'll be waiting for you, kid," he said gravely.

Buck gulped and went out.

Waller flashed a quick look at Clay. "Sore?" he asked curtly.

Clay shook his head. "Of course not. I'm eternally grateful, Bill. You're overlooking those saddlebags."

"I'm not overlookin' 'em," cut in the sheriff. "If Buck breaks his parole, it will be just too bad for him. But I'm playin' a little gamble, Clay. I still think Buck has good stuff in him, if we can only stir it up. I'm gambling that maybe, now that I've ripped the hide off him, his conscience will get to workin'. He'll start thinkin', realize that he's off on the wrong foot, and one of these days come through without any proddin' with all he knows about this arsenic business. Then I'll be able to clamp down on who is really responsible. Somehow, when he said he didn't poison that water hole, I believed him. But he carried that arsenic for somebody else, and what I want to do is find out who that somebody is."

Clay nodded. "I sort of figured you were up to something like that, Bill. I'll help all I can."

Before the hour of grace was up Buck Garrison was back at the sheriff's office with his horse. He looked considerably better. He'd had a good wash. It seemed to Clay that there was just a trifle more tilt to Buck's jaw than usual.

36

They rode out to the ranch in silence all the way. As soon as they arrived, Buck changed to a fresh bronco.

"Where are you going?" Clay asked quietly.

"Out to help the boys with the cattle."

Clay's heart warmed. "No need of rushing it, kid. You look pretty seedy. You better go lay down and get some sleep. Tomorrow morning you can dig in."

Buck shook his head. "Now's the time to start," he said gruffly.

"All right," said Clay. "We'll go out together."

The long, dusty hours in that feral sun did things to Buck. At first it nearly crucified him, with his aching head. But it also burned the whiskey out of him, and by sundown the puffiness had left his face and a clearer light had come into his eyes.

When supper was over with, Clay turned to Buck.

"I'm going up to the Orde place. Want to find out how Rock is making it. I think Leigh would appreciate it if you came along, kid."

"Sure," said Buck. "Let's go."

When they reached the RO Up and Down, they found Jerry Hyatt and Turk Conroy sitting on the ranch house steps, smoking. Their greeting was cordial.

"Rock's better?" Clay guessed.

"Shore is!" enthused Turk. "Never was enough lead mined to kill that old catamount. Doc Peets says he's amazed, but tickled pink."

"That," Clay said slowly, "is plumb great."

There was the *click* of a heel and the swish of movement and a slim figure stood on the porch. Clay heard Leigh's quick exclamation of delight.

"Buck!" she said softly, adding offhandedly: "Hello, Clay."

Buck went up the steps, and he and Leigh moved off around the porch. Clay stared out into the night, glad that the dark hid the wistfulness and pain in his eyes.

"Heard about Tinsley and Stinchfield, Clay?" asked Jerry Hyatt.

"No. What about 'em?"

"They sold out."

"Sold out! Both of 'em?"

"Yep, both of 'em. And I'll bet you can't guess who to."

"Not an idea," admitted Clay.

"Drew, Frisco Dan Drew. He bought 'em out, lock, stock, and barrel. This drought licked 'em."

"I'll be damned," said Clay slowly. "Tinsley . . . he don't surprise me. He always was a sort of weak one, always lookin' on the darkest side. But Bob Stinchfield . . . I always figured Bob as being too salty to quit under punishment."

"I've heard that Bob's been buckin' the tiger pretty heavy at the Humbug lately, and not winnin'," said Turk Conroy. "Maybe he got to owing Drew so much money he had to sell to get from under. I've known more'n one man who was stout in every other way to be the weakest kind of sucker over a poker table. I am myself, for that matter." Turk laughed cheerfully.

Clay thoughtfully built a smoke. "If Drew keeps on buyin', he's going to own most of this Buttonwillow range pretty quick," he said gravely. "That makes three ranches he's picked up in less than a week. Boley

Stevens's, Tinsley's, and Stinchfield's. He's takin' a long chance. If this drought don't bust right soon, it will bust him."

"Drew is a gambler," Jerry Hyatt said slowly. "I reckon he's got that figured out. On the other hand, if he can hang on now till the rain does come, he'll cash in heavy. Good times hit this range again and he'll have an empire with those three ranches."

Another horse came jogging up through the darkness. It carried Ben Cullop, Orde's neighbor and one of the bigger ranchers in the vicinity.

"How's Rock makin' it?" he asked.

"Fine," answered Hyatt. "Doc Peets is real pleased."

Cullop found a place on the steps. "Any line yet on who shot him?"

"Not yet. We're waitin' till he gets strong enough to talk. Maybe he knows something. If he does . . ." — Hyatt's lazy drawl crisped to ice — "some polecat is goin' to stretch rope."

Cullop mopped his brow with his neckerchief. "Sometimes I feel like stretchin' my own neck," he mumbled. "Just to get shut of this cussed weather. Sometimes I think there never was such a thing as rain. Two or three times I been half a mind to quit. Today I come near doing it. Had a chance to sell, but somehow I just couldn't bring myself to let go."

"Sell!" murmured Clay softly. "Who to?"

"Frisco Drew. He was out to see me. Offered me a pretty decent price. But I've worked so hard and long for that spread of mine, I decided to hang on a little while longer."

"Say," blurted Turk Conroy, "what does Drew want to do . . . make a king of himself over this whole danged range? He buys out Stevens and Tinsley and Stinchfield, and now wants to buy you out. That *hombre* shore is ambitious, either that or soft in the head."

"You say he bought out Bob Stinchfield and Tinsley?" demanded the startled Cullop.

"That's right. Got the word straight this afternoon."

"I'll be damned," said Cullop. "He's either a smart man, or a plain fool, I don't know which."

Clay got slowly to his feet. In his eyes a thin, strong flame was burning. "Tell Buck when he asks for me that I've drifted, chasing down an idea. Good night, boys."

The three on the steps stared after him as Clay rode away into the gloom of night.

"There goes a jasper I sometimes can't figure," said Ben Cullop.

"There goes one of the stoutest men, all ways, that I ever knew," said Jerry Hyatt. "Clay is deep. Not any for fuss and feathers or wild jumpin'. He's slow and quiet. Look what happened to Spike Kirby and Shell Ringo in the Humbug a few nights ago when Clay swung on 'em. Clay Garrison, Ben, is smart as a whip with the nerve of a lion. And if he says he's got an idea, you can bet he's got an idea."

"Right," chimed in Turk Conroy. "Right all the way, Jerry."

It did not take Clay Garrison long to reach town, and once there he headed straight for the sheriff's office. Waller was surprised to see him again so soon.

"You remind me of a danged grasshopper," said Bill Waller. "You're in and out, here and yonder all the time, Clay. What you got on your mind? Buck actin' up again already?"

Clay shook his head. "No. I think Buck is over the peak, Bill. He's different than he's been for a long time. No, it isn't about Buck that I'm here. It's about Frisco Dan Drew."

Waller's eyes narrowed. "What about Frisco Drew?"

"Today he bought out Tinsley and Stinchfield, and offered to buy out Ben Cullop."

"And the other day he bought out Boley Stevens," Waller murmured.

"After Boley's best water hole had been poisoned," Clay said softly. "And yesterday Rock Orde was mysteriously shot. Something vicious is forming on this range."

"I don't doubt it."

"What's more, Bill, Turk Conroy tells me that Stinchfield has been losing a lot at the Humbug. It was Turk's idea that maybe Bob got to owing Drew more money than he could pay."

Waller reached for his hat. "Think I'll go over and have a talk with Drew. I won't act suspicious. I'll just make it sort of casual-like and see how he acts when I tell him I've heard about him buying out these ranchers. Want to come along?"

"No. I'll be getting on home. Play your cards careful, Bill."

"Leave that to me." The sheriff nodded.

CHAPTER
FIVE

On the solitary ride back to the Sleeping G, Clay tried to keep his thoughts on the problem he had just brought to Bill Waller. But in spite of himself, those thoughts persisted in switching back to Rock Orde's spread, back to a slim girl who had appeared like a shadow in the gloom, and with that deep, thrilling note in her voice had called Buck's name.

Clay Garrison was not the sort to delude himself with false hopes and fears. He was a practical man when dealing with facts, whether those facts hurt or not. As far back, almost, as he could remember, the vision of Leigh Orde had been in his heart. The cool, pure honesty of her, the slim, gay grace, the fine, tempered courage — these things he had accepted as the certain attributes of the only girl. He knew that, in his eyes, there could never be another like her. When her father had first been brought in, dangerously wounded by some sneaking bushwhacker's bullet, she had sent for him. But that was only because, in her grief and shock, she remembered what her father had told her to do. It wasn't her heart that had sent for him; it was her numbed and distracted brain. Tonight, happy with the knowledge that Rock Orde was making a successful fight for life, she had thrilled to the knowledge that Buck had come to her. In her single word of greeting, there had been her heart speaking.

Clay shook himself savagely. He couldn't go on being maudlin over this thing. After all, Buck was his brother, his kid brother, and Buck needed someone like Leigh Orde. She could give Buck the background of moral strength he needed. She could make a man out of Buck. And she couldn't help where her heart led her. That wistfulness and ache within him — well, he'd just have to endure it and let the years mellow it. He had just as well set about subduing it right now. His face took on that craggy, indomitable look and he lifted his eyes to the stars.

A dry, parching wind was beginning to blow, a wind full of a strange kind of electricity that set a man's teeth on edge and made his horse irritable and nervous. Clay's mount took to shying at imaginary shadows. He quieted the edgy brute with strong hands and stern words.

He built a cigarette and twisted in the saddle to shelter the flame of a match from the wind. At that moment something struck him a terrific blow on the side of the head. The universe exploded in a burst of blazing, weird-colored lights. In a numb, stricken sort of way, Clay realized that he was toppling from his saddle. As he fell, it seemed that he heard, thin and broken in the wail of the wind, the fluttering echoes of a gunshot. The earth came up to meet him and he struck it soddenly. Then he was in blackness, drifting . . . drifting . . .

★   ★   ★

43

When Clay recovered consciousness, it was still black dark. The wind had died down. The stars seemed cooler, gentler. For a long time he lay as he had fallen, drugged with a numb lassitude. His brain seemed to have frozen, refusing to function. He merely lay there, looking up at the stars with dazed, uncomprehending eyes.

After a time the tide of returning strength that had brought him back to consciousness rose higher in him, gradually clearing his brain of shock. His senses began to function; feeling returned. He realized that his head was all one thundering ache. On one side of his face the night air felt cooler, because something wet and sticky was smeared there.

He began to hear again. Something was stamping the earth near him. Of a sudden he realized that it was his horse, restless but faithful, waiting for him to get up and ride. Instinct brought Clay up on one elbow. Just in time he locked his jaws to keep back a groan of agony. He flattened out again, for the stars had begun to dance crazily once more. He lay for a long time with his eyes closed. But that movement seemed to start his brain really to working. He realized now what had happened. Some bushwhacker along the trail had taken a shot at him, had bounced a slug off the side of his head.

In time Clay stirred once more and again got to an elbow. This time he stayed there, his jaw set to rigid whiteness, while he fought off weakness and nausea and that terrible, thundering pain. He got to his knees and put one exploring hand to his head. It came away sticky with blood. Clay tried to get to his feet, but couldn't make it. So he crawled slowly over to his horse, which snorted and stamped, but did not move away from him. He reached up, got hold of a stirrup, and pulled himself to his feet. But for the horse he would have fallen again. He leaned against the faithful animal, his wounded head dropping down to rest against the smooth, hard curve of the saddle.

He never did remember how he got into that saddle. Only sheer, stark will of the most indomitable kind could have been the answer. But get into the saddle he did, and, as he hunched forward over the horn, sick and dizzy, the horse struck out at a swinging walk.

Clay must have lost consciousness again, for he remembered almost nothing of the ride home. When he did come to the realization that his horse was standing still, he looked around, dazedly recognizing shadowy corral and bulked feed sheds. He slid to the ground, used the corral fence as far as he could for support, then struck out for the ranch house, weaving and stumbling like a man thoroughly drunk.

He had only one thought now — water to satiate his terrible thirst. He wobbled up the porch steps and over to the water olla. And then he drank. The water was only reasonably cool and it was hard and bitter with alkali, but it was nectar to Clay that night. It reached all through him, that wonderful water. It cooled his feverish blood; it drove the worst of the mists from his brain. And when his thirst was fully quenched, Clay poured dipperful after dipperful over his wounded head. The water stung that ragged wound, but it was wet and cool and it drove the mist in his brain away.

A floorboard creaked and out of the door stepped Buck.

"Clay!" he said sharply. "What the devil! Say, where you been? You . . . you're not drunk?"

"No, kid," Clay answered thickly. "But some polecat hid out along the town trail tried to blow my head off and blame' near succeeded. Help me inside."

Buck got him inside and onto a bunk. Then he lit a lamp. He caught his breath sharply at sight of Clay's head. He ran out of the house and down to the bunkhouse. Soon he was back with old Charley Curtis. Luke Pierce was already splitting the wind for the RO Up and Down to get Dr. Peets. Although Buck and Charley tried to mop some of the dirt and blood off that wounded head, Clay again lost consciousness.

The next time he opened his eyes, Clay found that his head was heavily bandaged, that he was between blankets, and that it was day once more. Sunlight blazed through the windows of the room and the air was hot and dead. Three people were in the room with him — Buck, Sheriff Waller, and Charley Curtis. Buck was mixing something in a glass. He leaned over Clay.

"Drink this, old-timer," he said gravely. "Doc Peets left it for you to take."

Clay downed the draught, shuddered, then managed a wry grin.

"Well, here we are again," he mumbled. "Hi, Bill."

The sheriff's face was quiet and grim. "You had one devilish close call, cowboy. Doc Peets said you must have a head like a rock. What do you remember about getting hit?"

Clay blinked. "I had just built a cigarette and was going to light it. There was a wind blowing and I turned in the saddle a little to shield the match. Then, *blooie!* It hit me. While I was fallin', I thought I heard gun echoes. That's all I know except coming out of it, getting into the saddle, and riding home."

"You want to bless that wind," growled Waller. "If you hadn't turned a little as you lit that match, that slug would have gone straight through your head. As it is, according to Doc, if you've got the same kind of grizzly-bear constitution as Rock Orde, you'll be ridin' again in a couple of days. Can you recall about where it happened, Clay?"

Clay squinted painfully. "Wasn't paying much attention," he mumbled. "Thinking of other things. I remember my bronc' acting kind of nervous, shying considerable. Yeah, I remember now, Bill. It was down on that little ridge. Reckon that polecat was hid out in some of that brush."

Waller nodded. "I'll have a look around when I'm headin' back to town. Remember what we were talking about last night? Well, I'm just about convinced we're right. Soon as I get a little more evidence, I'm calling a showdown."

"What are you two talkin' about?" asked Buck.

"Just an idea," said Waller. "Well, best thing we can do is clear out and let the old maverick get some rest. Best thing in the world for a sore top-knot."

"Reckon that's what Doc Peets figured," murmured Clay sleepily. "That medicine . . ."

He was asleep before he could finish.

The next day Clay was up and around again, a little shaky, but with the old strength surging stronger and stronger in him with every passing hour. His head was sore, but that terrible numb feeling had left it. Dr. Peets dropped over in the morning to put a fresh dressing on it.

"How you missed a bad concussion, I don't know," confessed the doctor.

"Just plain lunk-headed, I reckon." Clay grinned. "How's Rock?"

"Going to get well . . . and, when I first saw him, I wouldn't have given a cent for his chances."

"He able to talk yet?"

"Oh, yes. Bill Waller was out to see him. But Rock don't know who shot him. He was up along the river when it happened. One minute he was riding free and fine. The next he had a slug in him. That's all."

Clay squinted soberly. "Better lay in a lot of bandages and medicine, Doc. You're going to need them. There's a pot of hell's brew on this range and the lid is about due to fly off."

"So I figured." Peets nodded. "Men are the biggest fools. They shoot one another and I patch 'em up so they can go out and get shot again."

That afternoon Leigh Orde rode in. Sitting on the porch, Clay's heart took a truant leap at sight of her. Always she was like a sweet wind, cool and fragrant.

48

Clay wondered at the strange shyness that was in her eyes. She stood before him, slim and straight.

"If this shooting doesn't stop, I'm going to go crazy," she said soberly. "First Dad and now you, Clay. What does it mean?"

"That there is a rotten spot on this range that will have to be cleaned out. But don't you worry your pretty head about it. Here, sit down and let me look at you a while."

She gave a queer little laugh, but obeyed. "Anyone would think that was a pleasure."

"It is. You've got no idea how much it is."

She looked away, soft color beating in her cheeks. "You did a good job on Buck, Clay," she said. "He is almost like his old self again."

"You can thank Bill Waller a lot for that. I think it was a broadside that Bill threw at the kid that had the most effect . . . Doc tells me your dad is on the way up."

"That's right, and I'm so happy about it. Yet he's already making threats as to what he'll do when he's able to be up and doing again. And maybe the next time . . ." She broke off, shivering.

"I wouldn't worry none about that, were I you," Clay comforted. "By the time Rock Orde is ready to ride again, this range will be blown plumb to pieces, or it will be quiet and healthy again."

She looked directly at him. "Clay, I'm no child and I can be trusted. Tell me, who do you think is responsible for this trouble?"

Clay was silent for a moment, then he shrugged. "Remember, Leigh, what I think and what are the facts may be two different things. But you asked me who I think is responsible, so I'll tell you. Frisco Dan Drew."

"Frisco Drew!" She stared at him. "Why, I spoke to him this morning, in town. He . . . why, are you sure of that?"

"I only told you what I think," said Clay. "Oh, I'm not saying that Drew actually pulled the trigger on your father and me. But my bet is that whoever did it was under orders from Drew. Me, I didn't know you were acquainted with Drew."

He was looking at her thoughtfully. Silence between them grew strained.

CHAPTER
SIX

Leigh colored a little, for there was a certain censure in Clay Garrison's words. But she met the scrutiny of his glance without flinching. "I've known Mister Drew for a long time, Clay," she said finally. "Dad introduced us himself. And I hope I'll never be a snob. Frisco Drew may run a saloon and a gambling hall, but as long as he is a gentleman in my presence, there is no reason why I should ignore him, is there?"

Clay made an impatient gesture. "Oh, I suppose not," he grumbled. "But you're so clean and fine, Leigh. It just seems to me . . . oh, well, I reckon it's none of my business."

She looked at him guardedly, then laughed softly. "You men! You frequent the Humbug. You drink there and play cards there and think nothing of it. But if one of your womenfolk speaks to the man who runs the place, you're upset about it."

"Maybe you're right." Clay shrugged. "But a man tries to keep his ideals way up above, as far away from things like that as he can."

"Am I an ideal?" she asked.

Clay looked at her with strange intentness. "You are to me. I'd like to keep you away up on the clouds and sunshine, always."

Color fluttered in her cheeks; her laugh was a trifle shaky. "I'm not ready to be an angel just yet, Clay. And I haven't any of the qualifications. But coming back to serious things. Why would Frisco Drew want Dad and you shot?"

"Drew has bought out Tinsley and Stinchfield and Boley Stevens," Clay said gravely. "He tried to buy out Ben Cullop. For all we know Drew may be one of these jaspers who dreams of a range empire. Many men before him have. Yet, no man could fully control Buttonwillow range unless he also had control of the RO Up and Down and the Sleeping G. Your dad's spread and this ranch here are the heart of the range. Drew might have figured it that neither Rock Orde nor I would think of selling out. But if Rock and I were both dead, you and Buck might be persuaded to let go of the holdings."

Leigh went pale. "You make it sound awfully cold-blooded," she murmured.

"Men get that way when they play for big stakes. And Drew has always been a gambler. Me, I've studied Frisco Drew more than once. Looking at him, you get just as far as his eyes. There you stop. You can't see past them, or get a single hint of what is going on in back of those eyes. The man is deep and, I'll bet, ruthless."

Leigh got slowly to her feet.

"Now I'm scared, scared into fits," she said plaintively. "I know I'll have bad dreams."

"Remember you asked for facts," Clay reminded.

"I know." She nodded. "Well, anyhow, I'm mighty glad your wound wasn't too serious, Clay."

"Thanks. It was good of you to ride over, Leigh."

"Where is Buck?" she asked.

"Out with the boys, nagging those poor, tortured brutes of cattle around. If we don't get rain pretty quick, this Buttonwillow range won't be worth anything to anybody."

She nodded thoughtfully. Then she started briskly down the steps. She halted abruptly however, as a rider came cantering up from the creek. That rider was Frisco Dan Drew.

Drew sat a horse well. His dress, however, was somewhat dandified, being high, glossy Cordovan boots, riding breeches of dove gray whipcord, and a sheer, white silk shirt with a flowing gray tie. His Stetson was new and white and expensive. His only concession to the mode of the country was a holstered gun at his hip.

He dismounted, took off his hat, and bowed low to Leigh, his hard, black eyes running over her in a look of speculative admiration that made Clay grit his teeth.

"Miss Orde!" Drew exclaimed, in his softest, most slurring tones. "This is a pleasure. Don't let me drive you away. I have a little business I want to talk over with Garrison, then I am riding up to your father's ranch to congratulate him on his fortunate recovery. If you are heading for home, I'd enjoy escorting you there."

Leigh hesitated slightly, then shook her head. "I'm afraid I can't wait, Mister Drew. I've overstayed now. I've got to get right back."

She slid lithely into her saddle, turned, looked past and over Drew, threw up a hand in farewell to Clay, who waved back, a gleam of pride in his eyes. Then she was gone, swiftly.

Drew watched her out of sight, then climbed the steps to the porch. His face displayed no outward sign of his feelings over the snub, but Clay knew that inside the fellow was raging.

Drew spoke abruptly. "Sorry to hear about your accident, Garrison. And glad you are coming out of it so fast."

"No accident," Clay said. "Just some sneaking coyote who tried to dry-gulch me . . . What is this business you want to talk over with me?"

"Perhaps I should have said business with your brother, Buck," returned Drew smoothly. "I've spoken to Buck about it a couple of times, but he didn't give me much satisfaction. Now, seeing that I've made several investments in the past few days, I find myself forced to come to you, for I need every dollar I can get hold of. Coming right to the point, Buck owes me eighteen hundred dollars . . . poker debts. I have his I.O.U.s for all of it. Care to see them?"

Clay stared at Drew. "Eighteen hundred dollars! That's a lot of money, Drew."

"Exactly. And the reason I'm here." From a hip pocket Drew produced a number of slips of paper. "Look 'em over," he said.

There was no mistaking the authenticity of the I.O.U.s. Each was in Buck's handwriting and Clay found the accumulated total correct. Behind the craggy impassiveness of his face, Clay's mind was racing. These I.O.U.s could account for many things, primarily for that burst of strange activity on the part of Buck, his sullenness, his edgy waywardness. Clay got slowly to his feet.

"I'll go write a check for these," he said. "That satisfactory?"

"Perfectly."

When Clay returned with the check, Drew glanced at it, pocketed it, then tore the I.O.U.s to bits and tossed them aside.

"Sorry I had to press the debt," he purred. "Ordinarily I wouldn't have. Hope this won't change our friendship."

Clay laughed harshly. "Slow it, Drew. Let's take the masks off. You and I have never been friends, and never could be. You know that as well as I do."

Drew smiled thinly and shrugged. "All right with me, Garrison. You're pretty direct, but you're right. I'll go to my grave hating your insides. And for reasons I can hardly define. Queer, isn't it?"

"Maybe, maybe not," said Clay brusquely. "But you've called the turn. You're smooth, Drew, smooth as butter. But there are some of us along this river you're not fooling at all. Here's a tip. Don't let your ambitions reach too high. Else you'll have a longer way to drop. As far as Buck is concerned, I reckon he'll never flip a card across one of your poker tables again. Next time he plays, it will be in an honest lay-out."

Just a fleck of crimson showed in Drew's eyes, to be masked immediately. "Poker debts always do gripe those who have to pay," he said.

"There are other kinds of debts that gripe, too. And you're building up one of them, Drew. It will take a heap to square it, a lot more than will be pleasant to pay. But you'll pay, all right."

Drew's eyes narrowed. "What you driving at?"

"You guess. Now . . . drift. And don't come back."

For a moment their eyes locked. Red hate lanced back and forth between them. That hate had always been a living flame between these two men, but never before had it been in the open.

"I might add," went on Clay, "that, if I were you, I wouldn't bother to ride up to see Rock Orde. You won't find your welcome too hearty."

Drew whirled on his heels and walked down the steps. There was fury in the way he hit his saddle, the way he spurred his mount to movement. And Clay smiled grimly as he saw Drew head, not for the RO Up and Down, but straight back for town.

After supper that night Buck Garrison walked out and stood on the porch beside his elder brother, who sat there staring out into the hot gloom. The air was thick and lifeless in a man's lungs and had the smell of scorched, burned dust. Overhead, even the stars looked feverish. At intervals came the sound of cattle, bellowing mournful complaint against hunger and thirst.

"Clay," said Buck abruptly, "I've got something I have to get off my mind. Oh, I've been a plumb fool, and I wouldn't blame you none if you knocked hell out of me. Clay, I owe Frisco Drew eighteen hundred dollars in gambling debts."

Clay drew a deep breath in sudden relief. "Been waiting for you to come clean, kid. But you don't owe Drew a thing any more. He was out today. I gave him a check for those I.O.U.s."

"You did! He came out to collect them?"

"Yeah."

"That was a lot of money, Clay. I . . . I feel like a coyote."

"It was cheap enough," Clay said gently, "to get the old kid brother back again. We'll charge that off to experience, Buck, and forget it."

Buck blinked at the sudden blur in his eyes. Good old Clay, staunch and true and steadfast. "I'll go the rest of the way!" he cried hoarsely. "That arsenic powder . . . Drew sent me after that. Those two days I was gone I rode clear over to Maverick after that powder. I knew it was to be used for no good, but Drew reminded me of those debts. I was just fool enough to let him bluff me. So I went and got it. I know I was a yellow dog. Like a lot of other cussed fools I thought I could bluster my way through. And when I found out I couldn't, I hit the bottle. I wouldn't blame you if you took a quirt to me."

Clay stood up and put a big hand on his brother's shoulder and shook him slightly. "Your coming clean squares everything, kid. Who poisoned Boley Stevens's water hole?"

"Spike Kirby and Shell Ringo. At Drew's orders. Stevens wanted to sell, but Drew figured that by using a couple of dollars' worth of arsenic he could get the ranch for half what Stevens first asked for it. And he did . . . just about half. That Drew is crooked as they come. He's got ambitions. Two or three times I've heard him make little remarks which didn't mean nothing by themselves, but, putting them all together, they meant plenty."

"I'd already figured that." Clay nodded. "I don't like fighting any better than anybody else, but if I got to fight, I aim to get in the first wallop, if possible. Go down and throw your kak and mine on a couple of bronc's. We're riding in to see Bill Waller."

They did not take the usual trail to town. That bushwhacking shot that had come so close to costing Clay's life had made him wary. So he and Buck made a wide circle and came into Black Rock from the south. There was a dim light burning in Bill Waller's office. The door was closed, but not locked. When Clay pushed it open, he saw Waller at his desk table. The sheriff was leaning on the table, his head on his arms, as though asleep.

"Hello, Bill," said Clay. "Wake up! I got news for you."

Waller did not move. Clay walked over and took him by the shoulder, shaking him slightly.

58

"Wake up, Bill."

There was a flaccid inertness about the sheriff. Of a sudden Clay went cold all over.

"Turn up that lamp a little, Buck," he grated. "Something is wrong with Bill."

Buck turned up the lamp, held it high. Clay's face went into a haggard mask.

"He's dead," he said simply. "Look!"

There was a narrow slit in the back of Bill Waller's shirt. A spreading patch of soggy, sticky wetness clung about that slit.

"Stabbed," whispered Buck. "Stabbed in the back."

Clay was like a man turned to stone. Good old Bill Waller, as white a man as ever lived. Brave, four-square, tolerant, a true stalwart friend.

Buck drew a sharp, quivering breath. "That day, when I was seen riding out by the Lost Hills with Kirby and Ringo, Drew sent us out to make a range count of Boley Stevens's herd. That day we pulled in for a time at the water hole, the one Kirby and Ringo poisoned the next day. Ringo took his shirt off to douse his head and shoulders in the water to cool off. And, Clay, down under his left arm he had a knife strapped on. I saw it . . . saw it plain."

Clay nodded stiffly. "Turn the light down again," he said tonelessly. "We're going over to the Humbug."

They crossed the street, Clay stalking in front. It seemed to Buck that this brother of his was almost a stranger. Only his eyes seemed alive, and these were pinpoints of coldest ice.

Just inside the door of the saloon Clay stopped, his glance running over the room. There was quite a crowd present.

"What's all this?" murmured Buck at Clay's shoulder. "Most of these *hombres* are strangers. This is funny."

Clay didn't answer, although he had noted that most of the riders present, drinking and grouped about the poker tables, were strangers and a hard-bitten lot.

Frisco Drew, Spike Kirby, and Shell Ringo were not in evidence. But Ben Cullop was there, with Skeet Farnell, his foreman. The two of them walked over to Clay and Buck. Cullop was scowling in puzzlement.

"What do you make of this, Clay?" he asked in a low voice. "Where did all these jaspers come from, and why?"

"I think I've got the answer to that," Clay replied harshly. "Seen Drew or Kirby or Ringo around?"

"No, not tonight. Why?"

"Come outside," growled Clay Garrison.

CHAPTER
SEVEN

Farnell and Cullop sensed the savage tragedy of Clay's mood and followed silently. In the blackness of the overhang of Pete Flood's store, Clay halted.

"Buck and me just came from Bill Waller's office," he stated. "Bill is there, dead!"

Ben Cullop gulped. "Dead?"

"Stabbed in the back."

"That . . . that's terrible!" stuttered Cullop. "Who . . . why . . . ?"

"I think I know," rasped Clay, "but we've got no time to talk about it now. Anyhow, Buck and me will look after that. You and Skeet go down and get Jigger Dugan's buckboard. Drive it up back of the Emporium. Don't let anybody see you and don't make any noise."

Cullop was still stuttering, dazed by amazement and shock. Skeet Farnell caught Cullop by the arm. "Come on, boss. I reckon Clay knows what he's doing."

Farnell and Cullop hurried off.

Old Pete Flood's living quarters were in one of the rear corners of his store. He answered sleepily to Clay's knock on a side door.

"Who is it?" twanged the old storekeeper. "I ain't goin' to open up to sell some jug-headed cowpunch' a dime's worth of smokin'."

"This is Clay Garrison, Pete. It is smoking I want all right, but it ain't the kind you think. And it will be a heap more than a dime's worth. Open up."

Flood lighted a lamp and let Clay and Buck in.

"What's biting you jaspers?" he demanded.

Clay closed the door. "Turn that lamp low, Pete. And listen. Bill Waller is dead. Somebody stabbed him in the back."

Pete Flood's eyes stuck out, his jaw dropped. "Bill Waller . . . dead?"

"Yeah, Pete, and I want every gun, every cartridge you got in the store. Ben Cullop and Skeet Farnell are bringing a buckboard to the back door for the load. Come on, get busy."

"I got eight rifles and ten six-guns in stock," Pete said, trusting Clay's wisdom at once. "And about seven hundred rounds of ammunition for both kinds. Here, I'll break 'em out and you fellers lug 'em to the back door."

The transfer was soon made, and, when Clay opened the back door to listen, he heard the buckboard coming. "All set?" called Skeet Farnell softly.

"All set, Skeet," answered Clay. "Take this stuff out to the RO Up and Down. Turn it over to Jerry Hyatt. Tell him I'll be over in the morning to explain. Ben, you have all your riders up on their toes. Don't let a man leave the ranch without a rifle under his leg and a six-gun at his belt."

"What are you driving at, Clay?" Cullop asked.

"No time to tell you now, Ben. You'll get the whole story later. Only stow this under your belt. You, and every other decent rancher along the Buttonwillow, is going to be fighting for his life inside the next few days. All right, Skeet, roll."

The buckboard creaked away into the night.

Clay turned to Flood. "How much for all that stuff, Pete?"

"We'll let it ride for a time," Flood said. "We'll see if you put it to good use. If you do, then it won't cost you a cent. I don't know what this is all about, but if you're going skunk huntin' for the jasper who did for Bill Waller, I'm with you four ways from the ace. I'm goin' to get my old sawed-off Greener, load her up with buckshot, and get a bead on the sidewinder who killed Bill."

"You'll have to beat Buck and me to it," Clay said firmly. "In the meantime, keep your eye on Drew."

"Drew? Frisco Drew?"

"Right. And if you see anything going on here in town that strikes you queer, get word to me about it. And, Pete, will you and Jigger Dugan take care of Bill? Doc Peets will help you, I reckon."

"Yeah," Flood said soberly. "We'll take care of Bill. Good luck in your skunk huntin', boys."

Clay and Buck slipped around to the shadowed front of the Emporium. From there they had an open view of the door of the Humbug.

"Here we wait, Buck," said Clay.

Men drifted in and out of the Humbug, but not the two they sought. As the time dragged along until an hour had passed, Buck began to get restless, but Clay waited, motionless. It seemed to Buck that in this elder brother of his there burned a terrible and unquenchable purpose of stark retribution.

It was Buck who first saw Kirby and Ringo. They were on foot, coming from somewhere uptown. They were only dim shadows against the darker bulk of the buildings, but Buck recognized the truculent swagger of Kirby, the slouching shamble of Shell Ringo.

"There they are, Clay."

Instantly Clay was moving, silent and crouched. Buck, shaking with a cold excitement, followed. Kirby and Ringo stopped before the open door of the Humbug to make some remark to a rider who had just emerged. The rider laughed, made some reply, and moved on. Kirby and Ringo turned to enter.

"Ringo!" The harsh word rang along the street. "Ringo, I'm looking for you."

Ringo whirled, a hand darting to a gun.

"Who is it?" he blurted thickly. "What you want?"

"This is Clay Garrison. I want to see if Bill Waller's blood is still on that knife of yours."

Ringo's answer was proof of his guilt. He dragged his gun and began to shoot, shooting blindly, the act of a man with the ghost of cold-blooded murder riding him, the act of a man whose nerves were jangling and jumpy with the fear of retribution. The snarl of Ringo's gun was taken up by the roaring blasts of Clay Garrison's. Crimson flame lanced and stabbed through the darkness. Echoes rattled and clattered the length and breadth of Black Rock's single street.

Shell Ringo began to reel and jerk, as though buffeted by stormy winds. He spun wildly, tried to make for the shelter of the Humbug. But a terrific convulsion racked him and he fell limply, half in, half out of the door. As Ringo fell, Spike Kirby dived clear over him, to the safety beyond.

"All right, Buck," Clay said icily. "That's that. Now we're riding."

They stepped across the street, to their horses, swung into their saddles. Someone was shooting at them from the door of the Humbug. Clay turned in the saddle and dropped the fellow across the body of Ringo, then emptied his guns at the door and windows of the place.

Inside the Humbug men were yelling and cursing, but no other reckless one showed at the door until Clay and Buck had put Black Rock behind them and were spurring through the hot night beyond. Buck was aquiver with excitement and a strange exultation, but Clay rode grimly, stony cold. For Clay knew that, when he had downed Ringo, he had done two things. He had avenged Bill Waller, but he also had struck the first return blow in the rising war for the mastery of the Buttonwillow range.

Just after sunup the following morning, Clay led his outfit up to the RO Up and Down corrals. Every man of them was armed, every man grave and quiet. Clay had told them about Bill Waller, and how he had downed Shell Ringo. He had told them of what he thought was due to break on the Buttonwillow. Their response had been significant. They had quietly slung Winchesters to their saddles, and loaded their gun belts to the last loop.

Ben Cullop and his C Cross crew were already at the RO Up and Down. Cullop came out to meet him, along with Jerry Hyatt.

"On the way home, I got to thinking, Clay," said Cullop. "I figured that fighting alone we couldn't do much, but by combining our outfits, we can give out plenty of trouble. If you'll only let us all in on what you figure we got to lick."

"Fair enough, Ben. Call all the boys around. You, too, Jerry . . . get your crew out here."

Quickly the riders were all surrounding Clay, waiting silently.

"Maybe a lot of you boys got this figured out, same as me," he said as they gathered closely around. "But here is how I see it. Frisco Drew bought out Boley Stevens, Tinsley, and Bob Stinchfield. He tried to get Ben Cullop to sell, but didn't have any luck. He knew that Rock Orde and I never would. So Rock Orde is mysteriously shot and nearly killed. They try to bushwhack me. It adds up to Drew being out to grab all of Buttonwillow range. He knows the drought can't last forever, and, when the rains do come, the range will be rich, like it was before."

"How about Bill Waller being killed?" demanded one of the riders. "You figure Drew had a hand in that, Clay?"

"He was behind it. I'd gamble my life on that. Bill and I had more than one talk together. Bill was beginning to see through Drew's plan. Drew knew it, and he knew that Bill was the one man with the authority to make an arrest that would have spoiled his plan. And so Bill Waller was killed."

"And that's why I want to get a bead on Drew," growled a rider. "Any skunk that would use a knife on a man like Bill Waller . . ."

"Drew didn't actually use the knife, Chuck," said Clay. "Shell Ringo did, and Ringo is dead. Buck and I took care of him last night."

"What do you think Drew will do now, Clay?" asked Cullop.

"You saw all that crowd of strange, tough riders in the Humbug last night, Ben. Well, there's only one answer. Drew must have brought them in to fight. One thing is certain. Without the RO Up and Down, without the C Cross and the Sleeping G, Drew can never hope to control the Buttonwillow. The spreads he's bought up all lay around the edge of things. But these three big outfits are the heart of the range, and Drew must have them if he wants to make his play stick. I don't know where he'll hit, or exactly how. But my bet is that he'll hit somewhere."

"We'll give that whelp what for," Jerry Hyatt said.

"The time to start is now," said Clay. "Jerry, pick out four men and send 'em out to scout in all directions. Unless Drew is a bigger fool than I think, he'll know by this time that we're wise to him. He won't wait too long before he makes his next move, because the longer he waits, the stronger our hand will be. I've got a man in town watching, but we've got to have men scouting the range, all the time. Do that, Jerry."

"Right now, Clay. All for one, one for all."

Clay heard his name called in clear tones and he looked over to the ranch house to see Leigh Orde, standing on the porch. He stalked slowly over to her. She was plainly anxious, worried-looking.

"Clay," she exclaimed, "what does this mean? Why are you and Ben Cullop here with all your riders?"

"Remember what I was telling you about Frisco Drew yesterday, Leigh? Well, it looks like I was right. We all agree that he's out to gobble the Buttonwillow range. We're just getting ready for him."

"Then it means . . . fight?"

"It means fight." Clay nodded. Then he added harshly: "I should have gunned him yesterday, down at the ranch, when I had him face to face and dead to rights. If I had, it might have saved Bill Waller."

"Bill Waller? What about him?"

"You haven't heard?"

"I've heard nothing."

"Bill Waller was killed last night by Shell Ringo," Clay said somberly.

Leigh caught at a porch post, going dead white. "B-Bill Waller?" she whispered.

"Ringo killed him," Clay said with savagery in his tone. "Ringo's a knifer, and, another thing, he got panicky. I was able to even up some. I got Ringo. But Drew was behind it. I'm as certain of that as I am that he was behind the attempts to get your father and me.

We law-abiding folks have let a wolf run loose among us."

Clay saw tears well up in Leigh's clear, fine eyes.

"Dear old Bill," she choked. "He was so fair, so kind."

Clay put a hand on her shoulder. "It's tough, little pardner. Not since my father's death has anything hurt me as bad. But it's done, and we've got to make the best of it. But we won't forget."

Her head came up bravely. "We mustn't let Dad know yet," she said. "If he heard it, sick and weak as he is, Dad would climb right out of bed and buckle on his guns. He and Bill were such old friends. Oh, Clay, I'm so glad I didn't ride with that . . . that . . ."

"So am I. Remember always, Frisco Drew is a wolf. And here is something I want you to promise. Until this thing is settled, one way or another, I don't want you to ride a foot away from this ranch house unless one of the boys is along with you."

"I promise," she told him firmly.

CHAPTER
EIGHT

Slowly the hours wore away. Clay went over to the RO Up and Down bunkhouse, where the combined forces of the three big ranches, less the four men Jerry Hyatt had sent out as scouts, were gathered in grim silence.

Clay fell to wondering if he hadn't jumped the gun. Maybe Drew wouldn't show his hand for some time yet. And he might strike in a way totally unsuspected. However, cold analysis of the situation led to the inescapable conclusion that Drew would strike swiftly.

Trouble broke suddenly in a clatter of hoofs speeding down from the north. It was Turk Conroy, who had been out on scout. Turk came to a rearing halt, his mount foaming.

"Grab your guns and bronc's!" he yelled. "Trouble is a-rollin'. Looks like all of the T Bar and Circle S cows are moving down on us. And plenty of riders are drivin' 'em."

"Tinsley and Stinchfield cows!" exclaimed Clay. "It's Drew's first move, and a shrewd one. He owns those brands now and he's aiming to pour those herds down onto our range and water when we ain't got enough for our own stock. We got to stop 'em! Come on, boys, we ride!"

The concerted movement of the riders was almost like an explosion. They went into their saddles and pounded away into the north, Turk Conroy and Clay in the lead.

Within half a mile they sighted the rolling dust cloud of the approaching cattle. And within two miles more they sighted the herd. It came on slowly, spread in a wide front, for those cattle were weak and grudged the movement of the drive. Beyond, like phantoms in the dust, riders darted here and there, urging the cattle forward.

Clay, standing high in his stirrups, made a rough count of those distant riders. "About thirty of them," he told Jerry Hyatt. "We're outnumbered almost two to one. We'd be in a tight spot if these cattle were strong and well-fed. As it is, they can't stir that herd to a run. There ain't a chance for a stampede, so we don't need to worry much about holding the middle. We'll split up. You take half our boys and I'll take the other half, Jerry. You swing east. I'll go west. We'll get 'em between us. Open up as soon as you're in rifle range."

The ranchers and their men split up and swung apart at a driving gallop, and the wild bunch with the cattle threw men out on either flank for protection. But as soon as they did this, they found themselves with a white elephant on their hands. The cattle, weak and protesting of any movement at all, slowed to a stop as the pressure of the drive was taken off them. This nullified the best weapon the wild bunch had. For unless they could throw the cattle across the frugal range and water holes of the RO Up and Down and

Sleeping G acres, to overrun everything like a horde of locusts, the whole point of their attack would fail. The leader of the outlaw crowd drew his men back from the flanks to force the herd into movement once more.

The first rifles began to snarl and rap then. Hissing lead whined about the ears of Clay and his staunch little group. A slug told with a *thud* and a horse collapsed, throwing its rider headlong. The rider, jarred but unhurt, came up cursing, to begin levering shot after shot.

Clay did not halt in his ride until he was in a spot that directly flanked the men with the herd. Then he pulled up and jumped from the saddle.

"Down on the ground!" he yelled. "You can't do any good shooting from a running bronc'."

Boot heels bit into the earth all about him and rifles took up their wild song. And at this moment Jerry Hyatt and his men started in from the east side. They had the disconcerted wild bunch with the herd in a crossfire and the results were quick and deadly. Snarling lead raked the line of renegades from one end to the other. Men and horses began going down, scattering. Some leader among them, whose fury was greater than his judgment, rallied a small group and led them in a furious charge, right at Clay and his few valiants.

"Pick that *hombre* on the blaze-faced sorrel!" yelled Clay. "He's leading them."

The leader was riding high in his stirrups, exhorting his men on. He jerked this way and that as lead took him, and left his saddle in a whipping tangle of loose

72

arms and legs. The charge broke and scattered, every man for himself.

Of a sudden the entire group with the herd broke and rode for it, plainly without stomach for any more of the blazing wrath being poured in on them. Despite having lost several men, they still outnumbered the cattlemen heavily, but the set-up was such that those odds meant nothing at the moment.

"Hold it!" shouted Clay. "They've got enough for the time. Guess they didn't figure we'd be organized like this. Looks like they're pulling out completely."

This was true. The hired gunfighters gathered on a low rise, a good 1,000 yards away. For a time they grouped there, then in a dark, slow riding mass they vanished into the north and east.

Charley Curtis spat in huge contempt. "Headin' back for town to lap up booze and try and build up fresh nerve again."

A rider came swirling through the thick haze of dust — Jerry Hyatt, his bronzed face split in a cold grin.

"They got aplenty . . . quick," he said. "What next, Clay?"

"Make sure they've called it a day, then start these cattle back where they belong."

"Come on, Buck," said Charley Curtis. "You and me will ride a ways and check up."

It was on Clay's tongue to call the eager Buck back and send one of the other men. There might be an ambush out there, and Buck, his kid brother — Clay shrugged. Buck was one of them. He'd have to take his chances.

Clay's fears were groundless, however. Buck and Charley rode out past that distant rise, disappeared for a few moments, then came jogging back. Clay relaxed. "They've called it a day," he said. "We can start moving the cattle. Any of your crowd hurt, Jerry?"

"Stew Alton stopped one with his left arm and Jim Colyer lost his bronc'."

"Send Stew back to the ranch for attention. We'll catch up a riderless bronc' for Jim. Then for the cattle."

When Clay and the crowd rode back to the RO Up and Down, Leigh Orde came flying out to the corrals to meet them. Her eyes flashed from face to face as though she were counting noses, and she seemed to relax when she saw that all were there.

Clay's heart warmed within him. This girl had fought, also, fought in the terrible, slow stillness of being alone and not knowing whether faithful men were out dying or living as they fought for her, as well as for themselves. And she had had to wait until they returned to learn that there were, as yet, no deaths of friends to haunt her memory.

"We were plenty lucky, Leigh," Clay told her gently. "Stew Alton was the only one hurt. How is he?"

"Doing all right," she answered a little tremulously. "I bandaged his arm." She turned back to the house.

Jerry Hyatt came up to Clay. "Where do we go from here, cowboy?"

"Who knows, Jerry? I don't think we have much to worry about for a day or two. But we can't take any chances. I think Ben Cullop and I should send a couple of men out to our spreads to keep guard. Drew may

74

take it into his head to have a few matches dropped where they could do the most good."

"I'll tend to that right away."

"Fine. And maybe tonight you and I will drift in to look over the town on the sly and see what we can pick up."

Just at dusk Dr. Peets drove up in his buckboard.

"What happened out here today?" he asked. "I spent a couple of hours in town this afternoon patching up half a dozen gents with bullet holes in them."

Clay explained briefly. "Glad you came out, Doc," he said then. "Stew Alton is in the bunkhouse with a smashed arm."

"I figured I might be needed," said Dr. Peets. "Pete Flood, Jigger Dugan, a couple of other boys around town and I . . . we buried Bill this morning. And Frisco Drew was there, with his hat off, looking mighty grieved."

"The dirty, crooked hypocrite!" exploded Clay. "Doc, that whelp killed old Bill just as sure as though he had stuck that knife into him himself."

"Of course." Dr. Peets nodded. "Pete and Jigger and me all agreed on that. But we kept our mouths shut. Right now Frisco Dan Drew is high dog in Black Rock. The town is swarming with his gun bullies."

"Drew is open game to the first one of our boys who can get a bead on him," snapped Clay.

"Soon as I get through with Alton and have a look at Rock Orde, I'm going over that head of yours again," the doctor said. "You're looking plenty peaked and haggard. You're not made of steel, you know."

Clay went over to the bunkhouse and stretched out on a bunk. He did feel a little rocky now that the excitement had died out. Dr. Peets worked over Stew Alton and gave the wounded cowpuncher a hypodermic to put him to sleep. From this job Dr. Peets went up to the main house to see how Rock Orde was making it.

When he returned a half hour later, Leigh Orde was with him. While the doctor stripped the grimed, dusty bandage from Clay's head, Leigh stood beside the bunk and smiled down at him. It seemed to Clay that the combination of shadows and yellow lamplight filled her eyes with a certain vague mystery, the natural pity of a woman for a wounded man.

She helped the doctor put a fresh bandage in place. Here and there her fingers would fall, deft and gentle and cool.

"Hurt you, Clay?" asked Dr. Peets, as Clay's lips twisted and tightened.

"No, not a bit, Doc. I was just thinking."

After that, it seemed that Leigh's touch trembled, ever so slightly.

Clay went to supper with the boys. The men Jerry Hyatt had sent to the Sleeping G and the C Cross returned to report everything quiet. Walking back to the bunkhouse, Ben Cullop dropped in beside Clay.

"Reckon me and the boys can pull out for home for the night," said Cullop. "I'll leave one man here, Clay, to act as messenger if we're needed in a hurry."

Clay nodded. "I don't think a thing will break tonight."

It was while the C Cross outfit was saddling up that Pete Flood came jogging in from the night. Clay knew a quick alarm.

"Anything wrong in town, Pete?"

"Nothing, except that it's overrun with a flock of cussed coyotes," answered the old storekeeper tartly. "They're plenty warm under the collar, Clay. You shore hurt their feelin's today. They'd be out here after you in the dark, except for one thing. They're short of ammunition."

"What?"

"Exactly. Drew was in to see me late this afternoon. Said he wanted all the cartridges in the place. And when I told him you'd beat him to 'em, he was so mad he foamed. He made me write out a big order and he sent a couple of men with a buckboard hellity-pickety for Maverick after that order. Which means he's plenty low on shootin' lead. Does that suggest anything to you?"

"You old fox, what are you driving at?"

Pete Flood grinned bleakly into the darkness. "That crowd's lappin' up booze like prairie dogs, and they're short on shells. It just struck me that maybe was you to hit them, instead of waiting until they're stout and full of fight again, you might bust Drew wide open. Tonight would be a fine time."

For a moment Clay stood still. Then he whirled and yelled: "Ben Cullop, Jerry Hyatt . . . all you boys, gather 'round!"

Clay shared the import of Pete Flood's news and suggestion that they strike while the iron was hot with the listening group. Growls of enthusiasm answered him.

"A couple of hours after midnight will be just about right," said Charley Curtis. "A man who's been hittin' the bottle all night ain't much good about then. And that crowd seems to like their snake juice."

"It's settled, then," said Clay. "We go for them. Pete, we won't forget you for bringing us this word."

"Aw, shucks!" grunted Pete. "That's all right. Me and Jigger Dugan aim to pull a trigger or two ourselves tonight. We're both rememberin' Bill Waller."

"And we're not exactly forgetting him," Clay said grimly.

CHAPTER
NINE

It was near eleven o'clock before Clay and his men were ready to ride. Pete Flood had already returned to town.

Just before leaving, Clay had talked to Leigh Orde, telling her what they intended doing.

"I think we can win," he told her soberly. "If I didn't, I wouldn't lead the boys to town. But just in case I'm wrong, I want you to be on the watch tonight, little pardner. You stay inside. Lock all the doors. Don't let anybody in the house unless you recognize the voice."

Leigh quietly promised to do as he advised. As he turned to go, she made an impulsive little gesture that, in the dark, he could not see. Her hands fluttered out toward him, then were withdrawn, twisting nervously. She called after him, in a voice that trembled just the slightest: "Be careful, Clay, please!"

Clay and his men took a roundabout route to town. They came up on the far western edge of Black Rock and stopped a quarter of a mile from town. Clay dismounted and waited for the men to gather around him.

"You and me," he told Jerry Hyatt, "we'll go in and look things over. The rest of you boys wait here. And keep quiet."

Clay and Jerry went forward on foot. They came up in the black shadow of a building and paused there a moment. The night air was queerly thick, hot, and stifling, and there was an electric feeling to it that prickled the skin, laid heat along the spine, and set a man on edge. They moved out until they could look along the street. Most of the town was dark and silent. The Humbug Saloon, however, was lighted up, and hoarse bursts of laughter, drunken curses, and the quavering notes of a song sounded from it.

Clay and Jerry went on down the street, clinging to shadows. They passed the Humbug on the far side of the street. They passed Bill Waller's office, now dark and still. Clay knew a quick tightening in his throat, and the stark purpose of the night rose stronger and stronger in him.

At the lower end of the street they dodged across, to come to a halt by the yawning door of the livery barn. A low voice, thick with the brogue of old Ireland, came to them.

"Over here, ye terriers."

They found Jigger Dugan and Pete Flood there.

"We been checking up, Jigger and me," explained Pete Flood hurriedly. "They ain't scattered none. They're all of them at the Humbug, and most of 'em pretty drunk. You couldn't ask a better time, Clay."

"The town folks laying low?" asked Clay.

"You'd be surprised," answered Pete. "You're going to have plenty of help when things break, Clay. The decent folks here in town sort of tolerated Frisco Drew before, but they're plumb off him now, and that bunch of whelps he's gathered around him. Dave Granger's wife was talked to pretty insultin' by one of that wild bunch this evenin'. It was all Jigger and me could do to keep Dave from gettin' out his big buffalo Sharps and goin' huntin'. You'll hear that big cannon roar tonight. Right now Dave is layin' out on top of the old Sunset House, ready to go."

"Folks in this town thought plenty of Bill Waller," said Jigger. The little Irishman wriggled nervously. "What's it in the air tonight?" he complained. "I'm after being jumpy as a cat. Never did I feel so queer. Look, all the stars are gone."

"We're all on edge, Jigger," said Clay. "Well, we might as well open the ball. We'll hit 'em from two sides, up the street and down, with a couple of boys out back. Pete, this isn't any of yours or Jigger's chore, so you better lay low."

"That's what you think, me bhoy," retorted doughty little Jigger. "Don't you worry none about Pete and me. We got an idea or two, we have."

Clay and Jerry Hyatt moved off into the gloom. Jigger and Pete scuttled off, also, two wrinkled gnomes of the night. They went into the back door of the Emporium, soon to reappear, lugging something between them with special care. Up the back way they trudged until they came to the alley that ran between the Humbug and the White Front Eating House.

"This," muttered Flood, "is going to raise hell, Jigger."

"Hope it puts a rock under it," growled Jigger. "Always I'm thinking of Bill Waller, and that settles it."

"We might burn the whole cussed town down," said Flood.

"Let her burn," snapped the implacable Jigger. "We're going to run a flock of coyotes out into the open. Here, gimme that stuff. I'll lay it."

Pete Flood shook his grizzled head. "We're both in on this. Come on."

They ducked into the blackness of the alley while, in the Humbug, the revelry was still going at full blast. Of all that motley, tough crowd, only Frisco Dan Drew seemed not to be enjoying himself. He stood at the far end of the bar, his black eyes cold, his face a dark mask over his thoughts.

In a lull, the bartender, Dumpy Kling, sweating and fatigued, sidled up to Drew.

"The thirstiest bunch I ever see, boss," he mumbled. "This keeps up much longer and we're going to run low on likker. They lap it up like it was rainwater."

Drew's eyes flashed contempt. "Slop for the swine," he growled thinly. "Let 'em have it, Dumpy. A lot of them will be dead before this range is mine. Keep 'em drunk and happy until it's time for the big clean up. Poor tools to work with, but a coyote is a coyote, Dumpy, whether you buy it or hire it. Yeah, let 'em have all they want. It will burn up their consciences, if any of them own to such a thing. And I'm going to need men without consciences or hearts."

Dumpy gulped and moved away. Whenever he got a glimpse of the savagery that had been consuming Drew lately, it scared him.

The renegades clamored at the bar. Raw whiskey flowed, as Dumpy had said, like rainwater. The air of the place was hot, depressing, fetid. Tobacco smoke lay along the low ceiling like fog, blue and drifting, and through it the hanging lamps shone dully, like drunken eyes.

A man darted in at the door. It was Spike Kirby. He stopped beside Drew.

"Garrison and his crowd are in town, Frisco!" he panted. "They're surroundin' this place. I recognized two or three of 'em!"

For a moment Drew stood stone still. Then he cursed savagely.

"And all my fighters as drunk as dogs. I might have guessed something . . ."

Whatever Frisco Drew intended to say was lost in the flat rumble of a shot. One of the lamps dissolved in a clatter of shattered glass and a spray of oil. Before any man could think or move, that gun outside the door rumbled twice more and the other two lamps went to pieces.

For the moment the room was a black, stagnant pool of amazement and fear. Then came the roar of cursing, yelling voices, and the pound and trample of boots as the drunken crowd went berserk with stupefied fear.

Thin and harsh as steel, Frisco Drew's voice cut through the clamor. "Stay inside, you fools! They're laying for us outside. They'll shoot us to pieces."

Some of the more sober renegades heard, and began fighting the others away from the door. They managed to bring about a momentary quiet. As they did, from out of the blackness of the street, the voice of Clay Garrison rang, harsh with purpose.

"You got one chance to surrender, Drew. Take it . . . or the consequences!"

The iron self-control of Frisco Drew broke. Always he had hated Clay Garrison, hated him because he knew in his heart that Clay Garrison was such a man as he could never hope to be himself, hated him because he knew that Clay Garrison's had been the mind behind his initial defeat in the conquest to make an empire for himself along the Buttonwillow, hated him because he knew that such a man as Clay Garrison might win the affection of a girl like Leigh Orde, while he never could. And, lastly, he hated Clay Garrison because he knew that Clay had not been fooled, not from the first, and that again he had outguessed him, trapped him.

All the vicious nature in Drew surged up and overflowed. "Come and get us, if you think you can!" he yelled. "Before you do, you'll know what perdition is like! Come and get —"

The whole town shook before the roaring shock. A back corner of the Humbug seemed to lift and dissolve, while through the place where the walls had been drove a sheet of white, searing light. Soul-shattering concussion knocked men down as though they were matches. A giant, invisible hand lifted Frisco Drew clear off the floor and hurled him against an inner wall with crushing force. He sagged down, dazed and stupid with shock.

Men screamed like animals. Then they fought each other madly to get away from the tongues of flame beginning to creep through the wreckage.

Someone fell across Drew, cursing savagely. Drew recognized the voice of Spike Kirby. He caught at Kirby and clung to him.

"Spike," he gasped thickly, "this is Drew. Help me out! The back way. We got something to do."

Kirby dragged Drew to his feet, pulled him along with one hand, while smashing with a clubbed gun with the other to clear a way through the frantic tangle. Somehow they located the rear door, stumbled through to the outer air.

Out in front of the Humbug, guns were snarling. A gun flashed not far from Kirby and a slug bit into the shattered wall behind him. Kirby shot back instinctively.

"Come on!" he snarled at Drew. "Run for it!"

Drew stumbled along behind Kirby, mechanically keeping his feet. His brain was still numbed from the shock, and, as he drew each gasping breath, knife-like pains shot through his chest.

As they passed that point of pale light thrown by the rising flames of the shattered corner, a voice cried out in startled amazement.

"Kirby! Drew!"

That was all staunch little Jigger Dugan had time to say before Spike Kirby's gun crashed down on his head. Jigger wilted to the dark earth.

But the explosion of the dynamite that Jigger and Pete Flood had set off at the rear corner of the Humbug won the fight for the cattlemen almost before it started. Bewildered, terror-stricken renegades who charged out into the street like stampeded cattle had little fight left in them. A few threw guns wildly, but cold-eyed men in the shadows, fighting for their own range, cut them down mercilessly.

Soon there was no more resistance. The cattlemen, under Clay Garrison's orders, disarmed the survivors and herded them off up the street.

Flames were roaring and leaping in the Humbug now. The place was doomed and Clay's fear was that the rest of the town might go with it.

"Jerry Hyatt!" he yelled. "You and Ben Cullop and a couple of others take care of those prisoners. Buck, get the rest of the boys and fight that fire. It's liable to take the whole town!"

"Coming up, Clay!" yelled Buck. "We'll —"

The world shuddered again before another terrific rumble and roar, and another sheet of white light dissolved the night. But this was dynamite of another making. This explosion was the hoarse, crashing bellow of thunder, and that greenish white light was the awful lance of lightning. Hardly had the lightning gone and while the thunder echoes were still booming, the rain came down in a sheet. Rain, torrents of it, a battering sheet of water that washed away the stifling heat, cooling and flooding a parched and thirsty earth.

Clay Garrison stood rooted in his tracks. He lifted his face to the cool, lashing joyousness of that blessed rain. What matter that the thunder boomed anew and that the pallid ghost of lightning galloped here and yon across the heavens. Rain! It was raining! The touch of it and the breath of it cooled his blood, sweetened his throat, filled him with a new, exultant energy and hope.

Someone had him by the arm, shaking him. It was Buck, yelling joyously: "The drought's broken! Come on, you rain! Don't ever stop. And, Clay, it's putting out that fire!"

Clay came back to earth. He knew now what that strange sense of restless edginess had been this night. It had been the effect on human nerves of a world full of electricity that had waited overlong to be dissolved. And with that electricity, that gathering storm which had shut out the stars, had come this blessed rain.

Clay shook his head, looked once more at the ruins of the Humbug. Buck was right. Already the flames were dying, flickering down under the roaring deluge from the sky. And someone was calling him, thinly, faintly — the voice of Jigger Dugan.

Clay found the little Irishman, tottering queerly. He caught Jigger by the arm, steadied him.

"Where you hit, Jigger?"

"I'm not shot," gasped Jigger. "It was Kirby . . . he gun-whipped me. And Drew was with him. They got out the back way and I bumped into 'em. Clay, lad, you'll be ridin' fast. How do I know where those two devils are goin'? I can't tell you, Clay, yet I'm knowin'. 'Tis the Irish of me, Clay. The RO Up and Down where that sweet lass will be, with only her wounded father . . . that is where they'll be heading. Drew, that divil

87

was crazed after that lass. With me own eyes I've seen him watch her, and I know. You'll be ridin' out there, Clay, ridin' fast. You'll be . . ."

Jigger went out again, sagging limply. Clay lowered him to the soaking earth, yelling sharply for help. Clay did not know that it was Skeet Farnell who came running. He only knew what Jigger had told him, and somehow he knew that Jigger was right.

"Take care of him," he growled to Skeet. "I've got riding to do."

He raced away into the swirling night. He found a horse and was away at a lashing gallop.

CHAPTER
TEN

All through the rest of his life Clay knew he would remember this ride. There was something almost of destiny in it. If he won, he would win all, or nearly all. And if he lost, then, indeed, would he lose everything. The threat of Frisco Drew's dream of empire was shattered, just as the Humbug had been shattered by that charge of dynamite that Jigger and Pete Flood had set off, just as the drought had been shattered by that first roar of thunder.

When this rain ceased, the range that had been dead and burned and scorched would live again. Green grass would ripple and bend before the push of the four winds. The Buttonwillow would flow once more. Cattle would thrive and grow fat. The bounty of the earth and sky would enrich the lives of men. Yet all this would go for nothing if Drew and Kirby reached the RO Up and Down before Clay did.

Strange, Clay thought, that he did not question this premonition of Jigger Dugan's. Jigger was a queer, deep little cuss, with much of the mysticism of his race about him. Yes, Jigger knew, all right.

It was black dark, out there on the range. There were no stars, nothing to guide him, yet Clay sent his mount instinctively on a dead line for the RO Up and Down. The tocsin of the thunder had moved south and east, grumbling in the distance like some discontented giant. But the drive of the rain had a settled permanence about it. It would last for a couple of days, at least.

Clay pushed his craggy face against the lash of the storm. He was drenched, soaked to the skin, but his lean, rock-hard body felt cooled and refreshed and strong. Underfoot the earth was already soggy. The churning hoofs of the horse never varied from a driving tempo. The rain, so magic was its touch on man and beast, that it made the bronco strong and wild to run.

Clay's thoughts reached ahead. In his mind's eye he could see Leigh Orde. She would be out on the porch, drinking in the sweet breath of the storm. The wet wind would be whipping tendrils of hair about her soft cheeks, and those cheeks would be dewy with rain mist.

Clay fought back the wistful longing of his thoughts. It would be Leigh and Buck, which was all right. After all, they would both belong to him. There were more ways to show your love for a girl than by the privilege of taking her in your arms. You could work for her and plan for her future and guard her against the buffets of the world. And Buck was his kid brother. You couldn't regret the good fortune and happiness of your kid brother. Yes, Leigh and Buck would be happy, and in their happiness he would find some reward for his own loneliness. If he got there in time!

Clay's mood changed. Some of the old, hard savagery came back to him. He had to get there in time! Automatically he roweled his hard running mount and the horse plunged down a steep slope and Clay found wind-whipped alders and willow clumps all about him. It was the Buttonwillow. Already the river was running. Then the horse was into the rising flood, plunging belly deep, foaming along in short, heavy lunges.

Out and up the other side, with the warm, wet steam from the animal heavy and pungent in Clay's nostrils. A lashing, tearing gallop once more, rider leaning forward in the saddle, lifting the animal on. Leigh Orde was out there ahead — alone — caring for her crippled father. And somewhere in this drenched black world two human wolves were racing to hurt and maim and render all victory hollow and heartbreaking. Abruptly through the blackness winked a pinpoint of yellow light. The Orde ranch house.

All along Clay had heard nothing but the voice of the storm. The plunge and pound of hoofs on sopping earth would be muffled by the whipping wind. If he heard nothing of any other riders, it was fair to believe that they had heard nothing of him. His eyes, adjusted to the murk, strained to see ahead.

He passed the dim bulk of barns, feed sheds, corrals. The flare of light grew stronger, took rectangular shape, the shape of an open door. And there, silhouetted against the light, stood a slim figure, seeming to lean forward, as though to embrace the sweet magic of the rain.

It was Leigh, just as he had known she would be, tasting this blessed moisture that meant life to the range. And Clay, as he swung his mount to a halt, saw her suddenly give back, as a queerly humped figure took shape from the storm and lunged up the steps.

It seemed to Clay he could hear her cry of alarm as that humped figure caught at her, held her. Clay struck the earth running, his eyes fixed on those two struggling figures limned against the light of the open door. He drew both guns, pushed them forward in tense fists.

Then, close to him, loomed the bulk of two horses. A man snarled a startled curse. The blasting rumble of a gun sounded. A mighty blow struck Clay across the ribs, numbing him, sending his senses reeling. He almost went down. But he hadn't made this wild ride out here to go down before any man. He drove two shots in return, slamming them at that finger of crimson flame that had lanced at him. He did not know that Spike Kirby died suddenly and abruptly, with one bullet through his body and another just above the bridge of his nose.

Clay fought off the deathly weakness that dragged at him. The job was only half done. He lurched on toward the steps, a strange hoarse sound blurting from his straining lips. The numbness of that first blow in his ribs was gone, but a terrible white fire burned there, a fire that seemed to be slowly consuming him.

Strong as Leigh Orde was in her wiry slenderness, she would ordinarily have been no match in strength for this queerly hunched, snarling animal of a man who was Frisco Drew. But Drew was maimed from the injuries he had suffered in the explosion that had wrecked the Humbug. When he had been smashed against the wall, ribs had been caved in, muscles wrenched and torn. Only his feral hate, the madness of every evil passion in him that had been loosed, had enabled him to ride as far as the Orde ranch. And now he found a blazing-eyed fury in this girl he meant to take with him as he rode away.

The coughing bellow of those three shots, just below the porch, broke through the veil of madness that consumed Frisco Drew. Warning jerked at his twisted brain. As he swung his head to look, the struggling girl tore an arm free and one clenched fist pounded against the side of Drew's head. The blow caught him off balance, sent him staggering half down the steps.

Less than four strides away, Clay Garrison set his guns to snarling once more. Strange, he thought, how cut in half he felt. His mind, his head were icily clear. Yet his body seemed queerly useless. Only the indomitable, starkly savage purpose in his brain made his hands work with utter certainty.

Clay laced that wavering figure of Frisco Dan Drew with unerring lead, blasting the man through and through. Drew weaved from side to side, then fell backward, huddling, limp and dead, at the foot of the steps.

Clay dropped his guns. In slow, dragging, uncertain strides he moved to the foot of the steps and slowly up them. He moved half across the porch, where the lamplight from the open door fell full upon him. A stark figure he made, his soaked clothes molded to his powerful shoulders and chest. Slowly a smile touched his lips.

"Leigh," he said. "Little pardner. It . . . it's all right now. We win . . . all ways. Everything is all . . . right!"

And he went down, down, down, into a pit of roaring blackness . . .

Clay Garrison came back to the world of the living after a long, long journey through pits of everlasting blackness. For days on end he had hovered in those depths while the flame of life burned so low that several times Dr. Peets believed it had gone out altogether. The doctor would have given up Clay more than once if it had not been for the tragic-eyed girl who worked beside him. For each time he despaired, he would look at her, read what was in her eyes, then return to the battle, fighting back at the leering specter of death with every trick of science at his command.

Yet when the turn finally came, when that faint, flickering pulse grew slowly stronger and stronger, Dr. Peets knew it was not his ointments or his medicines that had won the fight. It was the unconsciously indomitable will of this wounded man to live, that and the faith of this girl beside him.

Came a day when Dr. Peets, worn and haggard and unshaven and near collapse himself, staggered out onto the porch, where a group of silent men had waited and waited. Buck Garrison, his young face turned old and lined with worry, looked up.

Dr. Peets nodded. "He's going to live," he croaked. "The man's iron. Iron, I tell you. He's made a liar out of medical science. He's going to live, when by every rule in the book he should have been dead days ago.

And now I got to sleep. I'm dead on my feet. Some of you had better see that great little girl gets some rest, too. She's been magnificent. It's been something between her and Clay that's pulled Clay through, something stronger than death itself. Something that makes me feel small and useless and old. I've had the feeling all along that, if he had died, she would have died, too. Gawd! I'm tired."

Men led the valiant little doctor away, undressed him, and put him to bed, where he was asleep before they could cover him with blankets.

Buck Garrison and Jerry Hyatt tiptoed into the sick room. Clay lay there, a wasted shadow of his old self, but alive and with just the faintest tinge of precious color showing in his haggard cheeks. He was asleep. And in a chair beside him, Leigh Orde was also asleep.

As gently as he would have picked up a sleeping infant, Buck Garrison gathered her into his arms and he and Jerry Hyatt carried her into her own room and tucked her into bed. The eyes of both were wet as they left the house.

For twenty-four hours both Leigh and Clay slept. And now soft, mellow sunshine lay over the Buttonwillow range. Under its touch, green grass would soon be growing.

The rain had gone, but it had brought the life the range needed. Down under the nodding willows and alders, Buttonwillow River ran bank full with sparkling, sweet water. And no longer did the mournful, tragic complaint of cattle sound through every hour of the day and night.

It was not long before Clay Garrison was sitting up in bed. An open window was at his side and through it came the warm benediction of the sun.

Clay looked up as Leigh Orde came into the room. Buck followed her. And the younger brother grinned widely.

"Looking plenty chipper, you old wart hog. Feeling pretty fine, eh?"

Clay smiled and nodded. "Be glad to get out of this cussed bed. Never was so sick and tired of anything before in my life. Doc says I can sit on the porch next week. And maybe, by the end of the month, I'll be able to sit a saddle again. How's things out on the range, kid?"

"Never better. Cattle fattening up in great shape. Here, give me your paw."

Buck took Clay's hand, caught one of Leigh's, and pressed them together.

"There." He chuckled. "Knew I'd have to do that to make you two idiots understand. Bless you, my children."

Clay stared. "Huh! Why . . . what . . . what . . . ? Say, listen . . ."

"You, listen!" Buck laughed softly. "You big-hearted old goat. You had it all planned out for Leigh and me, didn't you? And you never stopped to ask either of us. Time was when Leigh and me thought we were in love. But we found out different. Sure I love her, always will. She's the sweetest little sister any man could want. And she told me a while back that, if I behaved myself, not cuss too much, worked hard, and minded my manners,

96

she'd consider me as a brother. Which set-up suits both her and me fine. Now, seeing that I ain't needed around here any longer, I'll slope. There's calves to be branded and all kinds of work to be done by an ambitious gent like me."

Buck slipped out of the door and closed it softly. Leigh stood looking down at Clay. Those gray eyes of hers were soft, tender.

Clay cleared his throat. "I had it figured the other way 'round, Leigh," he said. "I thought it was Buck."

"So did I for a time," she admitted, with all her honesty and directness. "But I found out different, as Buck told you. When I heard how close you had come to being killed that night when they tried to dry-gulch you, then I knew, Clay. I knew then that it had always been you. And right now I'm cold with terror that you may not think of me as I do of you."

Her voice grew softer and softer, then sank away entirely while she stood, one hand pressed to her throat, her eyes like misty stars.

Clay laughed joyously. "Look at me and find your answer, sweetheart."

Looking, Leigh knew, beyond all doubt. She gave a little sob and dropped down beside him, her hands framing his gaunt, craggy face. Her head dropped lower until her lips, soft and warm and fragrant as the sunlight, came to rest on his.

Hell for Sale

by Tom W. Blackburn

Tom W. Blackburn was born on the T.O. Ranch near Raton, New Mexico, where his father was employed as an engineer. The T.O., which controlled such a vast domain it had its own internal railroad system, was later used as the setting for Blackburn's novel, *Raton Pass* (Doubleday, 1950). Blackburn eventually moved with his family to southern California where he attended Glendale Junior College and then U.C.L.A. In 1937 he married Juanita Alsdorf and, surely, she was the model for many of his notable heroines. Blackburn got his start "ghosting" stories for Ed Earl Repp and Harry F. Olmsted, prolific contributors to Western pulp magazines but mostly of fiction they did not produce themselves. For example, one of the last stories Blackburn submitted to Harry F. Olmsted was sold to editor Jack Burr at Street & Smith's *Western Story Magazine* for $425.00. It was showcased as the featured novel under the title "Guns of the Buckskin Empire" by Harry F. Olmsted in *Western Story Magazine* (3/2/40). Olmsted paid Tom 3/10¢ a word; Tom's share came to $75.00.

Among his finest short novels are several that first appeared in *Lariat Story Magazine*: "Mistress of Night Riders' Rancho" (9/43), "Bullets Sang in Siesta" (11/44), "Trigger Boss of Wild Horse Creek" (5/45), and "Town of Whispering Guns" (9/49). Also among them is "Renegade Lady of the Blazing Buckhorn" (1/44), which appears here for the first time in book form with the author's title and text restored. This was Blackburn's 141st story and was sold to Fiction House for *Lariat Story Magazine* on June 21, 1943. The author was paid 1¼¢ a word.

Blackburn's first book-length novel, and one of his best, *Short Grass* (Simon and Schuster, 1948), was an expansion of a short novel he had submitted to Fiction House titled "Man from the Short-Grass". The title was changed to "The Gun-Prophet of El Dorado" when it appeared in *Action Stories* (2/43). Blackburn later adapted this novel as a screenplay and it was filmed as *Short Grass* (Allied Artists, 1951). He was readily able to do this because, beginning in the 1940s, he worked as a screenwriter for various Hollywood studios. Blackburn's longest affiliation was with the Disney studio where, for a time, he became well known for having written the lyrics for "The Ballad of Davy Crockett", a popular television and then theatrical series based on the exploits of this legendary frontiersman.

In his Western novels, Blackburn tended toward stories based on historical episodes such as *Navajo Canyon* (Doubleday, 1952) or *A Good Day to Die* (McKay, 1967). Perhaps his finest achievement as a novelist is the five-part Stanton saga focused on the building of a great ranch in New Mexico from the Spanish period to the end of the 19th century. Tom W. Blackburn's Western fiction is concerned with the struggles, torments, joys, and the rare warmth that comes from companionships of the soul, the very stuff that is as imperishable in its human significance as the "sun-dark skins of the clean blood of the land" that he celebrated and transfixed in shimmering images and unforgettable characters.

CHAPTER
ONE

There were times when Russ Cameron had his belly full of his job. This was one of those times. Evening shadows were settling down on Taprock. The town was mellowing with the fading light. At the bar across the room from his table, men were gathering in friendly groups talking of today and planning for tomorrow. The pattern of their lives was secure, anchored to this valley and the country around it. They had their land or their place on another's and they were satisfied with it.

Russ thought of his own day. He had hit town last night on the stage. This morning he had risen early and ridden up the valley on a rough-gaited livery horse. He had jolted all day, riding the boundaries, checking the water, and roughly tallying the herds on Bert Orr's Harpoon. Hitting town at sunset, he'd gone into the telegraph office and handed the girl operator a message to John Shane in Chicago:

Harpoon as represented worth 20,000. Will buy tomorrow subject your approval and draft. Cameron.

By the time he had finished dinner, Shane's answer was back. Not as terse as usual:

Must have Harpoon. Buyer already available. If Orr stubborn, go 2,500 higher. Don't miss this one. Extra commission for you. Shane.

Chewing his cigar and shaking the saddle cramp out of his leg muscles by walking up one street and down the other, Russ had thought about that answer. Shane was the biggest broker of grass-grown real estate in the country. In three years of working for the man, Russ had never seen a trace of generosity toward any seller, buyer, or his agent. It was puzzling. And he wondered where Shane had uncovered a buyer so quickly. Usually Shane held a property Russ picked up for months before he could dispose of it at the rate of profit he wanted. Maybe it was a piece of luck and Shane was just passing it around.

He caught the bartender's eye and raised his empty glass. The man crossed the room a few moments later, carrying a bottle for a refill. Russ nodded toward a tall, powerfully built man with tawny hair in the middle of a weathered-looking bunch of riders about in the center of the bar.

"Who's that?"

The bartender's face twisted wryly. "That, my friend," he said softly, "is Ed Jarrett, the curly wolf of Taprock. I hear he was kicked off the Chain again today by Miss Rae Orr and it looks like he's drinking himself up to a good howl over it. Stay clear, stranger, and you will stay happy."

The barkeep's tones held no affection for the man about whom he spoke, but they were not without a grudging admiration, too. Russ nodded his thanks and watched the big man. He placed him, now. Out on the south boundary of the Harpoon today, Bert Orr had pointed over broken ground toward a house against the hill in the distance.

"That's the Buckhorn," Orr had told him. "And run by the crawlingest snake in the state! If you're doubtful the Harpoon's worth twenty thousand, ask Ed Jarrett what he thinks it's worth. He's offered me thirty, twice. But I'd see him in hell afore I'd sell him Orr land!"

It was a kind of a funny set-up. In between riding and appraising, Russ had picked up quite a few of the loose ends of it. Young Orr's old man had been bucking this Jarrett pretty steadily for about ten years — part of the time worried about his holdings and part of the time about his daughter. Jarrett apparently wanted both of them. When old Orr died, he split his big ranch squarely in two. The half nearest to the Buckhorn he gave to his son. The other half, with a brand of its own, he gave to the girl. The old man's idea appeared to be that Bert would be sort of a buffer between his sister and Jarrett. But Bert couldn't hold up his end. Jarrett was either a tough customer or Bert had a terrible string of bad luck. At any rate, he was selling the Harpoon, putting a stranger in as a buffer between Jarrett and his sister's Chain. With the cash from the

Harpoon, Bert apparently figured on going over to his sister's spread and trenching in for a finish fight.

Russ uncovered a lot of strange things in his traveling for John Shane. There never was a ranch put up on the market that there wasn't some reason back of its owner's desire to sell. Hearing hundreds of these in a few years, a man got a little callous. Russ finished his drink. Still, this time he felt a little sympathy for Bert Orr. The kid wasn't a heavyweight. But he was a fighter. And this Jarrett lad had a very nasty look.

As Russ came to his feet, the man with the tawny hair turned for the first time toward his table and saw him. The man's eyes ran coolly over him, crown to toe. His lips twisted a little, and he tipped his head toward a rider beside him. He said something. The rider knifed a quick look at Russ, and nodded. The twist on Jarrett's lips became a reckless grin. He pushed out from the bar and walked up a dozen paces to where a man with gray mustaches was sucking noisily at a tankard of beer. Jarrett gently touched this man on the arm.

He set the tankard down, turned, and looked coolly up at Jarrett. Russ recognized him as a hand who had been in the compound of the Harpoon when he'd ridden in for an inspection of the buildings with young Bert Orr.

"Seame, you finished with that?" Jarrett asked.

The old man obliqued a glance at the tankard and shook his head. "No, Ed, I ain't," he said flatly.

Jarrett put a huge hand against his shoulder and pushed with it. "Then take it outside till you are," he counseled wickedly. "I don't like your racket."

106

The expression on the old man's face didn't change.

"I allus do my drinking at a bar," he said quietly. "I'm too damned old to fight and too damned stubborn to scare. What you don't like don't interest me none, Ed."

Jarrett's face fined down. He took another step forward and one of his big boots came down with cruel savagery on the little man's foot. It happened quickly. The little man's shoulder swung through a small, swift arc. His right arm stabbed forward and the bony knuckles of his balled hand plunged smartly into the bulge of Jarrett's shirt above the line of his belt.

It was the quick, instinctive blow of a hurt man. Jarrett grunted, stepped back a little, and swung his own hand like an axe. It hit the little man fully in the face. The little man's feet skidded apart. He sprawled widely through the sawdust of the floor and lay, motionless, the muscles of his thighs quivering with shock for a moment. Then he slowly raised the ruin of his face from the floor. Jarrett backed against the bar and laughed at him.

"Keep your hands to yourself, Seame!" he snapped. "And a tighter halter on your talk. Your boss ain't sold the Harpoon yet. Before he does, he's got to find a gent wide enough across the breeches to outbid me. And he ain't!"

The old man on the floor swung his battered face around toward Russ. Jarrett, also, was watching him. Russ knew the whole thing had been braced for him. The man to whom Jarrett had earlier whispered had probably seen Russ riding with Bert Orr and identified him to his boss. Seame was merely bait to draw him in. He started a slow, deliberate movement toward the door. There was no profit for him in local wars. He tried to keep apart from it. But Jarrett was insistent.

"I made my offer in the open. I made it to Bert and I made it to his sister. Open and plain. Thirty thousand dollars. If I'm outbid, it'll be by a man that's got guts enough to be as open. He'll sing it out or I'll beat it out of him!"

Russ stopped and turned. Jarrett pushed out from the bar and crossed to him. Russ measured the man and his drunkenness and saw that whiskey didn't impair Jarrett's faculties — only heightening the savagery in him. The man was ruthless and completely dangerous.

"You might try to beat the wrong man, friend," he said quietly.

"Where is he?" Jarrett taunted.

Russ squared a little, setting his balance, and watched intention form in the big man's eyes. But before it shaped fully, Seame dragged himself up off the floor of the room. Blinded and dazed, he spilled against Jarrett's elbow in passing. Jarrett struck like a cat with the heel of his hand. The old man dropped and Jarrett shook him with a stabbing boot toe.

"Damn you!" he raged. "I told you to keep clear of me!"

Something snapped in Russ. Something born of inactivity and unsettled moving from valley to valley and an old anger for which he knew no name.

"All right, friend," he said. Jarrett wheeled back toward him. But before the fire in Russ reached his muscles, the door of the bar swung open and a man plowed through.

"Hold it!" he snapped.

Russ quartered a little to see the newcomer without losing sight of the man in front of him. The man inside the door was small in a way that did not detract from the silent force of his personality. He was a cold man, even before the blast of the anger that showed faintly behind the mask of his face. Unhurriedness hung as easily on him as the sag of his belted gun. His frosty eyes told no more about him than the iron graying his hair pronounced his exact age. A Tiffany-made star winked jewel-like from his vest. He was, Russ saw, a well-oiled, lethal legal machine and sheriff of Taprock county. Nothing else.

"Who slugged Pop Seame?" the sheriff said quietly.

"I did, Colson," Jarrett answered with obvious pleasure. "Too bad, but he let me have it first."

The sheriff's eyes swept the room. Here and there a man nodded unwillingly at the bare truth of this statement. For a moment, as his eyes touched Jarrett, a bitter promise flamed up in them. But when he spoke, his voice was still quiet and level.

"We'll break it up. Jarrett, you'd better start your boys for home. And somebody see Pop gets down to Doc Marple's. His face has got to be sewed."

Jarrett shrugged.

Before the man could turn away, Russ spoke to the sheriff. "What are you going to do about Seame?"

The sheriff showed no surprise. "You heard me. Have him patched."

"Nothing else?"

The sheriff shook his head. A thin, tight grin crossed Russ Cameron's face.

Ed Jarrett seemed to sense what was coming. He crouched, cocked his right hand, and smashed it forward. But Russ didn't have an old man's feet under him. They moved a fraction of a foot. His body swayed a little. And that lethal maul passed over his shoulder beside his ear. As he started his answering drive, he felt his heels bite through the sawdust into the solid planking of the floor for purchase. The blow started there on the floor in his heels and ran through his whole body like the snap running through a long drover's whip. It exploded in blinding speed in his arm.

His fist landed fully on the bridge of Ed Jarrett's nose. Blood spattered as far as the white front of the barkeep's apron. Jarrett's head went far back. He took a great, staggering backward stride and went down with a crash that shook dust from the beams overhead. He lay as he fell, limp and motionless and with his nose a ghastly, dripping ruin.

Russ rubbed his knuckles with his other hand and grinned recklessly at the sheriff.

If Colson saw a challenge in the thing, he ignored it. Russ waited a long moment, then turned out the door.

Russ crossed the walk in front of the *Tres Piños* Bar and pushed on across the street toward the hotel. Midway over, a low voice hailed him from the lamp-lit doorway of the telegraph office. The girl who had earlier caught his attention there stood in the opening. The light of her back threw her small, trim figure into soft silhouette. A vagrant wind slanting down the street wrapped her skirt about her and loosened a strand of her thick hair so that she raised one hand to sweep it back from her face. She made a suddenly sharp picture before the focus of Russ Cameron's mind, a momentary, vibrant personification of things for which he hungered and that his constant travel from place to place denied him. He remembered seeing her write her name across one corner of his message to Shane after she had counted the words. Sue McKenzie. He touched his hat as he stepped up onto the walk before her. She thrust an envelope at him.

"Another message for you, Mister Cameron."

It was early and the restlessness in Russ had been increased, rather than eased, by his tangle with Jarrett. He looked at this girl and a knowledge that had been rising within him for many months became a certainty. Someday soon John Shane was going to lose his ace field agent. All men are anchored to the earth when they are born. And the day comes when the most footloose must put down roots.

Russ thanked Sue McKenzie for the envelope. He would have stayed there, hat in hand on the walk, talking idly and breathing in an aura of her fragrance that drifted down to him, but she muttered a quick apology about a closing time long past and shut the door.

Russ reset his hat with a feeling of disappointment and stared off toward the hotel, reluctant, yet, to go up to his room. A quiet voice beside him broke through his patternless thoughts.

"Pretty woman, isn't she?"

Russ turned. Sheriff Sam Colson had crossed the street soundlessly and stood at his elbow. Russ let his face twist wryly.

"I like stronger words."

A shadow of a smile crossed Colson's lips, but he spoke solemnly enough. "Yes. I reckon a fair man would say Sue was beautiful. She's a fine girl. Look, Cameron, I dropped in on the register at the hotel this afternoon, so I've got your name. Come along up to the office and I'll trade you a cigar for half an hour's talk."

Colson's office was clean. Its floors were freshly varnished and the raw timber paneling the walls had been oiled; it took a deep luster from the lamplight. His desk was boot-scarred, but its top was uncluttered. Nowhere was there a trace of disordered files or the inevitable rogues' gallery of reward dodgers nailed up. In their place along the walls were gun racks filled with well-kept pieces. Russ recognized a silver-encrusted old Tower musket, a brace of Allen & Thurber dueling guns, and an exquisite Lee hunting rifle. It was a man's room, reflecting much of the methodical, unhurried surety of its occupant. And Colson's cigars were good. Russ began to revise the hasty opinion he had formed in the *Tres Piños*.

Colson seemed to sense the direction of his thoughts. He smiled without humor. "You didn't like that business of Pop Seame, Cameron," he said. "Neither did I. You thought I was crawling, and you were right.

But if a man's after a killer grizzly, he does plenty of crawling. He works on his belly till he's close. And he keeps on working on his belly till his sights are in the clear and he's got an absolutely clean shot. There's a reason for it. If he misses the first time, he never gets a second chance. I want you to know how it is."

The man spoke quietly, almost like a cracker-barrel expert explaining his pet checker move. There was no malice to it. Only business — cold and unhurried. Russ looked up into the unlighted eyes.

"Then you've got this Jarrett chalked up in your black book?"

Sheriff Sam Colson shook his head. "Personally, yes. My stomach's no stronger than yours. Officially, no. Ed walks almighty close to the edge, sometimes. But he doesn't go over. Till he does, I've got to stay clear. The law's a hard boss, sometimes, Cameron. But I've got to stick to it if I'm to make the valley do the same. You see that?"

Russ nodded.

Colson leaned forward. "Now, I want to know where you fit into this. You could be a commission agent. You've got a fist on you like a Shane man. Or you could be dickering with Bert Orr on your own."

"Does it make any difference?"

Colson rubbed his jaw thoughtfully. "I don't know," he said slowly. "If you're aiming to buy for yourself, I'll make an even bet that you, or Bert Orr, don't live long enough to sign your contracts. Ed Jarrett's been after that Orr grass for ten years. Ten years is a long time to fight and Jarrett's not a man to quit. If you're buying for a broker, it will be the same thing . . . unless Jarrett has commissioned a broker to try buying the Harpoon for him, and you're from that broker's office. How about it?"

"If you want to know if I'm dickering with Orr for an outfit that'll turn the Harpoon over to Jarrett after the deal's closed, the answer is no."

"You're sure?" Colson said mildly. "Sue McKenzie gave you a telegram while I was crossing the street. Have you looked at it?"

Russ thrust his hand into his pocket, brought out the crumpled envelope, and ripped it open. It was not a received message but one of the pencil forms on which a man wrote a message in a large, sharp-angled hand and it was dated six hours ahead of his own message to Shane. It was addressed to Shane's office:

Your authority to purchase Bert Orr ranch, Taprock County. Sale refused me. Buy in your name for later transfer. Price thirty thousand, less your commission. Another buyer on hand. Act immediately. E.J. Jarrett.

Russ understood what he saw. He didn't understand why Sue McKenzie had taken a confidential message from the files of her office and handed it to him. But there could be no doubting that this was the original of a message from Jarrett to John Shane. And it fully explained Shane's relaxing on his offering price, his boasting of an available buyer, and his promise of a bonus. Russ reached into another pocket and brought out Shane's message to him. He tossed both across the desk to Colson.

The sheriff didn't look at them. "Sue's in this fight, too," he said quietly. "I don't know about Bert and her for sure. But she doesn't want to see him whipped. She kept me up on what went across her wires all day. Bert's a good boy, Cameron. And the Buckhorn's crowded him a sight further than most men could stand. But he's kept his head. Where you going to stand, now?"

Russ stood up. He knew that either Sue McKenzie or Colson, possibly both of them, would make it a point to see Orr before he met with the rancher to close the deal. When Orr discovered that as agent for Shane, Russ was also agent for Ed Jarrett, the deal would be cooked. It was, then, as far as Shane's office was concerned, one of those that occasionally turned sour. His business in Taprock was over — finished. But Shane and the irregular pattern of his business for his employer were not on his mind.

"Where are you going to stand, Colson?"

The sheriff's expression did not change. "With the law, Cameron. There's no other place I'll fit."

"You won't move?"

Colson shook his head.

"Then I reckon I'll ride to the Harpoon in the morning."

CHAPTER
TWO

Russ Cameron rode out of Taprock shortly after sunup. He'd backed Jess Stone, the liveryman, into a stall, and had gotten a better horse than he'd had the day before. He held the animal to a brisk pace. The morning was fresh, and, as he lifted at the upper end of the irrigated valley into the benches and rolling breaks under the hills that sheltered both Orr and Jarrett land, he was enjoying the ride.

Just under two hours out of town, he rose through the saddle of a pass. Below him was spread out a rough twenty-mile square of as good cow land as he had ever seen. At the extreme end, where a spear of sunlight broke through the shadows of the slopes, he could see a light patch of meadow with the pinpoint of a building beside it. The Buckhorn. He thought about Jarrett and his nose and the sale the man still believed was pending and he grinned at the uneasy bed the Buckhorn owner must occupy this morning.

The Harpoon house lay out of sight down a slanting drainage bearing off to his left. Rae Orr's Chain lay back of this in another basin six or eight miles westward. Russ wasn't sure. But it didn't matter. He was in no hurry. He wanted to see Bert first, anyhow. They'd ride across to Chain together.

He gigged his mount forward and started down the slope of the pass, dropping in a few hundred yards into a flat covered thickly with lodgepole growth. He was well into this before he saw the man waiting ahead for him. For a moment a quick surprise and involuntary alarm stung him. The man's face was plastered with fresh bandaging. In evidence that Jarrett was close to the surface of his mind, his first thought was of the Buckhorn owner. Then he grinned at himself. The man ahead was slight and bent in his saddle. Jarrett was big as his ugliness. This would be Pop Seame.

It was.

"Where do you think you're going?" Seame barked while a rod of distance still separated them.

Russ held on and reined up beside the grizzled, battered Harpoon rider.

"The Harpoon," he said pleasantly. "Ride along?"

Seame spat, and Russ saw there was still blood in his mouth.

"I will not!" Pop said tartly. "Not the way you're going. The Harpoon, eh? Think you'll get there?"

"I usually do," Russ suggested.

"Then you ain't usually fair game for wolves! Come here. I want to show you something . . ."

Seame pulled his horse around and worked it off down the slope, away from the trail and deep into the lodgepole cover. Russ followed him for a handful of minutes, deeply puzzled. At the end of this time, Seame dismounted and thrust his way through brush to the lip of a high slab-rock overhang. He beckoned to Russ.

The shelf was 600 or 800 feet up the slope and looked abruptly down into a spring-watered meadow, through which the trail they had quitted wound. Cautioning silence, Pop bent over the edge. Russ bent with him. The meadow below was apparently empty. But to one side of it, standing in a brushy pocket that effectively screened them from the trail, were half a dozen horses. A moment later Russ caught the wink of sunlight on steel in the high meadow grass. At almost the same time, two other men showed themselves briefly, shifting positions. It was plainly an ambush — a brass-cased, sure-fire ambush. Pop looked at his companion in open triumph.

"Buckhorn," he said succinctly. "Waiting for you!"

"For me?" Surprise shook Russ. "Jarrett'd go that far to block Orr's sale to me?"

Pop Seame spat again and his eyes winked wickedly behind the swollen, bandaged puffiness of his face. "Hell, you're buyin' the Harpoon is past business now, Cameron. You must have left town without breakfast this morning or you'd have heard. Jarrett got Sue McKenzie out of bed last midnight and made her open up her office at gun point. He read your telegram and the answer you got. He slapped Sue around a mite and made her admit she'd showed his wire to you. Ed knows now he's got no more chance of getting the Harpoon through a broker than you have of getting it for your boss. So he's going after it the hard way. And the first step is to plow you right out of the way. You hit too hard and too quick to suit him!"

"Jarrett roughed Sue McKenzie?" Russ's voice turned ugly. "Where was Sam Colson?"

"Locked snug in his own jail! Buckhorn took care of that trick, first thing."

"He got out?"

Pop Seame looked scornful.

"Sam? How long you think bars could hold that man? Of course he's out, was before Buckhorn was a mile out of town! He dug me out at Doc Marple's, gave me the lay of things, and hightailed me out to block you afore you met Ed and his boys."

Russ nodded. "What's he going to do now?"

"Nothing." Pop's voice was flat. "Sam Colson can't be hurried no more'n he can be stopped, once he's started."

Russ looked down again at the death waiting in the meadow. Then he crawled back from the lip of the ledge and stood up. "I reckon this puts us about even, Pop. Last night at the *Tres Piños* against this, today."

The old man nodded. "I reckon," he agreed solemnly. "The trail's clear back to town. If you rode smart, you'd catch the noon stage afore it left. Sam told me to tell you."

"Orders, Pop? He wants me to go?"

"Sam didn't say that."

Russ swung up to leather with a thin grin on his lips. "Then let's get on to Harpoon!"

★　★　★

Several saddled, sweat-streaked horses stood at the long rail before the Harpoon ranch house. The building was large and weathered into conformity with the weathered hills about it. There was an air of solidness and comfort and permanence in the way it sat upon its land. Russ realized that Harpoon must have been the old Orr headquarters and that, when the ranch was divided at old Orr's death, a new building must have been built on the separated Chain for Bert's sister.

As he swung down in front of the vine-grown verandah of the old house, Russ had a flash of understanding in which he knew how much of a sacrifice Bert Orr was making to sell this place in order to strengthen his sister's grip on her half of their inheritance. Bert came through the doorway of the house as Russ touched ground. A girl followed him. Russ needed no introduction. Where Sue McKenzie's beauty was partially an inner thing, molded without attention to sharp detail much as Mexican *albañiles* raised the warm grace of an adobe *hacienda*, Rae Orr was fashioned of wire-cut brick, pressed and fired to flawless and tiered to a perfect line and balance. She was nearly as tall as her brother and had the same wide-set eyes. But there was a directness in her gaze that Bert lacked; there was a hungry restlessness in her eyes that startled Russ as he first met them. There was a flatness, a lack of depth in the changing expressions across her face that Russ had seen on another face in this valley. It struck Russ as odd that he should think of Sam Colson when he looked at this girl, but he did.

He lifted his hat as Bert made introductions.

"We've had word out from town this morning, Mister Cameron," Rae Orr said easily. "We hardly looked for you to ride this way."

"Ed Jarrett expected him to," Pop Seame grunted.

A quick look of annoyance flashed across the girl's face. "The man's a curse!" she snapped. "Can't one word come out of anybody without Ed Jarrett's name being hung onto the end of it?"

"I can't think of none," Pop murmured.

Rae shot him a cold look. He grinned feebly through his bandaging and started down toward the corral with Russ's horse and his own.

Bert Orr turned back into the house. Russ waited for his sister, then followed. The living room of the house was littered with scattered clothing and gear. He looked at it curiously. The girl saw the look and glared angrily at her brother.

"Bert got the word from town before I did. When I got here, he was packing to move out."

Her scorn was plain and unsheathed. Bert colored. "There's some places where a man's hand is better than yours, Rae," he growled. "This is one of them. I wasn't moving clean out. Only over to Chain. Jarrett's through playing. He means business, this time. And I can't watch two ranches!"

"So you vacate Harpoon and let him move right onto my back step!"

"I'm vacating Harpoon because I promised Dad I'd keep Ed Jarrett off of your ranch and away from you. I'm the one that's to do it. I've got to do it my way!"

Rae sat back and swung her legs angrily. Bert swung accusingly on Russ. "You must have heard what happened in town. Sam Colson maybe wouldn't do much else, but at least he'd tell you what was shaping. Or didn't you believe him, Cameron? I couldn't sell this place to the devil with the Buckhorn ready for the war Jarrett's been holding back on for ten years. This is no day for talk. I've got work to do!"

"You're whipped?" Russ asked.

Obviously badgered by the friction between himself and his sister and the knowledge that the thing his father had so long foreseen was at hand, Orr colored deeply and took an angry step toward Russ.

"You can't keep the Harpoon, I mean," Russ added. "I've got to know!"

Orr's head came up and he glared defiantly at his sister.

"No, I can't!"

"I'll buy it." Russ put the words down quietly in the room.

The Orrs, brother and sister, looked sharply at him.

"For myself," he went on. He pulled a letter of credit on a Kansas City bank and a checkbook from an inner pocket. "I can't make twenty thousand, Orr. But unstocked, Harpoon should be worth about twelve. I can cover that, and I'll gamble with you. You run everything afoot on Harpoon over onto Chain. I'll buy into your fight with Jarrett. What I win out of it is mine, so long as Chain isn't hurt. An' we'll write in a no resale provision to keep me from switching sides in the middle of the creek. That ought to cover everything. How about it?"

Orr grunted in astonishment, the protecting astonishment of a man who hears good news. "You haven't any better chance against Jarrett than I have and you know it, Cameron!"

"I said I was gambling," Russ reminded. "Besides, this way each of us will have just one spread to worry about."

Bert looked at his sister. She had stopped the swinging of her legs and was staring with intent calculation at Russ. Suddenly she shook her head emphatically. "No, Bert!" There was a flat, commanding finality in her tone.

Bert stood irresolute and troubled for a moment. Then a tight smile pulled across his face. "Dad gave Harpoon to me, Rae," he said slowly. "This is one time you'll keep your oar out of it. Make out your check and draw up your contract, Cameron."

Throwing his own crew together with Rae's, Bert Orr swept Harpoon grass, driving every hoof onto Chain range with the exception of a string of four saddle horses written into the contract. With Harpoon swept clean, Orr closed the gates between the two ranches and turned willingly to a business he knew — raising beef. Russ stayed at the Harpoon house or rode brief circuits about it, waiting for the pen work of title and credit to be complete and his land secure before he moved.

The desertion of Harpoon and the concentration of Orr strength on Chain must have been well known to Jarrett. Twice, when the combined Orr crews were working the bottoms, Russ had seen riders along the skyline toward Buckhorn. A sharp man there with a good glass would make out what was happening if he couldn't make sense of it. Russ thought it likely Jarrett knew of his own presence on Harpoon.

Regardless, he kept the details as quiet and unnoticeable as possible, believing Buckhorn would make an effort to stop any transfer of title to the Harpoon if it was known. He sent his draft into Taprock on the flagged-down stage, addressed to Sue McKenzie in a sealed envelope. With it went a note asking her to pass it along, with a word of caution, to the bank for collection.

This was done. Five days later, Sue rode to the Harpoon and, missing him, had gone on to Chain. The draft had cleared. Orr sent his deed back with the girl for recording. All this had been done silently and with smoothness. But the caution was unnecessary.

Ed Jarrett waited, apparently fully aware of every movement in both the basin and the town, until the ink was dry in the county book of records on the entry that made Russ Cameron legal owner of Harpoon acreage. Then he rode up the valley.

It was late afternoon when Russ saw him drop down from the ridge and angle toward the house. He was alone and in no hurry. Russ put a glass to low spots and the timber fringe around the open ground in which the house stood. Seeing no sign of a hidden crew, tension

124

ran out of him and he moved out onto the porch with a certain eagerness to meet Jarrett.

The man pulled up a dozen yards from the rail. Splinting was still tightly taped to his shattered nose and the bandaging heightened the predatory cast of his broad, boldly formed features. His eyes ran over Russ, a glint rising in them when he saw Russ did not wear his gun belt.

"This is the first time in ten years that an unarmed man has stepped out of that door when I rode into this yard!" he said. There was neither admiration nor censure in his voice. "You got more sand than the Orrs or less brains? Or are you ready to talk business?"

Russ shrugged. "What's on your mind, Jarrett?"

Pushing his hat back from the tangled mat of his tawny hair, Jarrett swung down and came up two of the three steps onto the verandah. "I don't know what your game is, Cameron. And I care a sight less. But I'll give you the same chance I gave Orr. My price has come down since you horned in. If you'll saddle up now, you can ride off of Harpoon without losing a cent . . . or your hide. And that's more'n you've got coming!"

"If I won't ride?" The question came softly from Russ.

Jarrett grinned surely. "You will, Cameron. You're too smart to stay."

Russ shook his head carefully. "No. I'm not going, Jarrett. I'm staying. You've had your say. Now I'll have mine! If you want Harpoon, come after it. But when you do, I'm going after Buckhorn!"

Coolly relishing the full knowledge that after this there would be war, Russ chalked his own lines across the grass of Taprock County. A man dug deeply in new ground if he wanted to flourish when his roots took hold there. He expected anger in Jarrett. He expected noise and malice and sultry predictions. But no violence. Not now. Not when the man came alone. And here was his mistake.

Jarrett raised his hand toward the brim of his hat again. But this time his fingers were wrapped around the butt of his gun. The weapon stroked savagely downward. Blinding pain flashed behind Russ's eyes. His legs slackened and he slumped, balancing stubbornly on his hands and knees. But the slackness spread. He felt himself collapse and roll loosely down the steps in front of him.

Stunned, without volition or sensation, consciousness clung to him like a shaft of light in a darkened room. He was aware that Jarrett had holstered his gun and was bending over him. He felt the man lock a twisting hand in the collar of his jacket and jerk him half to his feet. He saw Jarrett swing, felt the impact of his maul-like fist, and nothing else. Even pain was dead. But consciousness clung.

He tried to struggle weakly against the next hammer-like swing of Jarrett's hand. Realization penetrated that the man intended to do with his hands what he could not do with his gun and stay clear of Sam Colson's law. But after an interminable time in which Jarrett held him still firmly by his collar and worked him over thoroughly from crown to belt, he saw

126

he had underestimated the man. This wasn't a foolish thing. Not yet. This was only a promise. Jarrett was going to let him live. Jarrett was going to show him to Taprock — to the Orrs, to the town, even to Sam Colson — so all of them would know that Buckhorn was through playing, that Buckhorn meant business.

Jarrett let him go. He went down in a loose heap. The Buckhorn owner, heaving with exertion and his face paled as if even he himself was a little sick with what he had done, turned back to his horse. Russ heard leather *creak* as the man mounted. He heard the hoof beats of his horse fade as Jarrett hammered off at a full run in contrast to his deliberate approach earlier.

The shadows slanted long and Russ was aware of the fading warmth of the sun. After that, in the darkness, it was hard to tell when he slept and when he did not. Pain began a faint prodding that grew through a pair of hours to a full, roaring beat against which his mind could barely force its way. He moved, rolling carefully onto his back, then over fully onto his stomach where he could pull his hands and knees under him. But the movement made him sick. He lay in nausea, trying to think. And before thought could form, he drifted off again.

CHAPTER
THREE

Sometime near midnight, the webbing of haze in which Russ lay opened in front of him. Pain had settled into something clearly defined. He could sense its boundaries and its force. His face was, he judged, a ruin. Most of Jarrett's work had been done on it — work coolly calculated to reach through damaged flesh to strike hard at things inside his victim — pride and vanity. This damage Cameron discounted. He painfully flexed muscles in his body, found those of his belly and lower chest sore and protesting, but no indication of broken ribs or serious damage.

This survey over, he raised himself painfully and walked uncertainly down to the corral. He had a brief rest there, clinging to the bars and looking fixedly at his horse. The animal watched him, spooking nervously away. The blood, Cameron knew. And it made a problem. This was an Orr horse, part of the Harpoon deal. If he'd had a few more days astride it, there'd have been a bond between them and the blood would make little difference. Now, it did.

Rested, driven stubbornly by a will building up in him, he crossed 200 yards of open to the bank of the creek. Dropping down flat there, he slid out until his head and shoulders were in the water. The water was cold, but it made quick fire across his wounds. For a little it was enough to lie motionlessly, letting the flow wash gently at the angry flesh. But he knew this wasn't enough and he presently propped himself on his elbows and fought back quickly answering pain long enough to work the water across his face with his fingers, cleaning away most of the blood.

This done, he moved back to the corral. It was all slow. More than half an hour, he judged. But he had a lot of time. Plenty of time. He was into it now. He'd wanted his roots down in good land. He'd planted them. And now he'd fight for them. There was no regret. But there was impatience. He kept his mind away from the time and went after his horse.

He felt better. And he caught the animal. He got a bridle on and looked at the heavy saddle and came near to mounting bareback. But some vague pride came forward and wouldn't let him mount until he had leather under him. He had doubted his ability to get away from the Harpoon in the beginning. When he had the saddle up and cinched, he knew that he would make it. And he moved more steadily. A late moon shoved up out of the hills as he pulled away from the house, and its light brought the trail across the ridge to Chain out of the shadows for him.

The premature graying of false dawn lay along the summit of the hills east of the basin as he rode down toward the Chain buildings. There was a dog on the place. It set up a challenge, and he rode into it; light winked up in the bunkhouse and a man slid out, carrying a rifle. The man stopped on the shadowed side of the building and snapped a soft query.

"Who is it?"

Russ recognized Pop Seame's voice.

"Cameron."

The sound came thickly through his battered lips. Pop stepped out of the shadows and watched him ride in. As he came closer, Pop grounded the rifle.

Russ was suddenly filled with relief that the ride was done. And with that relief came a wave of nausea that suddenly bent him limply double in the saddle. Pop let the rifle on down flat and stepped forward, his arm and shoulder ready as Russ tumbled out of the saddle. The ground was steadier under him than his saddle had been. Russ straightened. Pop peered closely at him, then swore softly.

"Jarrett?"

Russ nodded. Pop swore again and started toward lights that had come up in the main house. Russ was aware that Bert Orr came out through the door and took his other arm. Then he was in a low, neat room, lighted by a pair of round-wick lamps at the far end. He was sitting in a chair with a clean cover on it and he was aware of his own grime. Blood and dust and the mud of the creekbank were thick on his shirt. A door opened in the far wall and Rae Orr came through it.

She stopped when she saw him. She paled at his appearance and a strange expression was across her face. Russ realized that it was fear. He wondered at it for a moment. And he stared at her fixedly. Obviously roused from sleep, she had drawn on a loose wrapper

130

no more revealing than a sack. Yet he had never seen a woman more beautiful than Rae Orr the instant she appeared in the doorway. He made a move to come to his feet, but she checked him.

"How close are they behind you?" she said tightly. And her fear was in her voice.

Russ shook his head.

"Jarrett would have gone home after he'd done a job like this," Pop Seame exploded assuredly.

The fear slid from Rae's face. A sharp calculation tightened her mouth and flattened her cheeks. "You bought trouble with Jarrett when you bought the Harpoon," she said quietly. "Why'd you come here? Do you want out of it now?"

Russ thought there was a note of eager hopefulness in her voice. He wondered about this, also, and was vaguely as displeased with it as he was satisfied by her beauty. Bert chopped a sharp reproof at his sister.

"The man's hurt! Why'd he come here . . . ? Rae, what the devil's the matter with you?"

Rae shook her head. "Men like Russ Cameron don't run for arnica when they're hurt. He didn't come here for hot water and a bed, Bert. Did you, Cameron?"

"No."

Bert Orr scrubbed his hand across his face in puzzlement. "Why, then?"

"I want help."

"Our crew!" Rae drew her face tighter.

"Just one man, Miss Orr," Russ said slowly. "Just one. Pop Seame."

"No!" she answered solidly. "You paid for what you could buy from Bert. He sold you all we could afford to sell. The Harpoon's your gamble. If you lose, then it's only the Chain left against Ed Jarrett. You've got a shelter here till you're on your feet. What we can do without weakening ourselves, yes. But not one man. We can't risk our chances on yours!"

There was no apology. There was inflexible steel in this girl and a cool sense of values. Russ saw the uselessness of protest to her, the hopelessness of making her believe in him. He swung his head toward Bert. Orr was angry and deeply troubled. It was plain that he felt shamed by Rae's selfishness. But even he could not deny the solid sense of it. He shrugged helplessly.

"I was boss on the Harpoon, Cameron. I had a say there. I'm just a foreman, here. Chain is Rae's ranch and Chain hands are her men. We'll keep Pop."

Seame's eyes swung from Rae to Bert and back again. "The hell you will!" he snorted. "Rae, I paddled you afore you rode your first horse. Wish I could do it again! When the Orrs quit helping a fighting neighbor that comes asking honest, I'm done. Cameron, you've got yourself a hand! Now, what's orders?"

Russ grinned. His battered features refused to move, but appreciation warmed his eyes. "There's places in the hill country where a man that won't ask questions can hire quick guns and restless saddles if the pay is right and he agrees to take care of the law. Know where one of those places is?"

Pop looked startled for a moment. Then approval lighted in his eyes. "I do. But it'll take three days for me to get there and back."

Russ reached into his pocket and brought out the last greenbacks left from the Shane expense account that had brought him to Taprock. "I'll look for you Friday night," he said.

Pop took the bills, pocketed them, and turned out the door without a glance at the Orrs. Bert shuffled uneasily.

"Know where he's going?"

Russ shook his head.

"The Needles. Not even Sam Colson will ride into that den. But he'll raise hell with any man that brings some of those wolves out of there onto our grass!"

"Then let him raise it!" Russ snapped. "When I fight a war, I like the best damned tools I can get!"

Russ holed up to lick his wounds like a wounded grizzly and to wait. He chose an abandoned line cabin on a ridge face, overlooking most of the basin from the far end of the Harpoon. He kept his horse in a sheltered pocket half a mile away and showed no light after dark. With a glass he watched Ed Jarrett begin the first rounds of his final play for the basin grass. The first day, a Buckhorn crew ringed the Harpoon house and Indianed up on it for more than an hour before they discovered that it was unoccupied and undefended. They milled about in the compound but did little apparent damage beyond scattering the corralled stock.

Early on the second day they reappeared, crossing the ridges toward Chain. Bert Orr and a group of

133

Chain riders cut them off at the boundary fence. There was a parley in which hostility was evident, even across the basin. Leaving the fence, Buckhorn swept down through a strip of rough country, and, flushing out about fifteen head of Harpoon stock Orr appeared to have missed earlier, they hazed them on back toward their own ground.

Russ had meant to stay holed up until Pop Seame had gotten back down from The Needles and he had a chance to measure what crew the old rider could round up. But his face didn't heal as well as he had hoped. There was a deep gash in his right cheek. This refused to close, and, during the second night at the cabin, a steady drumbeat of pain set up in it. By morning it was darkly colored and angry-looking and he could feel the first light-headed touches of a fever setting in.

He wasn't sure that Seame would think of the line cabin when he found his new boss missing from the Harpoon, and he was troubled by the prospect of Seame's leading whatever hands he had been able to scare up in The Needles into town on a search for him. But the fever made him uneasy and he didn't want to wait too long. Finally he left a note under the corner of a box on the cabin table:

Pop Sit tight. Cameron

And he rode for town.

He hit Taprock in mid-morning. His face was extremely painful by then, and he was sweating heavily, although the morning was cool. He rode in quietly and

134

turned up an alley leading past the barn behind Doc Marple's house. The main street was unusually empty as he passed through its upper end and he had an idea that with luck he could put his mount up in Doc's barn and thus successfully have slid into town without being noticed. He wasn't sure this was important. But the longer he kept Ed Jarrett in ignorance as to his whereabouts, the better pleased he would be.

In the further pair of minutes it took to finish the alley and get into Doc Marple's barn, Russ saw no other face. It was with a feeling of relief that he pushed through a screened back door into the kitchen of the doctor's house. Doc's wife was rolling out some kind of pastry dough on a breadboard. Marple was sitting at a table, watching the dimples in her flour-covered elbows and grinning without attention. He took one look at Cameron as he came through the door and reached for an enameled pan from a shelf behind him. Crossing to the pump at the sink under the window, he filled the basin wordlessly. When he had prodded the fire in the squat range beside the door and had pushed the pan of water over the replaced fire lid, he turned to his wife.

"Bring that in when it's hot, Martha," he said shortly.

His wife wiped abstractedly at her flour-covered arms and tried to keep the quick concern in her eyes turned away from Russ. Marple kicked a door open and motioned toward the front of the house. Russ stepped past him and down a hall to the office at the far end.

Much of what actually happened in that office was mercifully hazed off. He heard Doc's first words to him

— a quick, unwilling apology as he opened his instrument case before him.

"The stage driver broke a bottle of chloroform for me, bringing it in last trip. I'm clean out. This is going to hurt like Satan's corns, too! If I could wait a day, I would. But that's a bad face, Cameron. I've seen plenty corpses look worse than you do!"

Right after that Doc tipped him back on the table and a sliver of steel in Doc's hand dipped. It did hurt. Not the dull, surging nerve shock that comes with an injury when it's received, but a sharp thing, quick and piercing as a doctor's scalpel. Sweat drenched Russ and the room darkened.

The room steadied, later, only to go spinning again as Marple put corrective pressure on his hammered nose. And finally, when he thought it was all done with, Doc bent with a suturing needle, swore once more at the stage driver's clumsiness, and went to work again. It was well past noon when Doc pressed down the last strip of adhesive and backed into a chair to mop his florid face and the bald, shiny crown of his head with a generous handkerchief.

"Just one place didn't heal right," Russ protested. "Did you have to make me over?"

"Just one place!" Marple snorted. "There was enough bugs in that one place to have killed a horse! And the rest . . . sure it was all healing. But you'd have looked like the ghost of a dynamited morgue if I hadn't shaped you up. I'd feel a lot better if I didn't think I'll probably have to do it all over again. Were you seen coming in here?"

"I don't know. Why?"

"Jarrett's been boasting he whipped you privately and he's going to do it again publicly the first time you show in Taprock. Martha saw him ride up the street about ten minutes ago and he gave this house a funny look." He slapped his knee with an abrupt change of mood, and stood up. "Well, you rest easy, anyways, son. You've got a couple days in bed ahead of you. Enjoy 'em. I'll worry about Jarrett. If there's one place in town he'll let be, it's mine. A doctor's a damned poor enemy for any man to have."

Marple's heartiness was meant to be reassuring; it failed. He guided his patient into an adjacent hospital room, with a bed. Russ railed at the doctor's promise that he would have a couple days in bed. There was so much to do, so little time in which to do it. He had wide faith in Pop Seame. But there were limitations to the old rider's abilities. If he had the kind of recruiting luck in The Needles for which Russ hoped, the new Harpoon hands would need a tighter rein than Pop could draw to hold them. Seame had no way of knowing anything of the blunt plan crystallizing in Russ's head beyond the fact Harpoon was done with running, save toward a fight.

As soon as the door closed behind Doc Marple, Russ tossed his blanket aside and swung his feet to the floor. He sat up, gripping the bed on either side of him. But he couldn't make it. The sweat came back, moist and chilling, and the room reeled crazily. He lay back to think of this, letting the tenseness run out of his muscles. He slid into a deep sleep before he recognized its coming sufficiently to make an effort against it.

In mid-afternoon, he was roused by a hauntingly familiar aura in his room. He opened his eyes, but he was alone. Puzzled, he lay there. Presently an indistinct murmur of voices in the back part of the house separated themselves and he recognized the low-pitched softness of Sue McKenzie's voice. He grinned a little inwardly.

Somehow he had gathered that Sue was Bert Orr's girl. Yet, if she was here — and she had been in his hospital room, he knew — she'd come to see him, not Bert. Orr was out on Chain, protected, like his sister, from Jarrett by the barrier Russ had sacrificed the savings of half a dozen successful years with John Shane voluntarily to set up on the Harpoon. He wished he knew about Sue.

Then he wasn't thinking of her, but of Rae Orr. There was a flaw in Rae, a flaw in the way she thought — in the way she looked at her brother and her neighbors and her valley — a flaw that marred her beauty and made it impossible for a man to measure her womanliness. Rae wanted something from the world and the iron in her made her override everything else to reach it. That something was neither a man nor a home or security. The girl had scorned these in one way or another. Russ wondered what she was fighting for. If a man could discover that, he might find rich reward in Rae. He labored with the thought. The voices at the back of the house faded. Presently he slept again.

★   ★   ★

Russ wakened with his earlier queasiness gone and his head clear. He was aware of a weakness through him and he realized that Doc Marple had done much for him — that he'd had a close brush with serious trouble from infection. He sat up. Marple and Sue McKenzie were facing him. Two vertical creases of worry were stabbed up through the doctor's forehead from the bridge of his nose. The face of the girl from the telegraph office was pallid with an honest fear not far from panic. Marple's eyes shuttled repeatedly to the girl and an edge of annoyed disapproval showed through his concern.

"This is Sue's doing," he said abruptly. "I told her half a day's rest for a sick man was no substitute for two. But it was either let her in or she'd break down the door!"

The girl bent forward, seizing Russ by the shoulders as though her urgency could pour its vitality into him. "Can you ride?" she asked swiftly. She didn't wait for an answer. "It's no matter. You've got to! You've got to get out of town . . . now!"

"Jarrett?" Russ asked the question quietly.

She nodded sharp agreement.

Doc Marple spread his hands. "I told you he was in town, Cameron. I told you he's been promising to hand you a public beating the first time he caught you here. I've done what I could. I sent Martha for Sam Colson. He came up and looked at you. Before he left, he told me to keep you quiet as long as you needed . . . that he'd take care of Jarrett and the Buckhorn boys. But

139

Sue doesn't think that's enough. She thinks Sam can't handle 'em!"

Russ shot a quick look at the girl. She shook her head. "It's not that!" she said quickly. "Sam Colson's a match for any man in Taprock . . . at a square game. But Jarrett won't play that way. You know that! The Buckhorn is in town to the last man. Every one of them knows the sheriff will be on the look-out for a move toward Doc's house now. But none of them look worried about it. Least of all, Ed Jarrett. I tell you, there's something afoot to get the sheriff out of the way while they come here. And you're in no shape to take a chance on the sheriff seeing it in time to block it. I've saddled your horse. Get your boots on and we'll try to make it out the back way!"

Russ swung his feet to the floor. He grinned wryly at the doctor. "A bald-headed man hasn't got a chance against a pretty woman," he said. "I've been looking for a way to get out of here. This is as good as the best I could think of."

"Let me tell you something, Cameron," Marple said seriously. "You won't have a chance yourself, if you get your carcass any more torn up before you've built back what you've lost the past few days. I don't scare a patient unless I have to do it with the truth. But every now and then I run across one I'd like to tie down until I'm done with him. Take it easy, man." Marple turned on the girl. "I'm not so sure he's as tough as he thinks he is, Sue. You better go with him a ways. You can saddle my mare in the barn."

Sue McKenzie smiled. "She's already saddled, Doc," she said, and moved to the door.

As they crossed the rear yard to the barn, a stillness that lay over the town was suddenly shattered by a surge of angry voices, a shot, and the silvery sound of falling glass. Sue jerked the barn door open and pulled Russ inside. The tumult up the street rose in violence. Russ found his horse and led the animal toward the rear door. Footfalls ran across the yard and Marple breathlessly thrust his head in.

"Here's your chance . . . quick! There's a hell of a fight on up at the *Tres Piños*. A shot, too! Colson just ran past. I've got to go. Likely somebody's bad hurt or going to be!"

The doctor wheeled abruptly away. Sue McKenzie clawed frantically at the drop bar across the rear door. The portal swung open. The girl swung up and Russ hauled himself onto his own mount.

"That's it," the girl breathed. "That fight . . . it drew the sheriff just as Jarrett figured it would. I knew something was coming. It even drew Doc. But all of Buckhorn won't be at the *Tres Piños*. Some of them will be here . . . any minute. Ride . . . but ride easy till we're clear of town."

CHAPTER
FOUR

Aware that Sue McKenzie's capable mind had shrewdly anticipated Jarrett's dodge to keep Colson busy while he was springing his trap on the new owner of the Harpoon, Russ left the mechanics of the ride out of town to the girl. She appeared to have thought it completely out beforehand. She held down the alley from Marple's house until she was against the back of the bank. Turning through the lot beside the bank building, she rode boldly across the street and into the shadows on the far side. At the upper end of town, men were still running toward the square of light thrown by the windows of the *Tres Piños*. Russ caught a glimpse of a dark knot of men on the front porch of the doctor's house. 120 seconds earlier, they would have found him there on the bed in Marple's little hospital room.

The crossing of the street, being made at the downvalley end of town, was unseen. Once on the far side, Sue headed directly toward a dry wash that slanted against the first of the ridges sloping toward the upper basin. In half an hour they were in timber on a moonless slope above the valley trail and the girl pulled up. Cameron reined in beside her.

"Well, you're out of that trap, Russ Cameron," she breathed softly. "Now, I want to know something. Who's going to pull you out of the next one?"

"You, I hope," Russ answered lightly.

The girl scowled. "You still aim to fight . . . alone?"

Russ shook his head. "Not alone . . ."

He told her about Pop Seame and his errand to The Needles. Pleasure began to warm in his eyes.

"When I bought the Harpoon," Russ went on, "it was a gamble. A gamble that's cost me every hand so far, just as it did the Orrs. But I'm pyramiding my bets. In the last pot, there'll only be one spread left . . . the Buckhorn or mine!"

Sue nodded.

Russ leaned toward her. "There's something I want to know, too," he said gently. "When I took title to the Harpoon, did your help come along with it? Or is this for the Orrs . . . because you want to keep me between them and the Buckhorn?"

The girl looked evenly at him for a long time as though rigid honesty made her weigh her reply carefully. Finally she answered soberly, "I don't know."

Russ nodded. "Thanks," he said, "for this time, anyway. We'll split trails here. You've ridden far enough for one night."

She flashed a quick smile at him, wheeled her horse, and dropped down the slope. Russ watched her go thoughtfully. In this girl, as in Rae Orr, he faced the first problem he had ever known for which he didn't have a sure and ready answer by which he could stick. There was flint and steel and powder and blood involved when a man put down his roots. But there were soft things, too. He grinned and started his horse moving deeper into the breaks toward the basin and the ranch whose battle for existence he had bought with its empty acres.

It was with relief that Russ rode into the swale that held the Harpoon buildings and saw lights in the main house. There would be no more business of hiding in a forgotten shack, watching Jarrett ride, free and wide. There would be no more crawling uneasiness between his shoulders when he rode across open ground. A crew in a man's house was like a string of capped shells in his belt. He could make a fight with them.

Seame heard him ride in and came out onto the porch, shutting the door behind him. "Cameron?"

"Yes. You got 'em?"

Seame chuckled. "Or they got me. I ain't sure which. You sure you ain't aimin' to use a scatter-gun to kill flies?"

Russ swung down and stepped up beside the old man. "Why?"

Seame dropped his voice. "I've got four men in there. Any one of 'em would spit in Ed Jarrett's eyes first and ask who he was afterward. But I doubt like hell if a man alive could make 'em work cattle like forty-and-founders. And by the look of your poke when you handed me the bills I took with me, unless something's handled mighty fast around here, we're going to be a plumb hungry outfit."

Russ clamped a hand around Seame's arm. "We'll keep that poke under our hat," he said softly. "Keep a man busy enough and he won't know whether he's eaten or not. Harpoon's going to start handling . . . and fast. But if it's cattle, it won't be our own."

Seame swore admiringly. "Buckhorn?"

"Buckhorn," Russ agreed. "Let's get in and see the line-up."

As they stepped through the door, Russ swung on the four men sprawled about his living room. They rose, eyeing him critically, missing nothing. He saw that Pop had done a good job. Something was behind each of them, a something that prodded at them constantly so that their nerves were sandpapered thin and their reflexes tempered as spring steel. It might be the law for one and an old hatred for another. What it was made no difference. They were of the badlands breed, reckless, scorning all men but their own company, and eternally restless for strife in which they could pour out some of their bitterness.

Pop dryly made the introductions. Russ saw that the biggest of the four, Kimberly, was their leader. That was good judgment in Pop, locating a quartet that had already settled its own internal differences and in which each man already had his own place. It made it this easy, that Russ had no need to worry about the other three. So long as Kimberly was his man, the others would be, also. He liked the big, austere, frozen-faced man. And that made it easier, too. Pardee was a small man, faintly like Sam Colson, and probably far more dangerous than the sheriff because of a thinner temper and a complete absence of action patterns set by law on Colson. Meredith was a kid, but out of his youthful face stared the same wise eyes that were in Kimberly's head. The last man, Cable, was small and rotund, barely missing being fat. He smiled constantly. Laughter was close to the surface of his eyes. Cameron thought he was the least reckless of the three and possibly the most reliable.

"And this is the boss, boys," Pop finished his rounds. "Russ Cameron. I told 'em, Russ," Pop went on, "pretty much what the lay of the land is. They've got the Orrs tabbed and Buckhorn. And they know where you come in on the deal, but damned if I could tell 'em why? I told 'em the Harpoon was buying ammunition and pay was a hundred a month . . . to survivors. No use paying dead men. Make 'em go a mite easy, maybe."

Russ nodded. "There's just one more thing, then. Our game is to crowd the Buckhorn at every turn. The more we crowd, the better we'll do. But we've got to stay clear of Sam Colson. I'll watch that. And it's got to be understood when I say to let up or bear down, there's going to be no argument. The man that bucks that . . . goes!"

Kimberly moved lazily. "We hear things one time and another up to The Needles, Cameron," he said. "We've got a pretty fair idea of how things sat before you came. And any way you look from what we hear, Jarrett's going to wind up your sheriff before he gets the grass he's after. Why worry about crossing a man that's already got his ticket? If you aim to ride wide, count Colson out. It'd be easier."

"Got anything against Sam Colson . . . any of you?" Russ asked sharply.

His crew shook their heads.

"Then I'll tell you why we'll stay clear of Sam. Jarrett won't get him. And the fastest gun The Needles ever saw couldn't face him. I've got to have full saddles to beat Jarrett . . . not empty ones. And I've got to be square with Colson when we're through. I aim to stay in this valley."

Kimberly and the others looked unconvinced, but they nodded.

Russ kicked chairs up to the table and pulled a sheet of paper and a pencil from the drawer. "Tonight the whole Buckhorn's in Taprock. So we're going calling. Here's how the Jarrett place lays. We'll go in from the north . . ."

At three o'clock in the morning, Russ and his five riders pulled up on a knoll a mile above Ed Jarrett's headquarters. The buildings were dark. Below the house half a mile, several hundred cattle were grazing in a meadow along the creek. Seame pulled over close to Russ.

"If the whole place was burned, we'd have Sam Colson on our necks for arson, sure'n hell. But say the stable and the wagon shed butted against it went, it *might* be an accident. It'd clip Ed in the ribs and Sam wouldn't have an awful lot to go on. Reckon there's a couple of cans of kerosene in the wagon shed. We'll try it?"

"If you were playing poker with a man, would you burn his money belt up, Pop?" Russ asked quietly. "No! Now, look. How many head of Harpoon cattle you suppose Jarrett's run off from Bert Orr the last six months, one way or another?"

Pop's eyes brightened eagerly. "Countin' normal calvin' and some strays we was bound to miss in tallyin', Bert and me figgered out a couple of weeks ago that we'd lost around eighty head since spring grass. New stuff, mostly, carried off acrost a saddle."

"Eighty . . ." Russ said musingly. "And counting that bunch I saw them sweep out of the bottoms yesterday or the day before . . . make it a hundred. All right, then! The way we play is double or nothing, boys! Get into that herd down there and cut out as near two hundred head as you can. Take 'em right back up the middle of the valley. Don't worry about leaving a trail. Bunch 'em in that coulée just back of the house on the Harpoon. Then we'll see."

Even Kimberly grinned at this. Pop pitched his horse forward and rode recklessly down the slope, yipping with every jump. Russ stayed on the knoll, alert and tightly keyed, until Pop's yipping and the noise of the others had ample time to rouse anyone on the Buckhorn. He saw a light come on in a little room back of the kitchen. But it went off again after a moment, and there was no sound from the ranch. Russ nodded satisfaction. Jarrett's crew was gone — and he had a smart cook!

Remembering Doc Marple's caution and fully aware that the medico was in no way bluffing when he warned about over-exertion until the virulence from the infection in his face wounds was entirely gone from his system, Russ took no actual part in the raid on the Buckhorn. He was content to sit on the knoll above his crew, keeping a guard against the possibility of a dawn return of Jarrett's crew from town.

Actually his position on the knoll permitted him to do something else as essential as the watch he kept. He knew from experience with many men in a hundred scattered towns and valleys that very likely his crew, acknowledged outcasts and bluntly hired as such, would cleave closer to their hired loyalty than the average working crew picked up through a course of time. It was a point of honor a man who had never ridden dark trails could not understand. But it was a strong point and seldom violated by men like Kimberly and Pardee, Meredith and Cable.

It was good to feel a certain security toward them in this direction, but he had no way of knowing how able they would be in the work he had cut out in his mind until he saw them at it. For that reason, he watched the trail from town but little and the five riders below with fixed attention. After half an hour of this, a strong satisfaction was deep in him. Even Pop Seame fell under Kimberly's easy leadership. The five of them split the Buckhorn herd with little commotion and no lost effort. When the cut began to move freely of the herd, Meredith rode ahead and in five minutes put on the neatest exhibition of fence cutting Russ had ever seen. The other four put pressure on behind the cut, and in forty minutes from the time of their arrival at Buckhorn the driven cattle were on Harpoon grass.

By dawn, all of them showing the deepened lines of sleeplessness on their faces, they were back in the Harpoon house at breakfast. The cattle were bunched in a coulée back of the house half a mile. An old brush barrier that Bert Orr had used at one time or another was dragged across the coulée. There was ample water for the stock but little graze. Pop Seame was worried about it.

Russ chuckled at his concern. "They won't need grass," he said. "They won't be there long enough, Pop."

Seame scowled. "Where the hell they goin', then?"

"Back to Buckhorn," Russ answered.

"After that drive and stickin' our necks right down that curly wolf's throat, you'll let Jarrett drive them critters home again?" Pop bleated protestingly.

"Yes. Look, we've got two hundred head now. Right? If Jarrett takes them, how many can we run off from him next time? Remember . . . it's double or nothing with us the whole way."

A look of comprehension broke widely across Pop's face. "I get it! Four hundred next time. And we can keep right on building. That's why you took Orr's land and let him keep his stock. You figgered on building a herd out of Jarrett's stuff! So that's the plan . . ." Pop stopped and scowled. Then he shook his head and grinned admiringly.

"That's the plan," Russ agreed.

Kimberly pushed his feet out in front of him. "That's a lot of pressure to put on a man!" he said slowly. "You'll break him if you keep it up. Can you?"

Russ looked at the big foreman of his crew. "You know more about that than I do, Kimberly," he said quietly.

Kimberly nodded. "I wanted to know how you looked at it, Cameron," he grunted. "Remember our skins are worth as much as yours and you'll have a crew that'll stick. I reckon I like the way you pile your bets. We'll do. We're apt to have company afore noon. I've got a nap comin'."

Kimberly rose and, picking up his hat, stepped out into the compound and started down toward the bunkhouse, carrying his war bag with him. His three companions filed after him.

Pop watched Russ's face until the last of them was gone. "That settles the boys, don't it?" he asked. "I couldn't have done no better?"

"No," Russ agreed. "You couldn't have done better. They're what I wanted."

Pop stood up. "Then everything's settled on how you aim to make something out of Harpoon except Rae Orr."

"Rae?" Russ eyed the old man sharply.

"She won't like this business of Buckhorn stock on Harpoon graze. She'll like it less because you run it there than if Jarrett had!"

"Why?"

"I can't figure that gal any more than Bert can," Pop said. "So I'm not going to clutter your head up with a

151

lot of my guesses. But you watch her, son, and you watch her close. They's few gals like her. And if she wasn't plumb cracked when it comes to the grass in Taprock basin, I reckon she'd be the best. You'll have more trouble afore you have less . . . and it won't all ride over the hill from Buckhorn!"

Pop picked up his hat and went outside, also, in plain evidence he didn't intend to say more about Bert Orr's sister. Russ was puzzled. But he was tired and sore and suddenly in much need of rest. He went out onto the verandah, saw Pop had taken up a look-out position below the corrals where he could see all approaches to the ranch, and went back into the house to flop gratefully on a deep couch.

Russ slept lightly, keyed up to a pitch in which sudden word that Jarrett's riders were trailing onto the Harpoon on the trail of the cattle that had been driven through their fence would be no jolt. The coming of Buckhorn was something to which he looked forward, a second step in his planning. Thus, when he woke up to find Pop Seame shaking him with rough insistence, he listened to the man, not wholly understanding what he said because it was contrary to his expectations.

"What?"

"I said our company's here . . . but it's Chain, and primed for business!"

Russ swung off the couch. In passing, his eyes found the rotund Cable at one front window, Kimberly at the other. He caught Kimberly with a questioning look. Kimberly gave him his answer.

"Meredith and Pardee are down in the well house with a Thirty-Thirty apiece. From there and from here, we've got the compound quartered, if they make trouble."

Russ nodded, fighting off a feeling that he was only half-conscious. Both Seame and Kimberly spoke and acted as though Chain riders in the Harpoon yard was something grim, to be classed with an attack from the other direction. He glanced at his watch, saw he had slept only a few minutes, and realized that Jarrett had probably not yet returned from town with his crew. There was time to see what Orr's men wanted and to clear them away from the house before the Buckhorn arrived. He crossed to the door.

When he pulled the portal open, he saw the reason for the concern in both Pop and Kimberly. Eight riders from Chain were fanned out in the compound. They sat in their saddles just beyond effective pistol range. All of them carried rifles booted or under one arm. Bert Orr sat a little out ahead of them.

As the door pulled open, he sang out: "I want to see you, Cameron!"

Russ stepped onto the porch, keeping far enough back of the eaves to shield his eyes from the morning light. "What the hell is this, Bert?" he ground out angrily.

Orr's face was a solemn mask. "What you aim to do with those Buckhorn cattle in the draw?" he asked flatly.

Quick anger flared up in Russ. He steadied it. He had to give Orr some answer but be damned if he was going to let Chain, too, in on his planning. If word of his full intent ever reached Jarrett, its effectiveness would be lost. "Keep them!" he snapped. "They're Harpoon stuff now."

Orr shook his head. "Cameron, I don't like to tell you this, but you're not keeping that stock. We let you onto Harpoon to keep Jarrett off of us. But we don't know you. If you start running stock, maybe there might be a sudden day when you turned king of the basin. Who's going to say you'd be any better than Jarrett, then?"

Bert Orr spoke quietly. Russ thought he sensed a certain reluctance in his voice. But he was solid enough about what he said. "So what do we do, then?" he asked quietly.

"I'm glad you're taking it right, Cameron." Relief was honest in Orr. "It won't be too bad. It's just this . . . if there's gain made, Chain gains, too. You've got two hundred head, more or less, up there. We're taking half of them!"

Russ swept his eyes over the compound. Kimberly's swift parting of his companions, setting two of them down in the well house, made the main house safe from attack. Twice the Chain crew couldn't break that four-man defense. But Chain didn't need to attack to reach the cattle. He had left the way clear so Jarrett could reach them. Orr could reach them just as easily. He knew that his men could drop two or three of Chain's crew, but the rest of them could reach the draw and two or three men wouldn't stop them.

"This is your idea, Bert?" he asked suddenly.

With bland truthfulness, Orr shook his head. "No, I told you once I didn't do the thinking on Chain. But I'll carry out my orders!"

Wearily Russ nodded. "I reckon you'd try," he agreed. "You know this splits us wide apart. There'll be no more business of two irons sticking together against the third. It's every man for himself, from here on out!"

"It'd have to be something like that after this," Orr said.

Russ turned back toward the door. "Take your half, Orr," he snapped. "Take them and figure the fighting over them will come later!"

Orr spoke to men behind him. Like a troop of cavalry, Chain wheeled and rode a wide circuit of the house toward the draw and the bunched cattle.

As Russ stepped back into the house, three pairs of eyes fastened solidly on him. Cable's round face was openly accusing. Kimberly's was thoughtful. Pop Seame wore a warning look. "Now you know what I meant, son!"

Russ scowled. "I know," he agreed. "Rae sent Bert up here. She's afraid I'll turn as bad a wolf as Jarrett. She's hoping that Ed and me, bumping against each other, will kill each other off. To make sure I don't get any bigger than she and Bert are, she's making him cut me down on my first pot."

Pop snorted. "Son, you've got a lot to learn about that gal! She ain't afraid of you nor of Jarrett, either. What she's afraid of is that somebody else beside her will end up with the basin. That's where she's aiming. In her way, she's as bad as Jarrett. There's nothing half

155

about Rae. She wants all the grass and she always has. She's as hard as Jarrett and maybe she's as hard as you."

Kimberly spoke slowly. "Looks to me as though that girl and her brother have spread your hand down afore you could get your bets made. What you going to do when Jarrett comes smoking for his stuff?"

Russ grinned crookedly. "That depends on Jarrett!" he answered.

CHAPTER
FIVE

Kimberly had his answer as to what defense there was against attack by the Buckhorn little more than an hour later. Jarrett brought his crew up out of the south, keeping to the open and plainly riding up the track left by the cattle drive of the night before. He circled them wide of the Harpoon buildings and swung up the southern of the two ridges lying alongside the coulée back of the house. He bunched them there, apparently studying the herd. Then he dropped them back to the mouth of the coulée to look over the brush fence closing in the stock. Finally four men rode a quarter of a mile on up the valley, studying the track left by Chain when they took out the half Orr had demanded.

These things took long minutes in which Russ and the men in the house watched nervously. For a brief pair of minutes, the whole of the Harpoon crew was out of sight. Russ had been worrying about Pardee and Meredith, down in the well house with their rifles. He took this chance to send Pop down to them with a caution to hold their fire until the signal came from the main house.

But in the long run of events, the caution was unnecessary. Jarrett and his men were plainly a little

157

puzzled by the division of the herd and the intrusion of Chain into what they had fully expected was to be a private battle between the new boss of the Harpoon and themselves. They quartered about on the flat below the mouth of the coulée, often within rifle shot of the Harpoon house, for the better part of half an hour. Then Jarrett bunched them, barked swift orders, and they suddenly rode north.

Russ saw this with immediate alarm. The Chain's shake down and the subsequent disruption of his own plans to let Jarrett retake the entire herd, only to lose it again, doubled, left him with enough bitterness toward the Orrs to feel little concern over how they would fare in the face of a direct Buckhorn attack. What they got out of this now, they'd asked for.

But part of his planning was to keep Chain intact on the other side of him, so that he would have a source of reinforcements, if they were needed at the final showdown. Jarrett seemed to know this. Cameron wondered if the man also knew how much he was banking on drawing Sam Colson's inflexible law into it at the last, too. He wondered if Jarrett, during the night or as a result of the fake fracas at the *Tres Piños*, had taken Colson out of the running. He wanted to know this so badly that he considered sending Pop into town. But this would cost him a man long enough to make the round trip, and, if Colson was still at hand, he had no good cause that could be used to draw the sheriff away from his town.

At last he was forced to give over thinking about Colson. In spite of the trader's flint Rae Orr had shown, and her brother's stolid carrying out of her orders, he was certain Chain would buckle in front of Jarrett now. In the first place, Rae would be expecting Buckhorn to take the half of the herd left in the Harpoon's coulée before it came on after the half Bert had driven north. Chain wouldn't be expecting attack without warning, and expectation was half the play in something like this. He watched Jarrett's crew top a lift upvalley. Then he wheeled on Kimberly.

"Leather up!" he snapped. "We've got to ride!"

Russ's five were in saddle and on the Buckhorn's trail in moments. But Russ knew he rode with a divided force. Kimberly and the other three from The Needles looked at the whole thing purely on the basis of a gamble in which odds were the deciding factor. To them, pursuit of Jarrett at this stage of the game was doubly foolish. In the first place, the Buckhorn outnumbered them — probably outnumbered the combined strength of themselves and the Chain crew. Secondly the Orrs had forfeited any right to assistance when Bert made his demand for half the cattle cut. Pop Seame rode willingly. His strange loyalty to Rae Orr made him do that. But he didn't approve. He accepted the ride as a necessity and was bitter about it. These things were evident on the faces riding shoulder with Russ Cameron. His own reactions would not boil down so clearly. With Kimberly and The Needles men, he fully knew there was foolishness in pressing so closely on Jarrett's heels. He knew a certain amount of luck had fallen into their laps when Buckhorn ignored the half of the herd they were holding and went on toward

Chain. He knew neither himself nor his men were yet ready to make a final facing against Jarrett if for no other reason than the fact his hole card from the sheriff's office in town hadn't yet been drawn out onto the grass of the basin. These thoughts ran swiftly through a part of his mind that was cool and mechanical in his dealing with them — that part of his mind that had fostered his whole plan at once to clean the valley and win himself a foothold in it. But in another part of his mind was a picture of Rae Orr in a wrapper. A picture of a tousled-headed girl who tried to fight like a man, yet looked wholly like a woman. Along with that picture was recollection that Ed Jarrett had wanted Rae Orr as long as he had wanted the basin. It was this part of his mind that drove him, now, and he was helpless against it.

The Buckhorn had ridden fast. Rifle fire was angry at Chain as Russ lifted his crew over the last rise and tipped down at the ranch buildings below. Jarrett had struck as Russ had feared he would, savagely, with full force, and with the intent of wiping out one of his two enemies in the valley. Three men were sprawled in the dust of the compound, dropped as they had run from the sudden onslaught. A fourth figure, vaguely familiar, lay face down on the floor of the porch, about a yard from the main door of the house. One Chain man was apparently holed up in the bunkhouse. His rifle snarled with regularity there. But Russ saw he was about finished. Three Buckhorn men were angling in toward him under cover and the bunkhouse was too sprawled for one man to hold.

160

The rest of the Buckhorn was fanned out in the yard and outbuildings, driving lead into the house. Fire answered from windows, but it was sporadic and Russ judged there weren't above three or four men at weapons there. Jarrett was at the extreme wing of his crew, directing them coolly. Guessing that the attack had been in progress about five minutes, Russ realized another five would see it finished. Twisting in his saddle, he swung his arm with clear meaning. His crew split a little apart, forming into a thin line, riding abreast and about thirty feet apart. They burst from the timber of the slope in this formation.

Just as they appeared, the door of the house below suddenly opened and Rae Orr ducked out through it onto the porch. Jarrett raised from where he was crouching and shouted to his men. The girl bent untouched above the man lying on the boards in front of her, straightened with the weight of his shoulders, and dragged him inside. About the time the door closed behind her, Jarrett shouted again. He had seen the Harpoon line.

At extreme range, Kimberly slid his rifle from its boot and began to fire, sitting loosely in his saddle. Russ was about to stop the waste of powder when he saw a crouching Buckhorn rider jerk suddenly upright and fall like an axed tree. Kimberly grinned, spat, and swung to a fresh target. Russ saw dust leap sharply beside Ed Jarrett. The range was dropping. Some Buckhorn lead was beginning to reach back up the slope at them. It looked like it was going to settle into a pitched stand and Russ was guessing how close he dared ride his boys before he scattered them to cover when Jarrett suddenly howled at his own men.

They broke shelter, streaked back of the Chain stable, and reappeared in a moment, astride the horses they had left bunched there. They strung out in ragged file northward for half a mile before they began to bend around and line for home. As they reached the open, they split, each man taking a divergent angle. Russ watched them for a moment, grinned that Jarrett had enough respect for him to provide, like that, for pursuit. Then he signaled his own men to disregard the running Buckhorn and drive straight on to the Orr house.

Pop Seame saw the grin on his face as they flung down in a whirl of dust in front of the Chain porch. "I doubt Ed ran from us, son!" he said dryly. "Look!"

Eastward, where they would be carefully by-passed by the retreating Buckhorn crew, two riders were lining toward the Chain at a driving run. Behind them, hanging in the clear air, was a tracery of dust that led back to the point where they had deserted the trail from town for the short cut they now rode. Russ recognized them both. Sheriff Sam Colson and Sue McKenzie.

He shook his head. Kimberly came up, having already bent for a moment beside the three Chain riders in the clay of the compound. Russ glanced inquiringly at him.

"Dead," Kimberly said quietly. "And there's another one spilling out the door of the bunkhouse."

Russ nodded thoughtfully.

Colson had been waiting for the right sign from Ed Jarrett. The beating the rancher had handed Pop Seame hadn't been it, nor had Russ's being beaten. Locking Colson in his own jail hadn't been it, nor the fracas at the *Tres Piños* that had covered Jarrett's attempt to steal a patient out of Doc Marple's office hospital. Maybe this would do the trick. Colson was a deliberate man and cool enough when he waited for something. But four dead men would turn a pretty strong stomach, and there was the fifth man who had been rescued from the planking of the porch floor. Russ turned toward the house.

The door opened to his hand. Three riders were knotted at a front window, watching Kimberly and his three companions in the yard and, beyond them, the drumming approach of the two horses from town. Back of them, Rae was doubled up with a pan of water and a strip of white cloth beside a couch. Bert Orr was stretched out on the cushions. His blood was on Rae's fingers. Russ crossed to her.

She had been ineffectually dabbing at a big hole in Bert's chest. Russ pushed her to one side and stripped Bert's shirt away from the wound. Rae looked at him through eyes that floated in her pallid face.

"He's dead!" she said dully. "He's dead . . . I did it . . ."

"He's a long ways from dead!" Russ said sharply. "He'll stay that way if I can have some bandage and some hot water!"

The girl stood up, shook herself, and moved abstractedly off toward the back of the house. Russ

163

stared at her clumsy efforts to take care of Bert. She'd been cool enough, dragging him off of the porch under a fire none of her men had apparently been willing to face, and it struck him as strange that she'd crack now.

Bert appeared to have lost too much blood before he'd been dragged in, but the wound itself was clear and the girl's alarm was wholly unjustified. In a woman apart from these things, maybe, but in Rae, who had planned to trade violence with two men for grass, no! Russ sat back on his heels, waiting for the girl to come back and waiting, also, for Sam Colson and Sue to reach the house. While he sat there, Bert opened his eyes.

"I told Rae you'd come, Cameron," he breathed. He stirred a little and a worried furrow creased his forehead. "She's had enough. Remember that, Cameron. I couldn't make her see, but Jarrett's bullets did! Go easy on her, man!"

"Sure," Russ agreed gently. But he didn't understand Orr and was unwilling to pry deeper now.

Moments later, the door opened and Pop Seame came in. The sheriff of Taprock County was behind him. And behind Colson was Sue McKenzie. She ducked past both men as she passed through the door and ran swiftly toward Russ. He came to his feet, smiling uncertainly. But she never saw his face. Her shoulder brushed his chest and she dropped to her knees beside the man on the couch.

"Bert!"

That single word cleared many things in Russ's mind. Sue McKenzie was still a beautiful woman. She had been a help when he needed help, and there was understanding between them. But here was the trial and the proof. Friendship could be fashioned out of those things, nothing more. The rest belonged to Bert Orr. Russ thought there would be regret in this, but there was none. A moment later, he understood why. Rae Orr came back from the kitchen, steadied now, and carrying a folded sheet and a basin of water. There was a woman's plea for a man's helping strength in her eyes. The pride was gone and the avarice that had set basin grass above neighbors and above honor. She smiled and he met that before he turned toward Colson.

The sheriff was looking at Kimberly and Meredith and Pardee and Cable. They stood easily along the wall, watching him with neither defense nor concern. He swung back to Russ.

"Your crew, Cameron?"

Russ nodded.

"Sue told me you'd hired one. She was worried about it. Didn't say anything to me for a long time. But she couldn't hold it in. She thought maybe you were after the whole basin, yourself."

Russ looked at Rae Orr. The girl colored but said nothing.

"What do you think, Colson?"

"I don't know," the sheriff said quietly. "But that'll wait. Ed Jarrett has walked across the line. There's four dead men out in the yard and Bert Orr with a hole through him. I'm riding south for the Buckhorn and I'm looking for a posse. Your boys'll throw in?"

Kimberly's watchfulness faded. A wide grin creased his face. "It'd be a pleasure, Sheriff."

Dry humor pulled at Colson's lips. Russ cut through it, driven by a certain edge of fairness. "Jarrett was trailing stolen stock when he came here, Colson."

"I can't know that unless somebody kills a lot of precious time telling me about it, can I?" the sheriff snapped. "I can't know that any more than I can know where you got your men."

The way he said it, Russ knew that Colson knew fully about the raid on the Buckhorn herd, and that Sue, finally making up her mind between two men, had betrayed the confidence of one to save another from a possible menace. The way Colson turned to Kimberly and Pop Seame and the rest made it plain, too, that such things as riding with a posse padded with men from The Needles counted for little now, that there would be a later reckoning for them.

"We're riding to Buckhorn, boys," Colson said sharply. "This time we're after wolves, not stock. Ready?"

Pop Seame slid out the door. The rest followed. As Russ moved forward, Rae Orr caught his arm momentarily. "Come back, Russ Cameron," she said tensely. "Be sure. I want to talk to you."

"Business?" Russ asked wickedly.

"Business," she agreed. But there was more than that in her eyes.

Ed Jarrett had gone home to make his big fight for certain good and definite reasons. The Buckhorn house

166

was small, low-built, and solid timber. The rest of the ranch buildings were nearly a quarter of a mile distant, across the creek. The entire open about the house had been carefully cleared of anything that might afford attackers shelter. It was plain that an integral part of the man's plan had been to draw his foes in at the end to his own roost. Russ looked down through slanting afternoon sun at the stronghold and shot a black look at Colson.

"There's only one way," he said.

Colson nodded. "I've known that from the beginning. Every man fights differently. Jarrett likes to copper his bets as he goes. This won't be easy. Will you boys stick?"

Russ nodded. Colson glanced at the three Chain riders who had come with them.

"So will Orr's men. They'll remember their saddle mates, dropped in the grit of their own yard. That kind of remembering makes any man fight!" Colson broke off and turned to his posse. He broke it up into twos, spreading them so that they'd form a wide circle around the Buckhorn when the charge started. Then he put a hand on Russ's arm.

"We're not all going to pull out of this. That's all right with your boys from The Needles. They know that, if they ride through this, they've got clean plasters in my county as long as they ride straight trails, and there never was a man holed up in those hills that wouldn't like to ride easy again. It's all right with Orr's boys. They've got a chore to do. And it's all right with me. This is my business. But how about you, Cameron?

We both know Orr'd give you back what you paid for his spread, any time. We both know you haven't got enough cash to stock it or operate and no chance of getting stock from Buckhorn with me rodding this fight. What are you in it for?"

Russ shrugged. "I don't know, Colson."

He had owned reasons in the beginning, reasons sufficiently worthwhile to risk sinking the savings of half a dozen years of ceaseless traveling and to buck a man who had held even the law of the basin to rigid caution. They had been in part a liking for this land and a sudden realization that he wanted a place among neighbors and friends. They had involved visions of the growth of a solid ranch about the old house on the Harpoon and thoughts of two women. Visions, thoughts, and reasons were alike gone. They left nothing. He knew that when he'd finished this ride with Colson, if he was not planted under the sod of this valley, he was through with it. The Orrs had not been neighbors. Sue McKenzie had not wanted him. Rae Orr had paid him in suspicion and enmity. His careful planning by which he hoped to make Ed Jarrett stock his ranch had failed. He knew Sam Colson had kept him with him to give him this opportunity. He knew the sheriff was waiting for him to realize suddenly that no ties held him here. He knew that no man in the valley would condemn him if he turned, now, and rode for Taprock. Most would be grateful for what he had already done. He knew that Bert Orr would take back the Harpoon eagerly, possibly paying him a profit for his efforts, and, in Chicago, John Shane would be eager to rehire his ace agent. But he couldn't go.

"The boys are set," he said to Colson.

The sheriff grunted and raised in his stirrups, giving the signal. "Let's go!"

The sun was warm on Russ Cameron's chest as he started down the slope beside Sam Colson. Its gentle heat was on the back of his hands as he dropped his reins and began to shoot. He could see Kimberly and Pardee, Pop Seame and Meredith, stubby Cable and an Orr rider, and the other two Chain men, converging on the Buckhorn houses through its strong light. He saw smoke and heard lead in the air above him. But these things were dimmed by one thing in his vision. His eyes were fastened on the wide front door of Ed Jarrett's house. Beyond that portal was the man he had stayed in Taprock to beat. Whatever emptiness there might be in victory now, he knew pride would not let him go until Jarrett was done. Colson sang out warningly to him once as they raced through rifle fire so close in to the house that handgun slugs began their deeper howling about them, but Russ held on. His horse took two diversely angling shots at once and went down in a somersault that hurled Russ into the air. He quit the saddle gracefully, kept his feet drawn up under him, and hit the ground a yard from Jarrett's front step. He vaulted onto the verandah before he was touched. When the touch came, it was hot, sickening, and mercilessly hard. It spilled him flat, so that he lay as Bert Orr had laid on the Chain porch earlier in the day. With his head twisted to one side, he saw in odd detachment that Kimberly and his partner, together with two of the Chain men and Sam Colson, were driving in against the house in his tracks.

He pulled himself together, remembering that his charge against the door had not been for glory, but to open a way through. It must have looked for a moment as though he was going to make it or the others wouldn't be following the same line. He was dully aware that they had thought he was going to get the door open ahead of their rush, and that he hadn't now put them in a bad spot.

He shifted, his muscles slow, but steady enough, still, and rapped a pair of shots into thick pine planking near the hinge edge and at about the level at which he judged the inner bar to be. He lifted himself to his feet, then, squared, and drove the full impact of his weight in putting a boot against the portal. The shock took his breath, dazed him. He fell back and lunged again, more weakly. The bar within gave and the door swung suddenly wide. His weight had been against it and the sudden give flung him full length across the threshold. Buckhorn guns flung a leaden scythe through the opening, but, because they expected a standing man in the opening, they all fired at waist level. Prone, under their fire, Russ's eyes focused on one face. Jarrett's gun was dropping as he pulled gently at his trigger. His gun fired. So did Jarrett's; so did others'. Russ felt his body quiver beyond his control at fresh blows, but the feeling was abstract. What counted was a satisfaction that went through him like a drug. Jarrett was dead, dead on his feet. The work was done.

Russ was not conscious of the final, stubborn step Ed Jarrett took toward the man who had beaten him before he fell. He wasn't conscious of the merciless gunfire Colson and Kimberly and Pop Seame and the rest brought with them through the doorway he had opened. He couldn't measure the relentless thoroughness with which Sam Colson's slow-moving law did its work or the unhurried calmness with which his crew from The Needles won their promised peace with Colson or Chain crew's full revenge for their dead saddle mates. Nor was he aware of the changes that three days brought across the basin.

Doc Marple was asleep in a chair beside the fire in the wide main room of the old Harpoon house. Outside, Russ heard Sam Colson's slow voice and big Kimberly's chuckle. Turning his head, he saw through the window, beside Marple's dozing figure, a wagon rolling into the yard. It was loaded with trunks and boxes and Sue McKenzie sat beside Bert Orr on its seat. The girl was driving and Bert, one arm in a sling, was grinning at her.

Russ moved restlessly, shoving his memory back painfully to see if he had talked with Bert since the fight at the Buckhorn. He decided he had not and he was puzzled that Orr was moving into the Harpoon like this. He must have said something, for a quiet voice answered him.

"That wagon load is mine, Russ Cameron. Bert and Sue just brought it down for me."

Russ turned his head. The front door stood open and Rae Orr was beside the bed. He stared incredulously at her.

"Yours?" he said. "Yours, coming down here. Why?"

Rae smiled at him. "Because I sold Chain to Bert . . . for twelve thousand dollars. I thought maybe you'd let me store my things here for a little while."

$12,000! The $12,000 he had paid Bert for the Harpoon. He was thinking that $12,000 would be enough to stock Harpoon and put it on its feet. But it was kind of funny. Chain had been Rae's. Harpoon had been Bert's. Now they'd just traded around. He didn't understand it. Rae knew, of course, that she could buy him out for what he'd put into Harpoon. Sam Colson would have told her that. But why hadn't she stayed where she was and let Bert buy his own spread back?

He raised himself on his elbows, staring hard at the girl. She looked now the way she had that first instant he had seen her in her wrapper in the Chain house — that first instant before she'd turned hard. The notion had persisted since he'd seen her bent over Bert when he was wounded that Rae was done with trading and a man's business in the valley. He was troubled once more to think that she wasn't.

"Why do you want Harpoon?" he said carefully.

Rae dropped onto the edge of his bed. She was laughing openly, eagerly now.

"Who says I do?" she countered softly. "You don't know why I sold Chain to Bert and Sue? Maybe it was because Sue said she liked my house best. Maybe it was because she told me how you liked the old one here . . ." She stopped.

From across the room Doc Marple grumbled irritably: "Won't you two ever let me get some sleep? For three days Rae's kept me working at you like a crazy man, trying to save you from the trouble I promised if you got yourself torn up before that infection was gone! And now, when you're comin' out, you've got to play dumb! For Lord's sake, if you want this ranch and nothing else out of the smoking hell you bought yourself into, say so and let me get some sleep!"

Vague realization dawned. Rae colored deeply and shot an accusing glance at the grinning doctor. Russ stared at her, realizing again that here was a beauty as poignant as Sue McKenzie's and the more rare because the iron that had made Rae hard when she dealt in grass also gave her a strength Sue would never own. Russ shook his head in bewilderment and sank back. But presently he was grinning. He had boasted when he bought Harpoon that it was a gamble. It had been. Also he had not even known the stakes for which he'd play when he made that boast! Land, yes — and neighbors. Friends and a place in the valley. He had the wisdom to see these things. But not Rae. Yet, thinking of it, he saw how empty the rest would be without this last. This, then, was a gambler's luck!

Proud Rider

by Harvey Fergusson

Harvey Fergusson was born in Albuquerque, New Mexico, but left the territory as a young man to go East and returned only for brief visits. Of the fifteen books Fergusson wrote, critics have singled out five of them for special commendation, and those happen to be the five historical romances set in the Southwest. The first three, chronologically, are *The Blood of the Conquerors* (Knopf, 1921), *Wolf Song* (Knopf, 1927), and *In Those Days* (Knopf, 1929). These three novels were later reissued in a trilogy titled *Followers of the Sun* (Knopf, 1936). They embody, as do the last two Southwestern novels, *Grant of Kingdom* (Morrow, 1950) and *The Conquest of Don Pedro* (Morrow, 1954), the classic structure of romance as it has come down to us from the Ancient Greeks. There is an *agon*, or conflict, that requires a clearly defined hero to resolve it in the course of a *pathos*, or the passion portion of the story, resulting in a final *anagnorisis*, or recognition. Fergusson articulated the recognition to be found in all five of these novels in his Foreword to *Followers of the Sun* when he observed that "the pioneering past has now been diligently debunked, but as surely as the flavor of reality had been recaptured the quality of the heroic has been lost. I sought to unite them because it seemed to me the heroism of the pioneer life was genuine and had lost its value."

In terms of the internal chronology of the trilogy, *Wolf Song* comes first. It is a mountain man story and its hero, Sam Lash, was based loosely on Fergusson's impression of Kit Carson. The story concerns Sam Lash's impassioned love affair with Lola Salazar, a beautiful *rica* maiden, and his life and death battle — a *sparagmos*, or mangling, is also a vital ingredient of Classical romance — with a savage Cheyenne warrior. The Cheyenne is vanquished, of course, and Lash is united with Lola at the end. But such a bald statement of Fergusson's plot does not convey the remarkable lyricism of his style, an almost tactile sensuousness, or his gift for vividly characterizing the land in its many moods.

The Mexican heroine, of course, is another notable characteristic of Fergusson's Southwestern fiction. "Some of these Mexican girls took a powerful hold upon his flesh," the reader is told about Jean Ballard, the hero of *Grant of Kingdom*. "Many of them were pretty and they had a soft and voluptuous quality, a completeness of submission and response that made them wholly different from the shrill and nervous women, laborious and full of malaria, he had known in Indiana." Perhaps we might shrug our shoulders and say, well, all the Mexican women Ballard met really were this way, to say nothing of the "shrill and nervous" women back in Indiana. However, every character in the novel agrees with Ballard's experience.

Fergusson was close to his maternal grandfather, Franz Huning, who arrived in Santa Fé in 1850 and became a successful merchant in Albuquerque in the years after 1857. Huning left behind him a memoir on which Fergusson based, to an extent, both *In Those Days* and the fifth and perhaps finest of his Southwestern novels, *The Conquest of Don Pedro*. Robert Jayson is the hero of *In Those Days*, a man who comes to New Mexico, becomes a prosperous merchant, only to wind up a victim of change. This is essentially the same plot as *The Conquest of Don Pedro* in which Leo Mendes, a Jewish peddler, comes to New Mexico, becomes a successful merchant, and, finally, loses everything, including his young and beautiful Mexican wife who is attracted to, and won by, an Anglo-American, although for Leo "a man's destiny is a thing he discovers, a mystery that unfolds", and the end of the story can be interpreted as a new beginning. Robert Jayson is a victim — as is almost every sympathetic character in these five novels — to the encroaching Anglo-American invasion. Ideologically he fails because he must fail, because he is a victim; and he is a victim because the "historical" aspect of the romance declares that he must be a victim in order to make poignantly evident the moral message concerning the spiritual emptiness of Anglo-American materialism. Leo Mendes, on the other hand, is not so completely a victim because, while Leo may be "wholly unable to deal with the world that was creeping up on him, a

177

world in which men were always counting their dollars and their minutes", he is left with an option, namely to pull out and leave. "The West," James K. Folsom wrote in *Harvey Fergusson* (Steck Vaughn, 1969), "in [Fergusson's] fiction is a good place *to be from* rather than a desirable place to *return to*."

Harvey Fergusson's view of the American West and the frontier was, therefore, somewhat misanthropic, but even knowing that does not prevent a reader from being utterly charmed by his images, his characters, and the lyricism of his fiction. "Proud Rider" was serialized over two issues in *Blue Book*, one of the most sophisticated of the pulp fiction magazines and a companion publication of *Red Book*. For some reason Fergusson never chose to reprint it during his lifetime. And so, to correct what in my view has been definitely a wayward oversight, here is the short novel as Harvey Fergusson wrote it.

CHAPTER
ONE

One day Antonio Salazar, the old man who had charge of *Don* Pascual's stables, came and told him that one of the stable boys, a Navajo Indian called Juan, had been secretly riding the wild black stallion. Old Antonio was a *peón* who had been in the *don*'s service all his life. He was an excellent horseman, and like most good servants a merciless martinet in his own small sphere of authority.

"I think the boy should be whipped at the post," he told the *don*. "In the first place, the stallion might have been injured, and he is a priceless animal. In the second place, the slave could easily have been killed, and he is a strong boy of nineteen, worth five hundred dollars of anybody's money. Moreover, discipline must be maintained."

It was a strong argument, but the *don* was a horseman as well as a plutocrat. He wanted to see the stallion ridden. He went to the corral, called the slave, gave him a good scolding for his disobedience, and then commanded him to mount and ride Diablo.

The boy did not utter a word or bat an eye. He got a basket in which he had been accustomed to feed the stallion his oats, went into the corral, and whistled. The stallion came forward, nickering. While he nuzzled the basket, the boy slipped a hackamore over his head, swung quickly upon his back, and rode him several times around the corral. The stallion snorted, shied, and pranced, showing all his magnificent action, but he did not buck, and he responded easily to the rope against his neck. When the boy slid off, the stallion swung his head, teeth bared, but the boy stood his ground, making an almost imperceptible movement of the hand, and the stallion did not bite him.

The *don* went away without saying anything, but he was immensely pleased. Plainly the horse was afraid of the Indian, and the Indian was not afraid of the horse. He certainly had a fine horseman in the boy, and potentially he had a racehorse in the stallion. The animal was soft from long idleness, but he was not more than seven years old, and he could be trained to become hard. The *don* called Antonio before him and curtly ordered him to have the slave boy ride the stallion every day.

The *don*'s full name was Pascual José Montoya y Penalosa, and he lived in the Rio Grande valley north of El Paso when that region was still a part of the young Republic of Mexico. The valley had already been settled for 150 years. Aristocratic families had lived for four generations on great estates granted them by the King of Spain. These men of wealth owned not only the earth but also its inhabitants. Most of the common people they held in *peonaje* by bonds of debt, handed down from father to son, and they also had many Indian slaves, mostly Navajos, that they had taken in

180

war or bought at the animal fairs in Taos and Chihuahua.

The establishment of *Don* Pascual comprised nearly 100 persons, including slaves, *peónes*, and members of his family. His house embraced two large courtyards, and there was a third enclosure, surrounded by an adobe wall ten feet high topped with growing cactus, where some of his servants had their quarters and where his coach and his best horses were kept. His fields of grain and chili extended up and down the valley for miles. Besides his farm lands he owned many square miles of mesa and mountain, both east and west of the valley, and pastured thereon more than 10,000 cattle and a fine herd of horses.

Much of his range land the *don* had never seen, for it was always a precarious business to venture far from the valley. The Comanches to the east, the Navajos to the west, and the Apaches to the south all made war upon the Mexicans. These savage tribes took toll of the *don*'s sheep every year and almost at will. They made travel dangerous, and the extension of civilization impossible. In his great house and upon his own estates *Don* Pascual and his people were safe enough, but it was different with his *peónes* who followed his herds across the mesas. The Navajos killed a certain percentage of them every year, just as surely as the coyotes killed some of his lambs.

When a young man, the *don* had married a beautiful girl of fourteen belonging to one of the best families, and their union was prolific. His wife bore him fifteen children, and no less than nine of them survived — a high percentage for those days. For a while after his wife's death the *don* lived only in his grief, but he had a very strong sense of duty toward his God, his family, and the state, and all of these required of him that he should marry again. The selection of a wife was complicated by the fact that the *don* could marry literally anyone he chose. Marriages in those days were arranged by families. Although in some cases the girl's wishes might be considered, no mere feminine whim would ever stand in the way of an alliance with the family and estate of Montoya. The *don* had considered many possible candidates for the honor of his hand, but he had a strong predilection for younger girls in general and for one in particular. His selection was the *Señorita* Adelita Chacon, the sixteen-year-old daughter of a near neighbor, *Don* Ramón Chacon.

Adelita Chacon was the only girl in a large family of boys, with the result that she had grown up a little wild and hoydenish, sharing the sports of her brothers when she might better have been employed in needlework, music, and devotional exercises. She was a tall, slender girl with a charming figure and unusual grace and ease of movement. It was this that first caught the eye of *Don* Pascual. Like all true horsemen, he assessed every living thing in terms of action. Adelita had the quick, unself-conscious movements of one who has known the joy of physical freedom, which most women of her time and place had not. Her face was handsome rather than pretty, with heavy black brows, an aquiline nose, and a large but shapely mouth.

182

Their wedding had been a notable occasion. All afternoon a great reception was held, and the dancing after supper lasted until two in the morning. Adelita was as gay as any during the greater part of the dance. Only as it drew toward the end, she found it harder and harder to smile and laugh, although still it was easy to dance. She wished that she could go on dancing forever.

Don Pascual had one friend who he visited more than any other, *Don* Pedro Garcia of Albuquerque, a man of his own age who he had known since childhood, when they had both gone to a private school maintained by a priest in Santa Fé for the sons of the best families. Together they had raided orchards and vineyards, hunted quail and jack rabbits, lost their hats and spurs in horse races with the Pueblos at Isleta. In their early twenties they had twice gone together on the great community buffalo hunts that were held every fall. Those were times to remember, when they first crossed the mountains by way of Pecos and saw the prairies near the Red River black with herds of buffalo and wild horses. The *don* was too old now for that hard-riding sport of killing wild meat with a lance from the back of a horse, but he loved to remember it, and every one of those prairie campfires was bright in his memory, too. Merely to say the name of his old friend was to conjure up visions that made his life seem incomparably rich.

All of it came back to the *don* whenever he sat down to write a letter to his friend, and it filled him with a nostalgia for his youth. It was his chief sorrow that they lived two days' journey apart and both of them were busy men. Each year they exchanged a visit, and that was all they could see of each other, but they made the most of these occasions. Now it was *Don* Pedro's turn to come. *Don* Pascual sat down to write him a long, affectionate letter of invitation and, also in this case, of challenge. They were going to have a horse race. It would not be the first. They often celebrated their meetings in this way, the visitor bringing a gifted colt to try out against one of his friend's. Horse racing was the favorite sport of that whole country, for every man was a gambler by choice and a horseman by necessity. Moreover, speed in a horse was a dearer thing than gold. A horse that could carry a man away from pursuing Apaches or bring him alongside a running buffalo could both save his life and sustain it.

Don Pedro had been boasting for several years of a buffalo horse he had bought in Taos from some Comanches — an ugly, rangy, ewe-necked blue buckskin gelding. *Don* Pedro was entirely convinced that this horse could beat anything on four legs in a long run. In races over a three-mile course, most horses would lead him for a mile or more, and then eat his dust for the rest of the way. *Don* Pascual was delighted to believe that he had something just a little more remarkable than his friend's horse in the shape of the wild black stallion that his own men had caught for him on the plains several years before.

The whole of the prairie country then abounded in wild horses, descended from stock imported by the Spaniards. The catching of wild horses was a precarious and difficult business, although some men made a living at it, and any buffalo-hunting party might try to round up a wild herd if they saw a favorable chance. This usually occurred in dry years when some stallion and his herd of mares were using a water hole that could easily be fenced. It would have to be in a narrow rocky draw or in a patch of brush so that the trap corral could be disguised like a blind for wildfowl. The wild horses would be kept incessantly on the move and away from the water until they were gaunt and desperate. Then they would be rushed into the trap and the gateway closed.

It was in such a roundup that the *don* had caught his black stallion — or rather had watched four of his best men catch him at the risk of their lives. It was only by skilled and lucky roping that they did it, for they caught the fighting wild thing by forelegs and rear at the same time, then got a rope on his neck and stretched him helpless. They tied him between two burros, and he nearly killed one of them, but he was finally brought home and put in a paddock, convinced at last that ropes and walls were too much for him. He had not been submitted to human domination. That was proved when the *don* employed a celebrated horse breaker from El Paso to mount and ride him. He was successfully blindfolded and saddled, and for that matter he was successfully ridden, for like most horses of great speed he was not a powerful bucker. It is the short-coupled, thick-set horse that can lift a man into the air, and this stallion had the long back and tapering barrel of a racer.

It was after the rider had dismounted and the horse stood heaving and apparently beaten that he suddenly rose on his hindlegs and struck with his forehoofs like a boxer. A stable boy was killed, his skull crushed, and another man was painfully injured. A kicking horse is bad enough, but a striking horse is deadly. One can keep far enough away from a horse's heels or close enough to them to be safe, but one cannot keep away from his head. The wild stallions fight endless battles among themselves, and they often fight to the death. Moreover, they fight more with forehoofs and teeth than by kicking. It was in the deadly duels by which he ruled his range that the black stallion had learned to kill, and doubtless men looked like easy game to him.

The *don* made no further effort to have the animal broken. His chief value was for breeding purposes, anyway. He was kept most of the time in a small corral by himself, where he could not injure other stock, and at times he was turned out alone in a fenced pasture to stretch his legs and graze. So he had lived for three years an untamed captive — until the slave boy ventured what all others feared.

For months now the *don* had kept a casual eye on the training of the stallion. He knew the horse was in perfect condition and could run his three miles as the *don* had never seen them run by anything, wild or tame. When he had received *Don* Pedro's promise to come on a certain day, *Don* Pascual called the Indian, Juan, before him. Juan was tall, like most Navajos — a little over six feet. He was straight and lean, fairly broad in the shoulders and very flat in the hips. The *don*

186

wished the boy were smaller and lighter, but he saw at a glance it would be of no use to bant him. He was lean as a coyote in January now, and his weight was all where he needed it — in his arms and shoulders. His complexion was lighter than that of most peónes, and his eyes were gray. That was nothing unusual in a slave of Navajo blood, and the don vaguely remembered that this boy's mother was supposed to have been a white woman. What gave Juan a distinctive look was the fact that his eyes were deep-set and wide apart — generally a mark of intelligence in man, horse, or dog. This, together with his nose, that was high, thin, and curved, gave him an oddly aquiline expression. A hungry young hawk, he looked like, the don thought. He had shuffled in with his hat in his hand, like any other slave or peón summoned before the master — men raised in bondage, wholly at the mercy of their lord. Juan's manner was all right, but something in his look the don did not wholly like. He did not drop his eyes, but bestowed upon his owner a steady, unblinking regard. He was not a perfect slave — but a perfect slave would never have tamed the stallion.

"I am going to race Diablo," the don told him. He paused.

The slave said nothing, nor did a muscle move in his face.

"You will ride him," the don went on. "See that he is ready . . . and you, too."

Excitement showed in the boy's eyes, but his features remained wooden.

"Sí, señor," he said.

The *don* took a silver coin out of his pocket and threw it on the floor. It was the way he always gave money to his inferiors. It was the customary way. Doubtless this was the first time Juan had ever been given money. He stood for a moment looking at the fallen coin, and the *don* began to wonder if he could possibly not have enough sense to pick it up. Juan looked from the coin to the man and back at the coin. Then he stooped and picked up the money and walked out without a word of thanks.

The *don* shook his head. This was a strange fellow, somewhat in need of discipline. But he was not much displeased. He got more than enough bows and thank-yous from his retainers.

CHAPTER
TWO

Juan went back to the stables with a strange excitement thumping in his blood. He had been in the service of *Don* Pascual for nine years, and this was the first time he had been given anything except enough beans and chili to keep him alive, and enough clothing to cover his nakedness. It was also the first time he had been given anything to do except the dirtiest kind of menial work. Had he been born in bondage, his lot would surely have been better, for he would have learned to submit with a good grace, and that was usually all the life of a slave required to make it easy. But he was one of those Navajos who had been captured in battle. He was only ten years old at the time, but Juan retained disturbingly vivid memories of his earlier life, and these, together with a hot and rebellious temper, had made it hard for him to accept a life of work and obedience.

He had been taken in one of the few great government campaigns against the Navajos, led by one Colonel Vizcarra of the Mexican army. Vizcarra had a small detachment of Mexican dragoons, and was assisted by a great many local volunteers. It was a small scouting party of these that came upon an isolated Navajo camp early one morning before the Indians who

189

occupied it were awake. The Mexicans lay in wait until a man appeared at the door, shot him dead, and killed two others as they rushed out when they heard the volley. Charging the hogan, they found inside a woman of about forty years and a boy of about ten. The woman submitted quietly to capture, but the boy fought like a wolf cub until he was rolled in a blanket by his laughing captors.

This woman created a difficult situation when she was taken to Santa Fé. When captured, she was very dirty and looked much like any other Navajo woman, but her light eyes and yellowish complexion showed that she was at least partly Spanish, and a rumor got abroad that she was wholly so. It was remembered that a girl of the Baca family had been captured by the Navajos at the age of five just about forty-five years before, and this woman might well be the same person. When she was washed and dressed like a Mexican woman, she bore an astonishing resemblance to some of the Bacas.

The captive was bewildered and unhappy. She was dragged from one Baca house to another; she was examined and cross-examined; she was kept in stuffy rooms and given chocolate, wine, and many other things to which she was not accustomed. The Bacas split into two factions and quarreled dangerously. One of these accused the other of trying to foist a common savage upon the family, and the other retorted that their opponents were refusing a home and Christian salvation to an authentic Baca. In the midst of the rumpus the woman caught cold, as Indians confined in houses are apt to do, and developed a double pneumonia. A hard-riding Baca brought a priest in time to administer Extreme Unction, and the woman died in the odor of sanctity, to the great relief of all concerned, including herself.

As for the boy, presumably the woman's son, he was completely forgotten and came by purchase into the hands of *Don* Pascual, who admired his sturdiness and good looks. The *don* had him baptized and turned him over to the old woman who managed his kitchen, thinking to make a house servant of him. Juan hung around the kitchen for several years. He was well fed and grew rapidly, but as a scullion he was a complete failure. He resented orders and menial tasks, and was much inclined to fight anyone who tried to force him. He was cuffed and scolded, and his temper grew bad.

He was finally kicked out of the kitchen for stealing and eating a whole chicken prepared for the master's table, and relegated to the stables, where old Antonio was told to make what use he could of him. His life at once became much harder and less nourishing. He slept on a pile of straw under a couple of sheepskins, got only a daily dole of *chili con carne* instead of the rich pickings from the table and all the food he could steal from the kitchen. A rapidly growing boy, he was often hungry, and sometimes at night he was cold. Old Antonio, seeing that he had a surly and rebellious temper, singled him out for discipline. Juan worked hard cleaning stables, carrying water for horses, pitching hay, mending harness, and splicing rope. He was strong and good at his work, but he got no praise

— only a curse or a slap if he was slow. Yet he worked as he had not worked in the kitchen, because he liked horses. The very smell of a horse was good in his nostrils, and he had some chance to ride horses too when he brought them from pasture or took them back. Seeing that he had a good seat, old Antonio gave him the job of riding unbroken colts. Juan enjoyed this, but he carefully concealed his joy in this work for he knew that Antonio gave it to him as a punishment.

It was in exactly the same spirit that the old man gave Juan the care of the stallion. Daily Juan filled the haymow in Diablo's stall and gave him oats when these were ordered. He could feed the horse and fill his watering trough without entering the small corral where he was kept, but in order to clean his stall it was necessary to go inside. No one wanted that job. Juan didn't want it. He was as much afraid of the stallion as anyone, and always worked with one eye on the horse that had several times chased men out of his corral with his teeth bared, squealing with rage. But Juan took a fascinated interest in the stallion. When he had nothing else to do, he spent hours at a stretch sitting on the corral fence, staring at the great shining black brute that no one had ever broken. He finally came to know for certain that he would one day mount the stallion and try to master him. This was not a desperate resolve or even a plan. It was merely a part of his destiny previsioned and accepted with the deep unconscious fatalism of his kind. He knew he would try to ride the stallion one day, just as he knew that one day he would die — and he was aware that both events might take place at once. But he did not believe they would. He approached the horse gradually and with all of his cunning. In the fact that he fed Diablo, he had a great advantage. Deliberately he began half starving the horse, giving him less than his allowance of hay, secretly spilling part of his oats. When Diablo was always hungry, Juan began giving a peculiar whistle every time he fed him, and it was not hard to make the stallion come to the call. Neither was it hard to put a hand upon him when he first plunged an eager muzzle into his grain, and then to rub him with a handful of straw. All horses like being rubbed, once they are used to it. Soon the sound of Juan's whistle and the touch of his hand were associated by the ravenous horse with his only source of nourishment.

Juan had a primitive man's instinctive grasp of animal consciousness. He knew what he could hope to do by cunning and kindness, and where only force would serve. These blandishments were preliminaries of battle. They continued until he had accustomed the stallion to a hackamore on his head and a surcingle about his belly. He knew it was hopeless to try to saddle the horse alone, but that did not trouble him much. Nearly all of his riding had been bareback, and he did not doubt his ability to stick to the horse. The danger all lay in getting on and off.

He had necessarily sneaked out to the corral late on moonlight nights to work with surcingle and hackamore, and it was near midnight under a full moon that he went stealthily as a thief to his first encounter. As many times before, he put the hackamore over the stallion's head while he was eating, and buckled the broad grass girth about him from behind the side of his stall. He was tense with mingled terror and excitement as he led the horse into the middle of the corral. Diablo had been broken to lead with a breeding pole, and he followed quietly, but Juan knew it was a quiet that might at any moment explode into fighting violence. As soon as he was in the clear, he vaulted onto the stallion's back. It was no use being gentle now. He could feel the horse gather under him, and then he was lifted skyward as Diablo fought with lowered head and squeals of rage to rid himself of a burden that enraged and terrified him.

The stallion made a dozen splendid plunges, but, because he was above all a creature of speed, they lacked the powerful jerk that enables the most gifted buckers almost to snap a man's head off. These were long, smooth plunges, and Juan rode them with ease. The last of them brought the horse fully against the high pole fence of the corral. He came up short on his haunches, whirled, and ran, only to bring up again before the fence on the other side.

He never smashed into the barrier, for he had learned the fear of fences on the day he was caught after battering himself against them until he bled. It was the fear that made his conquest possible, for, if he had hurled himself against the fence, Juan would hardly have escaped without broken bones. As it was, after half a dozen rushes he came to a trembling, bewildered stop in the middle of the corral. That was the worst place of all to leave him. Juan kicked him with both heels,

194

lashed his rump with the rope end of the hackamore, but the stallion stood like a rock for terrible seconds. Finally he made a single plunge that brought him a few yards nearer the fence. Before he could gather himself again, Juan was off his back and running for the fence. As he went over it with an agility born of terror, the stallion rose on his hind legs, and those terrible forehoofs clattered against the poles in a double blow that would have smashed a man's skull.

Juan lay safely just out of reach, weak with fear and weariness. He knew that Diablo had to be cured of charging men, as he had been cured of charging fences. Man-killing horses are rare, but their ways are known to all who deal with the wild stock of the prairies, because a man killer always achieves wide fame. Juan had never before encountered a killer, but he had heard of many. He knew that killers nearly always were shot. In a country where horses were many and cheap, it did not pay to spend time upon them. Even if they were broken of fighting men, they were still a menace to other horses.

He knew, too, that the worst horse can be broken — that any habit in an animal can be destroyed. What he had to do was face the stallion's charge and break it. For the purpose he secured a long leather whip, its handle loaded with lead. He knew that any charging animal has a tendency to stop or swerve, especially on the first rush, if a man stands and faces it. To run is fatal unless cover is surely within reach. A charging bull will always go through with his rush, because he closes his eyes and charges blindly, but a horse charges with

195

his eyes open and his head up. He often turns or hesitates. He, too, may be dodged if he comes straight, but it takes quick dodging.

The next time Juan rode the stallion he slipped from the animal's back in the midst of its bucking, landed on his feet, and stood where he was. The horse made three more jumps, stopped, and turned. Juan stood his ground waiting, tense and ready. So did the horse — for a moment. Then he trotted forward a few paces and suddenly charged, neck outstretched, ears back, teeth bared in a killing fury.

Juan waited until the horse was almost upon him, then stepped aside and with all his force brought the loaded whip butt down upon that spot just behind the ears where the spinal column ends. It is the most vulnerable spot for a blow upon any vertebrate creature. A man can knock a horse down with his fist if he lands upon exactly the right spot, but if he is an inch too far either way, the blow is futile. By luck Juan landed his blow exactly right. The stallion went down with his nose in the dirt, half rolled over with all four hoofs in the air, and then lay flat upon his side as though he had been shot.

A cold sweat of fear broke out upon the boy. In his desperation he had struck with all his might. What if he had struck too hard? What if the stallion were dead or permanently injured? Then Juan would better have gone down under those deadly hoofs. It was probably not more than thirty seconds that the stallion lay there, but the time seemed very long to Juan. Then a quiver

196

ran over the prostrate horse, he raised his head, lifted himself stiffly by his front hoofs — and stood!

Juan was beside him at once, whistling softly in the way he did when he fed the horse, rubbing his neck and belly. This was an important part of the process. The horse did not know what had hit him. Only one thing would remain in that tenacious animal memory — that his charge had ended in a crash of pain and black defeat. Before the stallion had fully recovered, Juan walked quietly away.

Next time he rode the horse, Diablo bucked less, and, when Juan left his back, he faced the animal confidently. Diablo whirled and faced him but did not charge. Juan walked up to him, patted him, whistling softly, and, still whistling, walked away. His triumph was not yet complete, but it was assured.

How Antonio learned of those stolen rides Juan never knew, but one night, when he got off the horse and walked away, he saw the old man standing at the gate, waiting. They stood facing each other in silence for a moment. When first he had been sent to the stables, Juan had been much smaller than Antonio. He remembered how once the old man had given him a kick and sent him head over heels. Now he was nearly a head taller, a strong young man with a great loaded whip in his hand.

"So you have been riding the stallion," Antonio said.

"Yes," answered Juan.

"You know that nobody is allowed to ride him," said Antonio. He spoke quietly, but suppressed rage was evident in his voice.

197

"Yes."

Antonio looked at him in silence again for a moment. He knew this man was now wholly out of his control.

"The *patrón* shall know about this," he said.

" *'Sta bueno*," answered Juan, and walked past the old man.

What would the *don* do to him? He did not care; he was not afraid. He had conquered something besides the stallion. Some cringing fear in himself had also yielded.

The visit of the Garcia family was a social event that shook the house of Montoya like a storm. *Don* Pedro came in a coach drawn by four mules and containing, besides himself and his wife, three daughters and a niece, while his four eldest sons followed on their best horses, and three personal servants brought up the rear.

When all the Garcias had dismounted, the two families rushed into each other's arms like charging armies. Family meant everything to these people. The state was corrupt; the army was a joke; the wilderness pressed upon their valley; Indians menaced their lives and property; but the great families in their recumbent earthen castles stood firmly as mountains from generation to generation. A meeting such as this between two of the oldest and most aristocratic families had nothing perfunctory about it. It was inspired by genuine pride and affection. Everyone embraced everyone else. The two *dones* embraced, kissed each other on the cheek, and hammered each other on the back until the dust flew out of their jackets. The women all first embraced, and then shyly and delightfully the young men and women put their arms about each other, for this was proper in public, on such an occasion.

All of them talked and laughed at once, and finally the whole crowd poured, chattering, into the house where eager hosts led guests to the sumptuous quarters. All of the beds were pallets and the floors were earthen, but luxury lay in the beautiful old blankets of Navajo and Chimayo, the heavy linens, the lamb-fleece rugs washed snowy white, and the bowls and ewers of solid silver, burnished for this occasion so that the tiny hammer marks caught myriad highlights.

Don Pascual's servants had been busy for days making the house ready for these distinguished visitors, and their arrival sent a thrill of heightened activity into every part of his great establishment. In the kitchen the old woman who was his head cook shouted excited orders like a general going into battle. She had two women beating up thick chocolate in wooden bowls while she herself was making ready platters of cakes for the afternoon repast that would be served as soon as the guests had washed the dust out of their eyes. In the stable yard old Salazar had his boys jumping like frightened grasshoppers to care for the visitors' horses. Only Juan, the Navajo boy, was exempt from extra duties. He sat, motionless as a buzzard, on the fence of the small corral where Diablo was kept, watching him munch his oats. He had hardly taken his eyes off the horse for three days except to sleep, and he had slept beside the corral so that no one could possibly annoy or frighten the stallion. Everything depended upon the mood of that moody being.

At four in the afternoon the guests were lightly refreshed with silver mugs full of thick chocolate, and two or three kinds of sweet cakes, with wine and brandy for those who wanted them. They sat and talked almost the whole time until supper was served at eight, and then they faced a table loaded with boiled chickens, roasts of mutton, stews of buffalo meat with chili and several kinds of vegetables, with custards, fruit, and a kind of candy made with brown sugar for dessert. Red native wine stood on the table in silver pitchers, and they drank it as freely as though it had been water.

They dined at two tables, one for the elders and one for the unmarried youngsters. The *don* presided at the board of the elders, with his aged mother on his right and his beautiful young wife opposite him. He loved occasions such as this, and he had come to his seat in a mood of gregarious expansion, but with Adelita under his eye he became uneasy. Everyone admired her beauty, but her conduct now was not all that it should have been. She was visibly bored by a long story *Don* Pedro was telling her. She squirmed perceptibly in her seat, and more than once she threw a glance over her shoulder at the other table where the boys and girls were finding a great deal to laugh about.

The fact was that Adelita had never become a good wife or a proper hostess. She frankly hated needlework, and had little taste for anything about the house. On the other hand, she was interested in horses to the point of obsession. She would seize upon any excuse to visit the corrals and stables, especially when colts were being broken, and a good bronco seemed to give her more pleasure than anything else. All these things annoyed *Don* Pascual, but his unhappiness about Adelita lay deeper than a mere displeasure with her manners. Although they had been married now nearly a year, their marriage remained a sterile one. This not only defeated its chief purpose, but it was sure to cause a great deal of unpleasant gossip about himself.

The *don* was relieved when the meal was over and the elders sat around while the younger ones played games. His mother, enthroned in a great homemade chair that was the only one in the room, presided like a queen. Everyone deferred to her. Presently the *don* took his old friend, *Don* Pedro, by the arm and led him into another room.

"That wife of yours is a fine girl," *Don* Pedro told him. "A devil of a fine girl."

"For the love of God," *Don* Pascual begged him, "let us not talk of women. Women are a nuisance. Let us talk of horses. Now that blue nag of yours, he is going to eat dust tomorrow."

Don Pedro laughed delightedly. "He has never tasted dust in a race yet," he boasted.

"Well . . . a little bet, then," *Don* Pascual suggested. "I have a barrel of brandy twenty years old, and just to show you that I know what I am talking about, I'll put it up against a hundred pounds of your best ground chili."

CHAPTER
THREE

San Juan is the patron saint of horsemen, and the day of San Juan has long been a widely celebrated occasion in New Mexico. It came during the visit of the Garcia family, and *Don* Pascual appropriately chose it as the day for the race. This was a sporting choice, for it meant that a crowd would gather, and neither the *don* nor anyone else knew how a yelling crowd would affect the untried stallion.

On *Día* San Juan everyone mounts his best horse and goes for a ride, and all the people of a neighborhood gather to play games and watch them. The long straight stretch of road in front of the *don*'s house was a favorite place for all such gatherings. Here, as soon as early Mass had been said, horsemen began to gather. Such an occasion brought out all the humble folk of the neighborhood, and some from far away — horse traders, buffalo hunters, and obscure men on fine mounts who probably were bandits.

Before noon they were having a game of *gallo* with fifty riders in line. A live rooster was buried to the neck in a patch of loose sand, and the riders of opposing teams galloped one by one, swung low from their saddles, and tried to snatch the bird out of the earth.

202

When one of them succeeded, he rode away in a dead run, pursued by all of his opponents. If he reached a goal uncaught, he could present the bloody trophy to a lady of his choice.

Women, children and the old men formed a growing crowd on both sides of the course. The *don*, his family, and guests were out on the *portal* to see the sport. Servants and *peónes* crowded the flat roof of the house from end to end. Vendors of melons and wine built booths of cottonwood boughs and did a good business.

Adelita, seated on the *portal* between her mother-in-law and *Don* Pedro, was bright-eyed and restless with suppressed excitement. *Don* Pedro looked at her and laughed. He was a fat, good-humored fellow, and his admiration for Adelita was not at all soured by the fact that she took no interest in him.

"You love horses, *señora*?" he asked.

"Better than anything else on earth, *Don* Pedro!" she exclaimed — and then blushed.

Don Pedro laughed again. It was his secret opinion that his old friend had shown more daring than judgment in marrying so young a girl.

Don Pascual meanwhile was clearing the road for the race. Considerately he had waited until the game was over, although he had no need ever to wait upon anyone. He sent a man up the road and one down, shouting his orders, and the crowd fell back, and the way was cleared.

The famous buffalo horse was led out first. He was not an impressive sight. Raw-boned and ewe-necked, he walked as quietly as a plow horse being led to water.

His color was about that of a mouse, and a wide black stripe ran from his mane to his tail. In this gathering of horsemen none was deceived by the quiet and homely appearance of the horse. What they noted was the long back, the high and powerful haunches, the straight forelegs, set wide apart and powerfully muscled. They knew they were looking at a creature built for speed, and money was wagered that he would win.

Diablo was a spectacular contrast to his opponent. He was led out by two men who managed him with a breeding pole — a stick about twelve feet long fastened to his halter by a very short rope. So held, he could neither strike, bite, nor kick them, but he pranced and curveted, snorting his nervousness through wide-flaring nostrils. Sleek and perfect in coat, with a slim barrel, a full muscular arching neck, and the massive mane and tail of a wild mustang, he was a veritable dream horse. But he did not draw much money from the pockets of the spectators. They knew he was fretting away his energy. They did not doubt he could run, but they doubted whether he could be successfully ridden.

A boy who acted as coachman for *Don* Pedro mounted the buffalo horse and sat waiting while his mount placidly switched at flies. The boy was at least ten pounds lighter than Juan.

Juan followed his mount, carrying a loaded rawhide quirt. His buckskin trousers were belted with a strip of bright red wool, and another strip of the same stuff bound his long dark hair. He wore moccasins and no spurs. Despite his gray eyes and light skin, he looked all Navajo. He also looked frightened and confused, as well

204

he might, for never before had he faced a staring crowd.

Only the *Doña* Adelita was smiling. She looked straight into his eyes and smiled. It was not exactly a smile for him, perhaps, but it fell warmly upon his spirit, and he took it to himself as a freezing man claims a sunbeam. It was the only human and personal thing in that long row of handsome waiting faces. He stood awkwardly for a moment, staring at her, and then turned quickly away.

As soon as he had twisted his left hand into the stallion's mane, he felt better, and, when he sat his mount, he was a man made over, erect and alert, in complete control of himself and his horse. He had been furtive and awkward on his feet, but he was a proud rider. All good horsemen are proud men. Any man on a good horse feels an irrepressible thrill of pride, and looks down upon those who walk the earth. Deliberately Juan rode his fretting mount up and down before the *portal*, to show them all that he had the stallion wholly in hand. He was a stable boy riding a horse for his master, but he was also youth sitting triumphantly upon its first achievement. He was a slave, and he was also the son of two races in which pride is a passion. His blood pounded with the tumult of an inner conflict that this moment had brought suddenly alive. He surveyed the faces of all his masters again — the right people, the fine people, the rich ones. All these names had been given them, and yet not one of them would have mounted this wild horse, the horse that had killed a man. He looked again into the eyes of

Adelita. She was smiling still, but it was not a smile for him. She was a woman, like any other, but as far beyond his reach as the moon. He rode away toward the starting point, his mind filled with a confusion such as he had never known before. He felt like a man awakening from some long half-conscious drowse. He had always accepted his relation to the world as a matter of course. Now, for the first time, it occurred to him to question: why was he bound, and by what right or power? What if he turned his horse toward the mountains now and galloped away? Who could stop him? Who could catch him?

The starter lifted his hand and began to count. The race was on. Deliberately Juan let the blue horse take the lead, hanging back so that the stallion's nose was even with his opponent's flank. Diablo had a soft mouth and was not hard to hold, but the blue had a mouth like a rock, and he could see the light boy on his back sawing and tugging. Then he felt sure of what he had suspected. The boy had been told by his master to let the stallion lead and make the pace. Then, at the end, the blue would be given his head. He was a horse trained to chases and would show the best of his power in overhauling anything ahead of him.

This strategy Juan found easy to defeat. The pace was being made by the blue, and it was a slow one for the first three-quarters of the long straight run. Not until he could see the colors of skirts and shirts in the crowd gathered at the finish did Juan let out his mount. Then with an Indian yell he gave the stallion his head and wrapped the quirt around his rump. Before the boy on the blue knew what had happened, the stallion had shot into a lead of thirty yards and was running like a frightened antelope. Juan lay close to his neck and gave him the quirt at every jump. Looking back, he could see the other rider's legs rising and falling as he spurred the blue, and he knew that the buffalo horse was gaining. He was longer and better trained for such work than the stallion.

The race became a desperate chase, with the buffalo horse hanging at the flank of the stallion like a hound after game. He was gaining by inches, but he wasn't gaining fast enough. As the two horses thundered past the finish, their riders yelling, their hoofs pounding the earth, the stallion still had a lead of more than half a length.

It was a striking finish. The crowd yelled; even the dignified spectators on the *portal* came up standing, and *Don* Pascual gave a whoop of delight that sounded in his own ears like a voice out of his youth when he himself had known the thrill of sitting a winner.

Don Pedro congratulated him, all good humor. "We'll run that race again," he said. "Your boy was better than mine, but I still think I have the best horse."

Don Pascual patted him on the back. "We'll have many races, Pedro," he said. "I only wish that we were young enough to ride them ourselves. For us old fellows there is nothing left better than a good show."

The stallion carried Juan almost a quarter of a mile past the end of the course before Juan could turn him. He was ribbed and streaked with shining sweat, dabbled with his own foam, and blowing heavily when

Juan rode him back to the *portal*, but he was still high-headed and full of battle. Juan slipped off him and stood a moment uncertainly. Afoot, he felt embarrassed, just as he had before. All the fine excitement of the race oozed out of him as his feet struck the ground. He was about to turn away when *Don* Pascual called to him, and with a sudden flip of the thumb tossed him a coin. Juan, expecting nothing, made no effort to catch it, and it fell in the dust. As once before he stood a moment, looking down on it, glanced again at his master, then stopped, as though with an effort, and picked it up. He walked away without a word, dumb with astonishment, for the coin was an eight-sided golden ounce, worth about fifteen Mexican dollars.

Don Pedro shook his head. "You shouldn't let your excitement loosen your fingers so much, Pascual," he said. "That boy will be drunk every day for a week, and every wench in your kitchen will be running after him."

"Not that boy," said *Don* Pascual. "He lives for nothing but horses."

"He can surely ride them," *Don* Pedro remarked. "I wish he belonged to me."

"A year ago you could have had him for his keep," *Don* Pascual replied. "He was good for nothing until he began to ride that stallion."

"Where did you get him?"

"I bought him in Taos. He was one of the Navajos that Vizcarra caught. His mother was a white woman, perhaps of good family, but he was a well-grown boy when I bought him."

Don Pedro nodded knowingly. "You can never make a good Christian out of a Navajo unless you baptize him before he is six. That boy probably never learned the fear of God."

"I know it," *Don* Pascual agreed. "He is just like the horse he rides. He has good blood, but he was caught too late."

CHAPTER
FOUR

After the race Juan was even more markedly a rising man than before. *Don* Pascual gave him two colts to train, both of them sired by the stallion and showing promise of speed. He tended the colts with a devoted care and handled them with the intelligence that was rare among the many kinds of men who served the *don*. The *don* had no special liking for his sullen and impudent stable boy, but he could trust him with valuable horses, and he was always in need of men he could trust with anything. So, in addition to the stallion and the two colts, he presently gave Juan two fine saddle horses of his own use to care for, and a little sorrel mare that his wife sometimes rode.

Juan was now a sort of equerry to his master, but he did not seem to appreciate the personal element in his new responsibility. The *don* sent him a clean shirt now and then, and ordered his hair cut so that he would present a decent appearance before guests, but Juan gave no thanks for these blessings.

One day he was ordered to groom and saddle a horse for the *don* and one for *Doña* Adelita, who was about to be treated to one of her infrequent airings. He led both horses to the front of the house and left them there, but, as he was walking away, the *don* came out and shouted after him angrily.

"Hold that horse for the *señora* while she mounts," he commanded. "And hereafter always wait with a horse until it is taken by the one who has ordered it. You must learn some manners."

Juan silently returned and stood holding the little sorrel.

The *don*'s voice rose to a note of sharp irritation. "Help her mount, fool! Hold your hands for her foot. Don't you know anything?"

Juan, in fact, knew little about helping ladies to mount. He had seen it done, and he obediently cupped his hands. As the girl approached him, he looked up at her, and she smiled at him just as she had on the day of the race. He had never before been near a woman of the gentry, or any woman so clean and comely as she. His eyes dropped before the white flash of her smile, and he stared in amazement at the small foot he held in both his hands, and the ankle he could have ringed with his thumb and finger. She seemed to him a being of a perfection that seldom belongs to men. She was like a bird or a wild animal. He stepped back. As she turned her horse to follow the *don*, she smiled upon him again.

He stood looking after her for several minutes. Then he looked at his own hands. He felt as though her foot had burned its trace upon them. He noticed how dirty they were. He became suddenly aware that he was dirty all over, and that he smelled of horses. Although it was late September, he walked back to the great canal, where a large hole below a water gate was used by all the *peónes* for bathing and laundry, and there he washed himself all over.

From that day on he suffered a new and painful consciousness of himself. He became aware of his dirt, his ragged clothes, his long hair. For the first time in his life he wondered how he looked. He had never seen his own image except for an occasional glimpse of his face reflected in a burnished pot or a pool of water when he stooped to drink, but now he wished for a mirror. He spent his money for bright shirts and strips of red wool to belt his buckskin trousers.

All of this primitive adornment was for the rare times when he held Adelita's horse and helped her mount. It did not happen once a week, even in the best of weather, but it became the most important moment in his life. When the little sorrel was ordered, he groomed himself as carefully as he did the horse, and he stood waiting with a rigid face that hid an intense excitement. Adelita never failed him with her smile, and that smile and the pressure of her foot upon his palm was to him an intercourse that changed the very quality of his life.

Juan had never paid much attention to women, although there was a Navajo girl of fourteen in the kitchen who had been flirting with him for months. Now, however, he lost all interest in the girl, and she was not slow to see it. Neither did she miss the reason.

"*La patrona* rides today," she sneered when she saw him in a clean shirt, and some men working nearby heard her and laughed.

Gossip was going around, but Juan hardly gave it a thought. When next she went for a ride with the *don*, he watched for the time of their return, and was on hand to take the horses. This happened several times, and Adelita always found a chance to smile at him.

Juan did not miss the fact that this smile was always behind the *don*'s back. He stood with a rigid face, looking at nothing while the *don*'s eyes were upon him, but stared at the girl with hungry worship when the man of power turned away. Both of them were at the *don*'s mercy. Far apart as they stood, she was yet as much a slave as he, and this fact nourished the secret sympathy between them.

The *don* permitted the slave to help her mount her horse, for this involved only that she touch him with her foot, which was quite within the conventions. There were great ladies who used male *peónes* and slaves for footstools, and others who cultivated a certain grace in kicking recalcitrant menials of either sex. But no lady could permit a male of inferior birth to touch any other part of her body, so it was necessary for the *don* to help Adelita off her horse while Juan stood by.

Once, as he did this, someone called to him from the house that forty of his sheep had been killed by lightning while huddled under a tree. The *don* forgot all about his wife and walked away cursing his negligent men. Juan and his mistress stood facing each other for a moment, he at the horse's head and she with one hand still upon the pommel. His breath came hard; she smiled at him, and one of her eyebrows lifted, giving her smile an oddly mischievous, mocking quality. She stood a moment, laughed a little with a lift of her head, and brushed past him. He raised his hand, without knowing why, and her shoulder was briefly pressed against it.

Had he touched her or had she touched him? He didn't know, but the feel of her filled him with a frightened excitement. He was no coward, but fear is a flower of bondage. He lived in a world where men were whipped and killed for touching women beyond their right. The touch of his hand upon her left arm left him at her mercy. He turned and followed her with his eyes. She hurried, almost ran in the door, and then over her shoulder threw him a quick, unmistakable smile.

His first feeling was one of relief and gratitude. His touch was forgiven — it was accepted. He turned and walked slowly back to the corral. There he took his favorite perch upon the fence and sat staring at the stallion in long and moody meditation. It was hard for him to believe that this woman had chosen to favor him — and yet he knew she had courted his touch. Such things were rare, but not unheard of, for when they happened, they were widely told. Juan knew of a *rico* who had cut off his wife's ears for showing interest in a man beneath her in station. As for the man, he had disappeared and no one knew what had become of him.

A deep and fatalistic gloom settled upon the boy as he sat brooding. He knew that he could not turn away from this woman. He knew that, if she came near him again and smiled, his hand would go out to her. And he knew that for him death might be in her touch.

For a week he saw nothing of her — because the *don* had gone away to some of his distant ranges, and she could not ride alone. Then one day, incredibly, he saw her come through the narrow gate in the adobe wall that cut off the great house from the corrals and stables.

It was strange and wholly uncustomary for Adelita, for any woman from the great house, to come through that gate. He knew she must be using a liberty that had grown with the absence of the *don*. She went to the stable where her own pony was kept, fed the mare an apple, and talked to a man who was working nearby. The man stood respectfully with his hat in his hand until she had gone. She came then to Diablo's paddock, where Juan was working, and stopped to look at the stallion.

Juan wore no hat, but he returned her greeting and stood uneasily. His words sounded surly in his own ears, but she seemed not at all put out.

"Do you still ride him every day?" she asked, nodding at the horse.

"Yes, *señora*, every day." Her easy words made him feel easier.

"I would give anything to ride him . . . just once," she said.

"You wouldn't find him hard to ride if once you were on him," he said. "But his temper makes him hard to mount."

"How did you come first to mount him?" she asked, and he knew that she was not asking just to make talk. She was truly curious. But he found it hard to explain.

215

"I sat and looked at him," he said slowly, "for a long time every day, and finally I knew that one day I would mount him, even if he broke my neck." He paused, aware that he had not explained anything, and also that explanations were not within his powers. Then he tried again. "If you think about anything long enough," he said, "at last you must do something, no matter what happens . . ." He stopped, flushing and confused. It was perhaps the first time he had ever tried to phrase a general idea. But she nodded with solemn young wisdom.

"You must," she agreed. "But what if you can't?"

He laughed, beginning to feel unaccountably happy. "You ask me hard questions," he said. "You better go to the *padre*. I know nothing about anything except horses."

She laughed, too. "I better go somewhere," she said. "I have no business here."

He watched her all the way back to the gate, and every man and woman about the place watched her, too. That *la patrona* should come out to the corrals and talk to a stable boy!

One other chat across a fence they had, but it was not so successful. After the first few minutes neither could think of anything to say. They stood staring into each other's eyes, silent and embarrassed.

Nearly a week went by before she came to the stables again. He was not at Diablo's stall, but out upon the road riding one of his colts when he saw her, a bright, unusual figure. It was late afternoon, beginning to dusk, but he knew it was she by the height and motion of her figure. She stood out from the kitchen women like a creature of another kind.

He pulled up the colt and sat watching her as a hunter watches distant game, and his blood beat a quickened measure. He saw her feed her mare an apple, exchange a word with old Salazar, go to Diablo's stall, and look, then go on toward the narrow gate. She had sought him; she had come to see him! She should not come in vain.

With rising excitement he slid off the colt and tied it to the hitch rack before the house. He walked to meet her, slowly. He seemed unconcerned, but he was alert as a man walking to meet a deadly foe. He glanced back and all around, and saw that no one was near on his side of the gate. They drew closer together, and he knew that she saw him, knew they would meet. It was dusk; he wished it were darker.

As she approached, his knees seemed to weaken, and his breathing was hard. He was more afraid of this woman than of anything he had ever faced. Yet he could not turn back, and he despised his own fear.

In the gateway he stood aside to let her pass. If she had merely smiled and gone her way, if she had spoken a casual word, the crisis would have been safely passed. But she chose to stop, and once more they stood staring into each other's eyes, helpless and silent. Then she did smile, and with that challenging, mocking lift of the eyebrows, as though she were questioning his courage, daring him.

He watched his own hands go out to her as though they had been no part of his conscious being. He extended them toward her slowly as though asking her what she wanted, and she did not draw back. He laid hold of her arms and felt them unresisting in his hands, saw the quick blood leap in her face and neck, and the lift of her breathing in her bosom. Suddenly she stiffened. He could feel the tendons harden in her arm. And she was looking not at him, but past him at something — something that suddenly filled her eyes with fear. Then she pulled away from his hands, brushed quickly past him, and hurried toward the house. He turned and looked after her. It was nearly dark but unmistakably he saw a dim figure turn the corner ahead of her — a furtive figure seeking to escape unseen.

For a long time after she had left, he stood motionless, bewildered. Why had he done this insane thing? He knew only too well that *Don* Pascual, like every other *patrón* of a great estate, practiced a restless espionage. There were trusted men and women set to watch over all the others. What more likely than that Adelita was always watched? What more certain than that they would be seen?

He walked back to the corral and stood staring at the great black horse again. And again that impulse toward flight possessed him. He could mount and go — where? He knew no world but this one of his master's stable yard. And here he was at their mercy — at her mercy. Whatever she chose to tell now, that would be believed. And whatever the *don* had decided, that would be done. He knew disaster hung over him. For a moment he was afraid; he was a wretch. Then his courage rose

— the fatalistic courage of his kind. He lifted his head and squared his shoulders. Every man must be tried in fire soon or late.

CHAPTER
FIVE

The *don* walked up and down the hard earthen floor of his room, smoking a cigarette furiously, his brows knotted into a pattern of troubled thought. He had been very angry at first, but he was a man who had learned to control his temper. It was necessary to make a decision and to make it with the best of his intelligence, not in a blind rage.

What did he know for sure? That his wife and the stable boy had been seen standing in the gateway together. Old Salazar, who had long been his most trusted spy, assured him that they were standing very close together. Well, if they were both in the narrow gateway, that was inevitable. And it had been near dusk. And he knew that Salazar hated Juan. He had got little satisfaction out of Adelita. She admitted that she had gone to the stables to feed her mare an apple, and that she had stopped in the gateway to exchange a word with Juan, who she had met there accidentally. Had the slave laid a hand upon her? Had he been in any way impudent? If so, Adelita wouldn't admit it.

Salazar was convinced that something was going on between the two. Did *Don* Pascual believe it? He didn't know whether to believe it or not. Concerning all things on earth *Don* Pascual was a skeptic. His faith reposed only in heaven. He was skeptical about men and still more so about women. Whatever else Adelita had done, she had committed a grievous fault in going to the stables, in chatting on familiar terms with her inferiors. A woman had no business outside the house except when accompanied by men of her own family. The *don* had scolded his wife as she deserved to be scolded, and she had taken his hard words with her head lifted and her eyes dry. His interview with her had not improved his temper. Neither had it shed any light upon his problem.

He knew but one thing surely. Gossip had been going the round of the whole estate. It was the gossip that made it necessary to do something — something drastic, public, and unmistakable. Otherwise discipline was endangered.

Don Pascual was a good disciplinarian and one who firmly believed in authority. He had long since discovered that discipline had nothing to do with justice. It was generally impossible to find out the rights of a case, and quite frequently it was inexpedient to act upon them if they were known. So now he did not hope to find out, but he knew that he must make an example of the boy. Otherwise, gossip would multiply; disrespect for his authority would grow.

For the same reason it would not do to punish Adelita. His house was full of ears. If it got about that he was in a rage with his wife, it would be assumed that she had done wrong. But it must be assumed that the Indian had committed some act of impertinence, and it must be seen that he was terribly punished for it. He would make the man admit it if he could. If not, he would have him whipped anyway.

Of course, there was nothing to be done except to whip him. How else could one punish a slave or a *peón*? Every one of the great estates had its whipping post and some of these might be abused. The Spanish blood is cruel because it despises pain. But most *patrónes* were reluctant to whip their men because this incapacitated them for work.

Don Pascual called before him two *peónes* who were employed for the most part in cutting and hauling wood from the mountains twelve miles away. One of them, Lorenzo, was a huge man, weighing 200 pounds without any fat. He was a first-class axe man and a very simple fellow who would carry out any order like a well-trained dog. The other was his brother Adolfo, who was not so strong but equally docile. The *don* had used these two for the same purpose before. He now directed them to bring Juan before him.

A few minutes later they returned with the boy. Juan stood before his master with a face like a rock, set and expressionless. It was very noticeable that, when this boy smiled or laughed, he looked like a Spaniard, but, when he shut his mouth and set his jaw, he was all Indian. His face then had all the inscrutable look that belongs to savages. The *don* had seen Navajo captives stood up against a wall to be shot, and they had faced the guns with just such an expression as Juan wore now. No Indian ever showed fear of death or of pain as long as he remained wholly an Indian. Make a good

Christian out of one of them, and you might inspire him with the fear of hell, but to an Indian, death was a thing to be accepted when it came, and pain was a thing to be endured with composure. Many an Indian had burned at the stake without opening his mouth.

He knew at once that this boy, whatever his descent, was too much an Indian to be frightened. He did not waste much time trying. He walked up to Juan and looked him hard in the eye.

"You laid your hand upon your mistress," he charged. "Do not deny it. I have witnesses."

Juan did not deny it. He looked through and beyond his master just as though he neither heard nor saw him.

"You know well that you have committed a wrong that must be punished," the *don* went on, speaking in his most impressive tones.

The Indian stood mutely. It was even worse than the *don* had feared. It was customary for a slave or *peón* accused of any wrongdoing to fall upon his knees, to deny his crime, and to beg for mercy. This, in fact, was almost a matter of etiquette. It was an acknowledgment of the fact that the master was the regent of God and could dispense a divine mercy. If Juan had fallen upon his knees and begged, *Don* Pascual might have mitigated his punishment, but now that was impossible.

"Take him out and bind him to the post," he said.

Juan was led to the large enclosure behind the house. In the center of it was a timber of yellow pine a foot thick that was often used as a snubbing post in handling horses, but a hole bored through it about four feet above the ground testified that it had been planted for another purpose. Juan was forced to his knees before the post; his hands were bound together and the rope tied through the hole in the post so that he hung helplessly. His shirt was stripped off his back, and the huge Lorenzo grasped his whip as calmly as though he were getting ready to fell a tree. Adolpho stood by, but not another human was in sight except the *don*.

Lorenzo laid on several slow, measured blows, and each time lifted a long red welt.

"Harder," the *don* ordered. He spoke without anger. He knew exactly what he wanted. The skin must be broken so that there would be a permanent scar. That was the real punishment for a slave or a *peón* who had offended against a woman, unless his offense merited death.

Lorenzo laid on a blow with all his strength, so that blood followed the lash from end to end.

"Not so hard, fool!" The *don* was becoming irritated. "I want to mark him, but I don't want to kill him."

Lorenzo laid on a dozen more blows that seemed to satisfy his master.

"Stop!" he ordered.

The lash hung limply and so did the victim, his weight sagging heavily upon his upstretched arms. The two *peónes* unbound him and lifted him to his feet, not unkindly. He hung between them for a moment, then shook his head and freed himself of their support. Alone he walked away slowly, staggering a little, toward the room where he slept. Just before he reached it, he fell to his knees, rested for a moment on all fours, then crawled through the door.

CHAPTER
SIX

An old man who had some local reputation as a healer came to Juan soon after the beating. He bathed the lacerated flesh with warm water in which a certain weed had been boiled, and rubbed the wounds with a salve made of buffalo grease. When he had gone, a woman came from the kitchen and left Juan a large jar of fresh water, a stack of tortillas, and an earthen pot full of beans cooked with mutton and chili. She touched him gently on the back to express her pity.

Juan mumbled his thanks but did not look up. He felt very sick, and he did not know whether he was more ill of his wounds or of the rage that seemed to be burning him up. Repeatedly it stiffened his whole body, and his hands clenched hard as though upon the handle of a weapon or the throat of a foe. Later in the night his face and head became hot with a fever, and he was very thirsty. Repeatedly he drank water and splashed it on his face and brow, but the fever grew upon him, and he felt like a man who is getting drunk in spite of himself. When he sat up, he was dizzy, and, when he lay down upon his face again, the room seemed to rock and roll. Things he imagined became more vivid than real ones. Sometimes he had his hands at the throat of his master and they closed upon it with the convulsive force of a great rage, and sometimes it was the image of the girl that haunted him. He saw again her smile with that mocking lift of the eyebrow. He was close to her again and smelled the fragrance of her hair. It was she who had sent him to the whipping post with a treacherous word and she who bent over him and whispered her pity. At other times the drumming of blood in his ears became the drum of hoofs and he was riding the stallion in some great race or flight.

Every Indian is a mystic for whom vision is as real as what he touches with his hands. Warriors and lovers fast until visions come to show them the paths they must follow, and medicine men in ecstatic dreams see the destinies of tribes. This is the logic of the primitive man who knows instinctively that his spirit contains the event that shall befall it, and that an inner eye can see impending doom or triumph. So, when his fever died and he lay weak and cool again, Juan knew what he would do. He knew that he would run away, and that, if he lived, sometime he would return. It was not a plan but a revelation.

He did not even know for sure how to reach the Navajos. He knew only that they ranged far to the west, and he had never been more than twenty miles from his master's house. He knew that to the Indians he would be only a Mexican boy on a good horse. Perhaps they would kill him and take his horse. This possibility troubled but did not deter him.

It was easy to plan his flight. He could rise in the night and go as easily as not. Taking a horse was another matter, but not a very difficult one. He would take the stallion if he could find him, because no other horse could overtake him. He knew there would be a pursuit as soon as he and the horse were missed. Now that he knew he was going, he became all cunning. He pretended to be more ill than he was and rolled and groaned when anyone was about. But he ate eagerly, and he was gaining strength.

One night he rose after midnight to make his preparations. Weapons he needed and food. There were several short Apache bows and a few arrows in the room where he lay. He chose the best of the bows, testing each of them carefully, and hid it in his bed, together with all of the arrows. Guns were scarce in New Mexico — few besides *ricos* owned them, but almost every man used a bow, and Juan could shoot well enough to hit a bird. He found, also, a long heavy knife of the kind used for cutting corn in the fields, and this he carefully whetted and hid.

He had chosen the next night for his going. It was necessary to start as early as possible, so that he might be far away before he was missed, but he had to wait until the whole great *hacienda* was soundly asleep. In the early evening there were many voices of men, women, and dogs, some near and some far. He heard music of a fiddle and laughter where some *peónes* were dancing, and from another part of the wide sprawl of adobe rooms came the voice of a man singing, and somewhere else he heard a child cry and a woman

227

scold it. Slowly the noises dwindled and died as the night deepened.

Alert and aware he stood erect in the courtyard, everything forgotten now except what he must do. For a long moment he listened to make sure nothing moved. Then he made his way out, by well-known gates and pathways, slipping from shadow to shadow.

In the pasture the horses were grazing, as they nearly always do in the early part of the night. He spotted the stallion with ease and walked toward him, whistling softly. The horse lifted his head and looked and snorted. Juan trailed a lasso on the ground, loop ready. If the horse once broke and ran, he was lost, and another would have to serve. He didn't try to come too close, but made his throw from a distance of twenty feet. The stallion made one jump, and stopped short as the rope tightened on his neck. He swung his head and nipped at Juan, but once he was mounted, he went quietly. Out the pasture gate Juan rode, and into the low dense forest of cottonwood that lined the river on either side. Now he was safe. He forded the stream, which was worn small by summer drought, stopping to let the stallion drink his fill, and drinking deeply himself.

On the crest of the few hills beyond the river he stopped and turned to look. There was less than half a moon just risen. By its light he could just discern the buildings of the *hacienda*, wide flat roofs washed in the pale light, walls black in the shadow. There was the only home he knew — more than that, the only world.

CHAPTER
SEVEN

Until near dawn Juan rode westward on a well-known trail. It led to the Pueblo of Laguna, thence to Acoma, and finally to Zuñi. It was the trail followed by all who went to trade with those western Pueblos and also by the expeditions that set out against the Navajos, for their country lay south and west of Zuñi. Juan's plan, so far as he had one, was to follow this route, traveling for the most part at night, living off what he could kill. If hard pressed for food, he could beg of the Pueblos, who were always friendly, and, if this seemed too dangerous, he could perhaps steal from their fields. If he reached Zuñi, he knew he would find Navajos, for they came there often to trade. As a Navajo, he could ride into Zuñi — and perhaps ride out as a member of a Navajo band.

But it would not do for daylight to find him on the trail. When the east began to fade, he turned due south, choosing a rocky bit of ground where a horse's tracks would barely show. He planned to ride southward for an hour or two, spend the day in some hidden arroyo, letting the stallion graze, and then late in the afternoon to strike west again so he would be back upon his route by dark. He knew the country only vaguely, but he had a sure instinct for finding his way. Water was the problem that worried him. It was September of a dry year.

Before him as a landmark rose the outline of the Ladrone Mountains. The range consists of a single pointed peak in striking isolation, its deeper slopes broken into foothills. Juan knew that a cañon on the western side of the mountain contained a spring that dripped a pool of good water even in the driest years. He also knew the mountain had been used for years as a hiding place by bandits. Few travelers ever went near it for that reason. Twenty years before, a famous bandit had lived there, a brave and terrible man who raided towns and carried off women as well as cattle and horses. He had been killed at last by dragoons from Mexico City. People still loved to tell his story, and there was a song about his exploits. For the bandits all were heroes to the poor, as they were a scourge to the rich.

More recently it was said that one Guadalupe Lopez now used the spring in the cañon as a place to gather stolen stock. This Lopez was the most notorious horse thief north of El Paso, and he had a price on his head for murder as well as for theft. He ranged widely, and no one ever knew where he was. Juan knew that he might be picked up by Lopez and his men, if they were about, but the spring in the Ladrone cañon would be a good place to hide. If the bandits were using the spring, tracks would be all around it. Tracks to him were ample record of everything that moved on feet, and one that he noted as a matter of course and without conscious effort. Before daylight he chose a place to hide. He picketed the stallion on good grass in a little hollow where he could not be seen from any distance. Then he took his bow, climbed to the top of a low hill and sat down to wait for light. It was the moment before the dawn when the hunting creatures bid the night good bye. A lone coyote gave three short barks and a long thin whining howl. He heard the cry of a bobcat, and a great owl uttered a deep *whoo-hoo*.

This solitude filled with inhuman voices was not a depressing place to Juan. He squatted on his heels, alert and absorbed. It was the first time in many years that he had been alone in the wilderness, but it seemed a familiar place to him as though he had come back here to some dimly remembered home. All he had left behind was for the moment forgotten. He lived now wholly in his senses. He was aware of sounds and odors and of the widening day; he was aware of his hunger, of the weapon in his hand, and of little else. He, too, was a hunting creature now, one who hunts by the sun.

The dawn rose over the black jagged edge of the mountains in a flare of rose-colored light that widened and faded, killing the stars, revealing the earth. The country thereabout was one of low reddish hills, bearing a scant and widely scattered growth of dark-green juniper bushes. The watercourses between the hills were streaks of white and edged with the delicate green of sage and the yellow of blossoming rabbit brush. It was a land of little water, and therefore of little game. Only the desert rabbits that live without drinking could survive here. At dawn they all move, and

Juan could see now both jack rabbits and cottontails, lifting their long pink ears above the brush, bobbing across perilous opens.

A young jack rabbit hopped toward him, pausing to nibble. Juan set an arrow and waited until the nibbling head went down, then sent his game rolling and kicking with the arrow through its middle. He ran to it eagerly, finished it off with a blow on the head, and walked back toward the arroyo, peeling off the tender hide as one peels a peach. He dressed his game with the big knife, eating the liver raw, built a fire, and broiled the tender flesh spitted on a green twig. He sprinkled it with salt from his pocket, and ate it to the last morsel, feeling his strength and courage rise as his belly filled and warmed. He killed his fire as soon as his cooking was done, and then lay down in the shadow of a cut bank where the afternoon sun would wake him like a warning hand.

He mounted and rode so as to reach the Río Puerco just before dark. At sunset he tied his horse and climbed a hill to survey a stretch of the sandy riverbed. The smallest pool of water just then would have flashed in the light like a jewel, but in all that long stretch of sand not one drop of water showed. Juan sat a long time looking at it, discouraged, undecided. He could follow the watercourse for miles in the hope of finding a shallow seepage pool. It would probably be a hopeless quest. He could push on toward Laguna, hoping the stallion's strength would bear the strain, but already he could count ribs in the horse's flank. And if he reached the Pueblo, he and the horse would both be exhausted and at the mercy of men. He turned back toward the mountain, which was only ten miles away.

Dawn again, and nearly thirty hours since he had tasted water, found him peering down upon the water hole from a hilltop. Unable to find it in the dark, he had spent another night without water. His throat was so dry he could not spit, and his tongue was beginning to swell, but he had not lost his caution.

Nothing living showed, and he rose and walked toward the spring that dripped from under the roots of a lone cottonwood in a narrow sandy gorge. In the sand near the pool were tracks of every wild thing — the sharp, heart-shaped prints of deer, the round, padded ones of cat and panther, wolf and coyote, the delicate traces of quail and dove, but not a track of men, and none of horses except very old ones. He looked all around once more, then threw himself flat on his belly and buried his face in the cold clear water, drinking in deep delicious gulps.

When he brought the stallion to drink, he had to drag at the horse with all his strength to get him away from the water before he foundered. He led his mount back among the juniper bushes and tied him there. He knew he ought to go farther, but now that he had drunk, a great weariness came over him. His knees twitched; his vision blurred so that he blinked to see. He crept under an overhanging rock, curled up, and went almost instantly to sleep.

What awakened him was a hand upon his shoulder. He looked up into a face, very swarthy and pockmarked. He tried to rise, and reached for his knife at the same time. The man pushed him down, saying: "Keep quiet!" His knife was gone, and he saw that the man had it, and had also taken his bow and laid it on the ground.

About forty paces away Juan saw three more men grouped about the stallion and looking him over with great interest.

"I am Guadalupe Lopez," he said quietly, "and you are my brother. Who are you, and where do you come from?"

Juan stood silently.

"Oh . . . you have no tongue perhaps! Well, I will make you talk later . . . ¡Vamos!" he added, addressing the others. He turned to Juan and smiled, showing his teeth. "If you try to run away, I will have to shoot you," he said pleasantly.

All of the men had good horses, large and fat. Juan mounted one of them, and they all rode up the cañon.

Juan felt little fright but a great disgust. He had been a fool to stay near the water. A mile upcañon they came to a house, or what was left of one. It had evidently been deserted for many years, and one end of it had fallen down, but there were two rooms intact, and a heavy door made of cedar posts had been recently built into one of these. On the ground in front of the house was a rock fireplace, blackened by much use.

It was near sunset when they reached the place, for Juan had slept most of a day. The men unsaddled their horses and hobbled them. One of them unwrapped a quarter of beef, which he had strapped on behind his saddle, and another produced a sack full of tortillas and

234

some cones of the brown sugar called *pelóncillo*. A great fire was built.

A handsome young man, dressed like Lopez, came and stared at Juan, laughing. He turned to Lopez. "Shall we feed this boy before we shoot him?" he asked. "What do you say? Christ had a last supper. Why not this fellow? In the prison in Mexico City, where I once spent a month, they always feed a man before they shoot him."

Lopez laughed. "Sure," he said. "We will feed him so he will be fat for the coyotes."

Juan grinned at him but said nothing. He did not think they would shoot him. Moreover, when he leaned back, fully fed, warmed, and almost numb from the power of the tequila, he did not care much what happened next.

CHAPTER
EIGHT

In the morning Juan squatted on his heels with his back against the wall and watched the bandits lead the stallion into camp and prepare to put a saddle on him. One of the *peónes* held him by the rope while Lopez put a bridle on him; Juan could not but admire the immense strength of the man, and the quick adroit movement with which he forced the horse's jaw. Then three of them held him while the fourth put on the leader's great Mexican saddle.

Lopez was not afraid of the horse. He was not afraid of any horse. He swung easily into the saddle, and the others loosed the stallion's head. The horse made three mighty plunges, squealing and snorting every time he hit the ground, putting all his fury into every jump. He had not fought like that since the time when Juan rode him secretly at night.

Lopez never fully gained his seat, and at the third jump he lost it, turning over in the air and coming down heavily with a *thump* that could be clearly heard, while the stallion made a few more jumps and then ran.

The two *peónes* stood with grave faces, but the young man laughed with delight.

"What a devil horse!" he shouted.

236

Lopez sat where he was a full minute, regaining his wind, then turned and looked at Juan, as though he had for the first time recalled the boy's existence.

"By God!" he said. "How does this boy ride him?"

"Perhaps he knows how to ride," suggested the irreverent one.

"Boy," Lopez ordered, "go and catch that horse and ride him. And if you try to run away, we will have a rifle ready."

Diablo had stopped not far away, and, giving the low whistle he had taught the horse to know, Juan walked up to him, mounted him easily, and rode him to the camp in a gentle canter. There he dismounted, dropped the reins on the ground, and returned to his former seat.

Lopez looked from the boy to the horse. Then he nodded to Juan. "Come with me," he ordered.

He walked a little way from the camp, and squatted on his heels in the position a Mexican can hold all day. Juan squatted opposite him, while Lopez took out corn husks and tobacco, rolled two cigarettes, and offered one to Juan. The youth inhaled luxuriously, waiting. He understood that he was being treated with great respect.

"Again I ask you," Lopez said, "who are you and how do you come here?"

For answer Juan pulled up his shirt and showed his back, striped with red wounds barely healed. He turned back to face his captor. "I was a slave and they whipped me," he said.

He could see by the other's expression that he was greatly pleased. "You are Indian?" he said.

"I was born Navajo," Juan replied.

"And your *patrón*?"

"*Don* Pascual Montoya."

Lopez nodded deeply.

"Ha! That old son-of-a-goat! May his liver rot! And why did he beat you that way? It must have been a woman."

Juan took a deep puff and blew smoke. "It is not a thing I like to talk about," he said. "I think she had me beaten to save her face. Anyway, you know why I am here. You can see that I was beaten. The rest makes no difference."

"Where are you going?" Lopez asked.

"Back to the Navajos," Juan said.

Lopez was silent a moment. "I have nothing against you," he said at last. "You can go if you want to. You cannot take that horse. I need him in my business. But I will give you another horse . . . a pretty good horse. You can go to the Navajos if you want to. They will not only take your horse, they will also take your hair and hang it on a pole and dance a dance around it." He paused.

Juan said nothing.

"Or you can stay with me," said Lopez. "I need good horsemen. I like men who hate the *ricos* and will not take the lash. I will give you work to do, and, when I make money, I will give you money."

Juan sat silently a long time, his face expressionless.

"Come," Lopez demanded. "What do you say?"

"All you say is right," said Juan. "I will go with you."

They shook hands and walked back to the campfire.

"*Compañeros*," said Lopez, "this man is an Indian who was beaten and ran away. He hates all *ricos*. He is one of us."

Guadalupe Lopez was one of the hundreds of bandit leaders who have always ranged Mexico, where banditry is a profession. Lopez had been a horse breaker on one of the great estates in Oaxaca, held in *peonaje* by debt. While still a youth, he had fallen in love with a pretty brown girl who worked about the estate of his *patrón*. Because of her good looks, she was taken into the house and became the personal maid of the great man's wife. For the same reason she was taken as a mistress by one of his sons. Lopez should have accepted this with resignation, but, instead, he went on a profound drunk. Meeting the young *rico* who had taken his girl, he stood before him and called him by every insulting name in his vocabulary. The man of gentle birth drew a silver-mounted horse pistol; the *peón* sprang like a panther. The pistol went off in the air, and a fourteen-inch blade severed the jugular of the proud one. The blood of the aristocracy made a dark blot upon the ground, and Lopez reached the mountains, riding bareback on a stolen horse. He lived like a wild animal in the wilderness for months, then joined with other outcasts in banditry and soon became their leader.

Riding southward with his newfound friends, Juan felt happy. True, he had dreamed of being free and he was not free. He had only changed one master for another. He had to do what Lopez said, and he knew that Lopez would shoot him if he tried to run. Nevertheless, his spirits rose as the world widened before his eyes, and what he left behind, although never forgotten, became remote.

They made forty miles a day and kept it up. Once they killed a deer at a water hole where they camped, and again an antelope. There was no coffee and only a little salt, but they always managed to find meat, if it was only a prairie dog or a rabbit.

Juan was seeing a new country where the mountains dwindled to arid hills, the levels widened and mesquite grew tall as a man. In the evenings, when they sat beside their fire, he was also learning of new and almost incredible worlds, from the young José Padilla. Padilla was a rebel by profession, almost by heredity. His father had been a follower of the inspired priest, Hidalgo, who led the Mexican peasants in their first great uprising against Spanish power. Independence from Spain had come, and with it an even worse tyranny. Young José, filled with the doctrines of freedom and equality preached by Hidalgo and taught to him by his father, had been engaged in revolutionary intrigues since the age of eighteen.

Like all zealots, José Padilla yearned for disciples, and in Juan he found one. José began by telling Juan about the revolutions that had been, and about the great revolution that was to come and destroy forever the tyranny of man over man. Juan, struggling with ideas wholly new, asked questions, and José's answers threw him into confusion worse than before. He

240

learned for the first time of cities that covered leagues, of oceans and ships, of a whole vast world beyond the reach of his imagination. Padilla laid new worlds at his feet, but more than that he offered Juan a new conception of himself.

"You are no slave," he told Juan. "The Mexican congress long ago passed a law against slavery. All the *ricos* break it. They hold captives and sell them, and a *peón* might as well be a slave. But if you go away to the south, you are free. No one can take you back."

All this was hard for Juan to grasp. He had seen life only as a hierarchy in which some were born to high places and some to low. Yet he began to think of himself in a new way — not as a slave or a refugee, not as an Indian or a half-breed, but as a man who would be whatever his skill and courage made him.

In the south this nascent idea found nourishment. Lopez sent Padilla and Juan to the town of Casas Grandes. They were to locate good stock that might be stolen, and above all they were to buy guns and powder. These things were hard to get and of great value, not only to use but even more to trade with the Apaches.

Lopez would not have dared to enter the town himself, and it would have been useless to send any of his half-wild followers, but in Juan and Padilla he had two young men of good appearance, wholly unknown in that part of the country. They could pose as stock buyers from El Paso — adventurous young men bent on making money by a bold ride across the Indian country. They had to look their parts and went dressed in good shoes and leggings, in buckskin vests with fancy foxing and wide sombreros. They traveled at night and camped one morning at a water hole outside the settlement to shave and wash themselves and put on clean shirts. Padilla was gay and delighted, for this was the kind of trick he loved. He slapped Juan on the back, spun him around, and looked at him.

"*Compañero*," he said, "remember, you are a *rico* now. As God is my witness, you look like me . . . proud and solemn as an *alcalde* sentencing a *peón* to forty lashes. Keep your mouth shut and leave women alone, and you will go far."

They came first to a good-size *hacienda* some miles from the settlement, and Padilla decided they should approach it. They rode up to a long house, washed white after the fashion of the south, with a row of pepper trees before its door, where mockingbirds sang, and women worked over *petates* in the shade. A young man came out of the door, greeted them, and asked them to dismount. He listened gravely to Padilla's long and facile story of whom they were and what they wanted.

"For all you know, *señor*," Padilla said, "we may be bandits. We do not ask you to trust us or give us your hospitality. We only ask you to sell us a cheese, some honey, and a few tortillas, and, if you have a horse to sell for not too much, we can pay for him in silver."

While he was speaking, the whole of the household came, one way or another, to get a peep at the strangers. Three more men came out and stood listening, one of them an elderly white-haired fellow of great dignity. An older woman appeared in the doorway; two younger ones stood behind her, and several small children peered from behind the women's skirts, their large brown eyes filled with shy interest. Meanwhile, a hurried, whispered conference was going on in the background. It was not hard to guess that the men were suspicious of the strangers, but that the women, full of curiosity and eager for new voices, wanted to ask them in. Finally the old man stepped forward, shook hands, and presented them to the whole family.

"*Caballeros*," he said, using the invariable formula of hospitality, "enter! My house is yours!"

The two of them spent the night at the *hacienda* and rode away in the morning well fed and rested, cheered by kindly voices bidding them return, wishing them good luck. They had learned, moreover, of an old man in the town who had guns to sell, and they had been told just how to reach his house.

Padilla was impressed, and he was excited over their success.

"We are a good team," he said. "One to talk and one to listen. And you are a devil with the girls . . . or might be if you were not afraid of them. You could stay around here, marry some girl, and get your foot on the land. But what are women to us? A baggage we cannot carry. We are dedicated to the liberation of man!"

Juan and Padilla found the man who had guns to sell and succeeded in buying several rusty army muskets, a keg of powder, some lead in bars, and one fine Hawkins rifle — a great prize. In the evening they camped on the

243

edge of the town, but they only waited until it was dark and the town was asleep. Then they started back.

They traveled only at night, for they feared a meeting with either Apaches or soldiers. Just before dark they would build a small fire, cook, and eat. And one evening beside their fire Padilla gave Juan his most complete confidence and broached to him a plan. He told Juan that he would not ride north again with Lopez. That he told Juan this was the measure of his trust in him, for it would never do for Lopez to know he was going. Padilla would simply disappear someday. He was going back to the state of Sinaloa, where his father and his four brothers were all small owners of land and cattle. They were men of humble birth who had freed themselves from debt, gone to the wild country, and built their houses with their own hands. They had acquired cattle as all poor men did, by putting a brand on a calf or yearling when and where they could. They were in constant danger from the Yaquis, but held their own because they were a large group, nearly all related. Padilla wanted Juan to go back with him. Juan, too, could build a house and file a claim to land. As for livestock, they would gather it on the way.

"You will be a free man, a *ranchero*," Padilla told him. "Perhaps someday a *rico*. There is silver in those hills, and you and I will find it. Everyone there will welcome you. Good fighting men are what we need. As long as you can sit a bronco and shoot a gun, nobody there cares where you came from or who you are. And we have pretty girls, spoiling for marriage. You will not be lonely, *amigo*, and, when the day comes, you and I will ride out together to fight for liberty!"

As Juan listened, he was aware of a conflict within him so intense that he felt it as a physical pain in his chest and throat, and it was hard for him to speak. He wanted to go, and he knew that he could not go — yet. "*Compañero*," he said, "I will come if I live. But not this spring. I have business first in the north."

Padilla was half angry and much excited, as always when he talked. "I know what you mean," he said. "It is that girl. You will say it is also the *don*. You will say that you want revenge. And so you do. But you are in love, my friend. You can't fool me. When a man wants to kiss a girl, he is in love a little, but when he feels as though he would like to choke her or beat her, then he is very badly in love. Then he has a sickness that is more dangerous than smallpox. The sure way to forget one woman, my friend, is to find another. Come with me, and I will promise to find you one of any shape or size you like."

Juan was in misery because he could not argue, and could not convince his friend that he must go back to the north. He sat, silent and unhappy, and for all of one night ride the friends said little to each other. Then tentatively Juan tried to persuade Padilla to go north with him. José would have none of it, but he relented toward Juan. He drew a map in the sand, showing him just how to reach the settlement on the Rio Balsas. Then he gave Juan a knife he carried — a Mexican knife with a fourteen-inch blade in a carved leather scabbard. Etched upon one side of the blade was a motto that read: **Do not draw me without cause nor sheath me without honor.** On the other side was the name: **José Padilla.**

"This knife will be like a letter to all who know me," he said. "I may not be there when you come, but I will tell them all that you are coming, and they will treat you as a brother."

Juan put the knife into his belt and gave José his own.

"I will come if I live," he said.

CHAPTER
NINE

With Padilla gone, the stealing of the mule herd from the leading *rico* of Casas Grandes became an enterprise depending wholly upon Juan. He knew that Lopez only half trusted him, but in this case the chief had everything to gain and nothing to lose by sending him. To Juan, this was a great business opportunity. In the Mexico of that day the stealing of livestock was a profession by which a man might rise to power and wealth — even become a figure of legend.

It was Juan who led five men south, placing two of them one-third of the distance to Casas Grandes, and another pair two-thirds of the way. Alone he rode on to make the capture and the first dangerous drive.

For two days and nights he hid in the hills, waiting for the dark of the moon, hoping for storm. On the third night he got it, and rather more of it than he needed. The first heavy downpour of the spring came riding out of the north on huge black clouds that were split wide open by chain lightning and sent down water in torrents. It was an outlaw's night — a night when no other would be abroad. As he rounded up the nimble half-wild mules, the rain changed to hail that pelted straight in his face. The mules refused to travel against it, turning back upon him again and again. He was drenched and almost frozen. A serape was no protection against such a storm as this.

His horse was exhausted by the struggle with the floundering herd. He roped a range horse, changed his saddle, and returned to the attack. When the storm abated, and he finally had fifty mules headed north, he was a nearly beaten man. His hands were so numb with cold that he could barely hold a bridle rein, and another horse was weakening between his knees. Again he roped a loose mount and shifted his saddle. This time the strange horse bucked, and he lost his seat, too stiff and weary to ride his best. But he held onto the bridle, remounted, and pushed on. The temptation was almost irresistible to dismount, build a fire, and rest, but that would have been defeat. He must get the mules to his first relay by dawn.

Every man periodically must face a decisive trial, and Juan knew this was one for him. Drenched and frozen, covered with mud and bruised, he clung to his saddle, resolved to ride as long as he could sit and see. The storm was ebbing now, but broad flashes of lightning still came to gleam upon the wet backs of his running herd, to show the greening hills livid as a dead man's face, and streaked with shining waters.

Once started, the mules held to the trail. There were leaders in the herd that had come from the north, and this was fortunate, for they knew where they were going. Just before dawn Juan saw the gleam of a fire that he knew was the camp of his men. He tried to shout, but had no more voice than a fish. He drew his pistol and fired a shot. Within ten minutes the two Sanchez brothers came to meet him and took over the herd, to rush it on northward as long as the mules could trot. No mounted pursuer could travel as far or as fast as these loose animals driven by relays.

Juan rode to the deserted camp, fell off his horse, ravenously devoured the beans and mutton he found on the fire, then rode into the hills to hide and sleep until another night, when he would follow north.

When Juan reached the ranch near the village again, the mules were there, and Lopez came forward to congratulate him.

"We will go back to Tomé as soon as these mules can travel again," he said. "You will help me sell them through the Pueblos. Half of what we get is yours."

Juan put no great faith in the word of Lopez. This man inspired no such confidence as Padilla did. Yet he felt sure he would get his money if the mules were successfully sold. Lopez needed him now. Moreover, he had a pistol of his own upon the horn of his saddle, and a smoothbore gun in the boot under his stirrup.

The mules were footsore and half starved and needed a week upon the spring grass, but their going north was hastened by an unexpected event. On the fourth day a man rode into camp. He was dressed like a *peón* and armed only with a knife. He told a plausible story of having run away from a *hacienda* far to the south because he had stolen a silver dish and they had found him out. He begged for food, and he was genuinely famished. Lopez welcomed him, fed him, and asked him a few questions, but not enough to alarm him. Meanwhile, he sent the eldest of the Sanchez brothers to pick up the man's back track. This Sanchez was a gifted tracker, one who could trail a deer over dry ground. He was gone all one day and part of a night. Then he came back and reported to Lopez. He also told his brother what he had found, and soon all the seven bandits then in the band were in on the secret. The trail had led to a camp where three armed men waited. The stranger was a spy.

Juan now looked to see the man shot in his tracks, but that was not the way of Lopez. That night one man was started north with the mules, moving slowly. The rest of them sat about the campfire for a while without speaking. Lopez wore a gloomy, preoccupied look.

The stranger felt a sudden change in the atmosphere. He tried to talk; he tried to tell stories. No one responded. Fear became visible in his eyes. Fear made his fingers restless. Fear finally stopped his tongue, and he sat looking at the fire with the expression of a man who sees the vision of his doom.

Once he rose and walked into the dark a little way. A man with a rifle in his hand silently followed him. Presently he came back and sat down again. His eyes roamed the group, looking for succor, looking for mercy. No one met his look. Lopez after a little while glanced at him and uttered a short harsh laugh. He sprang to his feet.

"¡Vamos!" he shouted.

They all swung into their saddles and rode at a hard gallop toward the town of Ascension, the stranger in the middle of the group. In Ascension was a saloon kept by an old woman. The saloon was one room in a large adobe house built about a courtyard. The rest of that house kept secrets.

It was this saloon and its proprietress, more than anything else, that bound Lopez to the town. There he went for his periodical sprees. Every once in so often he must get very drunk, for only in drunkenness did he escape the tension of fear and suspicion that ached in his nerves, and only in this house did he dare get drunk.

In the saloon all lined up before the bar and drank tequila from earthen cups. Juan watched the face of Lopez. It was undergoing a transformation. A heavy scowl deepened between his eyes, and these, when he glanced up briefly from his drink, were narrow and wicked as the eyes of a fighting wolf.

Juan watched him in amazement. Sober, Lopez was usually quiet, rather good-humored, always a little worried. He seldom shouted orders or tried to bully his men. He would endure with apparent good-humor much raillery from a man such as Padilla. Yet Juan knew that he had once, when drunk, drawn a knife on Padilla for little cause or none. He knew that all of his men dreaded to go on a spree with him.

It was plain that Lopez was drinking himself into a killing mood. He drank cups of tequila one after another, and, as he drank, all human expression seemed to drain out of his face. His eyes now were the eyes of a fighting animal, and his mouth worked strangely under his heavy mustache.

Suddenly he walked up to the stranger, seized him by the shoulder, and spun him around.

"So you are a *peón* who stole a silver dish!" he said. "How is it that you came with three others, all armed, who wait at the Río Puerco for you to return?"

The stranger was no coward. He knew his time had come. He took three quick paces backward so that he stood alone, facing the men lined up at the bar. His right hand fell to the hilt of his knife. With the other he swiftly crossed himself, and his lips formed a silent prayer.

Lopez sprang at him suddenly. Two knives flashed from their sheaths. Lopez was incredibly quick. Some feeling long repressed seemed to burst forth in that savage leap. It was a single movement that drew his knife and drove it into the man's body with a deadly upward sweep of the right arm, while his left, thrown up as a guard, stopped the other's stroke in mid-air. As the man fell, someone knocked over the candle that lit the room. The darkness was filled with the rasp and thud of feet as all rushed for the door. In another moment they were all mounted and riding hard on the trail of the herd.

For six weeks after his return Juan was a busy man. He rode as far north as the pueblo of Santa Domingo, only forty miles from Santa Fé, and as far west as Laguna, using Ladrone Mountain as a base. On each trip he drove from three to five mules before him. He traveled at night across the mesas, avoiding the valley and all roads and trails. At each pueblo he was instructed to ask for a certain Indian by name. This man would come forward and take the mules. Sometimes Juan was instructed to ask for a certain amount of money, and, when he did, he always received it and put it in a money belt he wore under his shirt. At other places he merely delivered the mules, and nothing was said about payment.

Only in the pueblo of San Felipe did he make a friend. Here Juan delivered his mules to a young man who smiled at him and spoke good Spanish. This man, who called himself Pablo Guiterrez, was probably of mixed descent. At any rate he wanted to talk. When Juan had been given a room, he came climbing down the ladder with a jar of red wine in his hand and a broad smile of hospitality upon his face. The two young men sat talking and drinking for hours. They did not confide in each other, but chatted in the Mexican fashion of weather and women, of horses and hunting, and food and wine. Nevertheless each was intuitively assessing the other. Both knew that they were making an alliance that might have many uses. When Pablo rose to go, he held out his hand.

"You are my brother," he said in the Indian fashion. "My house is yours when you want it."

He gave Juan an uncut but perfect turquoise, and Juan gave him a cupful of powder and a bar of lead.

That night, when the moon rose, Juan rode to the top of the western mesa and headed north, riding without a trail across a barren country. He was filled with the sense of confident well-being that belongs to a man whose course in the world is upward. A little less than a year ago he had been a ragged hatless Indian, running away on a stolen horse, with a sore back and a bitter spirit. Now he sat upon a good saddle that he owned. About his middle he wore a belt heavy with silver, and half of it was his. There was a pistol beside his saddle horn and a rifle under his leg. He wore a good buckskin suit dyed black, heavy silver spurs upon his heels, and a sombrero with a silver band. His serape was new and would turn a heavy shower. He was a man of substance — an armed and formidable man.

For him hope lived anywhere but in this country where he had been a captive Indian, a beaten slave. And yet he could not leave it yet. His next night's ride would bring him to Tomé, within a few miles of the *hacienda* where he had lived. He knew that day was a feast day in honor of the patron saint of the old Tomé church. He was almost sure the *don*'s carriage would be there, and Adelita would be in it. The place where she was drew him as though by a physical magnetism, although whether he hated or loved her, he did not know.

As he rode toward the town next morning, he pulled his hat low over his face. He knew that he looked a different man, that his mustache was an effectual disguise, but he also knew that he was taking a great and unnecessary risk. He drew the pistol from his saddle holster and put it in the band of his trousers where it would not show.

In the dusty plaza, mingling with many other horsemen, he felt a growing confidence that none would know him, but he tingled with the alert aliveness of those who go into danger. He stopped a moment to watch a game of *gallo*. He stooped from his saddle to buy a bunch of grapes, and, whenever anyone looked straight at him, he would raise the grapes to his face and bite off a few. Both men and women he saw who he had known, but none of them looked him in the eye.

Soon he had ridden all over the plaza, seen everything there was to see — everything but what he was looking for. He was about to turn away in disappointment, when he saw a cloud of dust far down the road. Watching it narrowly, he discerned the lines of a coach, and knew it must be the Montoya coach.

Juan pulled up beside the road and watched the approaching coach. As it drew nearer, he could see that it contained only women, save for the driver and one man riding beside it as an escort. The women at first were only a bright pattern of color in the sun. Then he could distinguish faces, and finally one face emerged brightly for him.

Adelita passed within ten feet of him. She was turned toward him, laughing and chattering with a girl who sat beside her. The sight of her sent a pang through his body, as sharp and physical as the thrust of a blade. After she had passed, he sat his horse for a moment, bewildered. Well, he had seen her — and now what? There she was, and as much beyond his reach as if she had been in those countries across waters a month wide that Padilla talked about.

He turned his horse and followed, not knowing exactly why, but with a vague hope that by looking at her he might free himself of the spell that bound him. She was, after all, just one girl like a thousand others, he told himself. For all her money and her silks and the coach she rode in, and the thick walls that surrounded her life, she was not different from other women.

He pulled up beside the coach, only a few yards away. Her back was toward him at first, and he sat, saying to himself that, when she turned, he would look at her once and ride away. He had dreamed of a meeting. He had believed it must happen. This would be it! This would be the end!

She turned at last. Her eyes roved the plaza; they came to him. He knew she was looking at his horse — a fine roan mare he had brought from the south. And then she stared curiously at the rider.

For a moment they looked into each other's eyes. Unmistakably he saw recognition, and amazement. Her lips parted; her eyes widened. She looked just as she had that day when he had laid his hand upon her, and he remembered the feel of her arm, the fragrance of her hair. Suddenly he wheeled his horse, glancing back just once, and rode away. As soon as he was out of the crowd, he spurred into a run and never spared his blowing horse until he was clear of the valley and riding up an arroyo toward the mesa. Like a wild animal he felt safe only on high ground, where he could see far, and away from roads.

He jogged slowly, shaking his head, cursing softly to himself. What a fool she made him! This was a thing that affected his head as well as his body. He was like a horse that has eaten locoweed. He might have ridden back into bondage just for a look at her. Well, but for her he would never have ridden out! The thought struck him with sudden force. She had made him what he was — had given his destiny its decisive push. And he knew that she ruled it still.

It was after dark when he reached the camp on Ladrone Mountain. A man lying by the fire asked — "*¿Quién es?*" — and he spoke his name, then picked up his blanket and buffalo robe and walked away in the dark to lie down. Like Lopez, he preferred to sleep alone and in the open.

CHAPTER
TEN

In dusty dignity the coach of *Don* Pascual Montoya rolled along the valley and toward Santa Fé. Much of his household goods and many of his servants had already gone ahead of him. He was going to the ancient capital of his province to accept a position under the new government that had recently taken power, and his going was a momentous and significant thing. Not that his position was an important one, but it was a matter of great importance that a man of his standing had chosen to identify himself with a government that was secretly opposed by so many of his fellow *ricos* and by almost all of the poorer people in the upper valley.

The *don* had taken this step only after prolonged meditation and earnest prayer. He did not like the new government much better than did his fellows. Neither did he like the governor, Albino Perez, who had been sent from Mexico City to administer the province, and he doubted very much the wisdom of the new system of excise taxes that had been imposed upon the people. They were accustomed to pay only a tariff on the goods they imported from Chihuahua, and, although this was a robbery, it was at least one of a familiar kind. Now the whole country was filled with taunts and whispers of rebellion, and they were the more alarming because it was so hard to trace them to any one source.

There was a tradition among the Pueblos that someday they would drive the Spaniards out of the valley, and that they would be aided by an invasion from the east. The Yankee trappers and traders who came in growing numbers every year to Santa Fé had given new life to that savage hope. If ever the Pueblos made common cause with the *peónes* and the small landowners, and then called upon the Yankees and the Texans for help, the best people would be doomed.

This journey to the capital of his province was for *Don* Pascual a sad one. For one thing, it was a dry year, and drought meant suffering and discontent. If revolution came, it would come with drought such as this. At Isleta the Pueblos were dancing the corn dance, which is a pagan prayer for rain. Half-naked brown men with fox skins and bells of horn at their girdles, bare-legged women with sprays of evergreen in their hands, they danced in two long lines to the heavy rhythm of drums and chanting. In such perfect time they danced that their feet shook the earth. Their sweating bodies gleamed in the merciless sun, while they chanted to gods of thunder, lightning, and rain. They were a splendid sight, but they did not please the *don*. Dancing half naked in the sun, calling upon their savage gods in deep chanting voices, they made the *don* feel anew that he lived in a world of terrible and hostile forces.

All along the road, too, he heard of the ravages of the Navajos. They were becoming bolder every year. They

259

had boasted that they could take every sheep in the province if they chose, but that they would rather leave a few for seed. It was lucky that both Pueblos and Mexicans hated and feared them.

The *don* rode grimly. More than once he looked to his pistols. Sitting at home in his great house, he could feel secure. There was nothing like a good house, well stored with food, well filled with arms, to give a man a sense of power. But here on the road everything that he saw filled him with a sense of doom impending.

The days of travel were long, hot, and dusty, but the nights a social ovation. Hospitality was a sacred rite among the *ricos*. Even men who differed with him in politics were proud to entertain the *don* and his charming young wife. Each night the *don*'s carriage rolled up to one of the great houses, and he was received by his peers and treated as though he had been a royal personage. Most notable was his visit at the house of *Don* Leandro Perea of Bernalillo, the only man in the lower valley who might have been accounted wealthier than the Montoyas.

Three of *Don* Leandro's grown sons rode to meet the Montoya carriage and escorted it to the door of his house, where he was received by fifteen or twenty members of the family, while as many *peónes* and Indians took charge of his horses and his baggage. That night there was a feast, and afterward dancing with many of the Chaveses of Corrales and the Romeros of Alameda present. Adelita was bright-eyed with excitement. For her the whole journey was a lark and a welcome break in the boredom of her life. She danced with abandon.

The *don* was intensely jealous of Adelita, but except for the almost forgotten incident of the Navajo boy who had run away, his suspicions had never found any nourishment. Now he watched his wife for an hour or two reducing young Severino Chaves to a state of hopeless infatuation. The young man's eyes followed her about the room; he lived only to dance with her — and all because Adelita incessantly laughed at him. The *don* grew tired of watching, and went to sit over many cups of brandy with *Don* Leandro, to discuss the corruption of the state, the decay of morals, the menace of Indian warfare and rebellion. These two agreed perfectly about everything. Mellowed by good grape brandy, they sat long after the dancing had stopped and most of the household had subsided into silence.

When Adelita had gone alone to her room, she heard the rattle of a handful of gravel thrown against the shutter. She opened the shutter and looked down into the imploring eyes of young Severino Chaves, who stood just outside her window. He was a handsome fellow with an especially fine nose and a very pleasing voice. Like nearly all the young *ricos* of his day, he devoted his life to cock fighting, hunting, and the girls. He was a lover famous for his daring. For him to come to her window this way was a daring thing, although he had carefully noted where the *don* was, and had posted a trusted *peón* to watch him. After all his careful planning there was still a great deal between them — a wall three feet thick and a window set with heavy wooden bars. They might have touched hands if she had been willing, but that was all. The privilege of speaking to her alone was all he gained, and all, on this occasion, that he sought.

"*Señora*," he said, "since I laid eyes upon you, I have seen nothing else. I will think of nothing else until I see you again."

"That is a nice speech," said Adelita, smiling. "How many times have you made it?"

Severino was irritated. That was no way for a girl to talk. Like all Mexicans, he was a romantic lover. Love making was an art that he respected. "*Señora*," he started again, "it is only my misfortune that I must creep to your window like a thief and beg for a smile. If you were free, I would offer you my hand, my all. I would devote my life to your wishes."

"But I have been married now for over two years," said Adelita, "and I am so bored that I bite my fingernails and weep at night."

"What would you like, *señora*?" asked the bewildered youth.

"I would like to go somewhere," said Adelita, and she spoke for the first time without mockery, with passion. "I would like to see something, do something . . . I don't care what. I would like to ride a horse and feel the wind in my hair as I did when I was a child. I think that was what spoiled me for being a lady. They let me run when I was a child, and now they expect me to sit still for the rest of my life. Can you wonder that I am bored? I wish I had been born a man, to ride and wander."

262

Severino was shocked, but he was also impressed. He had never heard a girl talk as this one did. To be sure, the lives of women were stupid enough, but few of them seemed to know it.

"*Señora*," he said almost apologetically, as one who offers what he can, knowing it is not much, "if you are bored with marriage, how would you like to have a lover?"

Adelita again considered, and again she smiled with a lift of the eyebrow. "That might help," she admitted. "But I would always be afraid my husband might shoot him, and then I would feel badly."

"I would gladly risk my life to touch your hand," said Severino, who felt that he was getting back to familiar ground.

"Thank you," said Adelita. "But a lover would be, after all, only one more man to wait for, and that he came through a window instead of a door would perhaps not make much difference."

Severino felt that his approach was countered again. He was gathering breath for a new start, when his faithful body servant whistled from the corner of the house. At the same time Adelita very gently replaced the shutter in the window, for she heard a firm familiar step in the hallway.

CHAPTER
ELEVEN

In the dusk of an August evening Juan, Lopez, and three others were sitting by a fire at the camp on Ladrone Mountain when the messenger of rebellion came. He was not unexpected. In primitive countries news travels fast and quietly to those who it concerns. For months it had been known to every bandit, to every restless and discontented man who could use a weapon and keep his mouth shut, that forces of rebellion were astir. It was known that war captains from all the northern Pueblos were going secretly to Taos, and that drums were rumbling and councils were being held in the black secrecy of the kivas. It was known that some sort of agreement had been reached between the northern Pueblos and the poor *rancheros* of the northern valleys — the owners of a few acres each, who nearly all hated the *ricos* even more than their own *peónes* did.

The *clink* of a shod hoof on rocks far down the cañon announced that someone was coming. The rocky trail never failed to warn. The bandits all moved back from their fire into the shadow, and Lopez cocked a rifle. A man rode into view and, as he came near, lifted his right hand, palm forward, which is the sign of peace. Lopez went forward to meet him. He dismounted, and they squatted on the ground, rolled cigarettes, and conferred long and earnestly. After half an hour they both came to the fire, and the stranger ate beans and tortillas and talked of indifferent matters with all of them. His name was never given. He was a small dark man with narrow eyes that gave him a look of cunning and a great black mustache that concealed his mouth. When he had finished eating, he remounted his horse, and saluted them all with a grand gesture.

"*Compañeros*," he said, "*adiós* until we meet again to fight for God and liberty!"

"God and liberty!" Lopez echoed.

The man spurred away. Almost before he was out of sight, Lopez burst into a great guffaw.

"God and liberty!" he repeated, and laughed again. "He invites us to fight for land and liberty! All these revolutionists are alike. I have listened to them before, in the south, where they have a revolution every year. All revolutions are for God and liberty, and those who win get money, mules, and women. Revolution . . . hah! I am a revolution all by myself. I also take money, mules, and women, and without hiding behind long words."

"What did you tell him?" asked Juan, trying to conceal his eagerness.

Lopez jerked his thumb. "Come, *compañero*," he said, "we must talk of this."

The two walked away and squatted alone. It was a conference of leaders, for Juan was now the acknowledged lieutenant, second in command.

265

"Listen, *compañero*," said Lopez. "I told him, sure, we are all ready to fight for God and liberty. We are ready to die for God and liberty, but what we need is guns and powder. I told him, if he will send me ten guns, then, when I am called, I will come with twenty armed men, and all of them will be men who have nothing to lose but their lives. They need us, *compañero*, much more than we need them. They can find many men, but most of these *rancheros* cannot fight any more than a cow."

"What did he say?" asked Juan.

"He said that they are going to gather at Santa Cruz, north of Santa Fé, and then they are going to march on Santa Fé and take it. They are going to kill the governor and everyone else connected with the government, take their houses and their money and everything else they have, and then, after they have gathered up everything in sight, they will proclaim a new government in the name of God and liberty."

"What did you say to that?" asked Juan.

Lopez laughed, delighted with himself. "I did a little piece of private business for us," he said. "You know that *Don* Pascual Montoya has gone to Santa Fé. He is part of the government. I said to this man that I will come with twenty men, and we will all fight to the last drop of our blood for God and liberty, and I said that our reward must be that we can sack the house of *Don* Pascual Montoya, because he is the man we all hate, the man who has wronged us, the man who laid a lash on your back."

Juan could feel the blood pounding in his temples, but he spoke quietly: "Do you trust this man to keep his word?"

Lopez snorted. "Trust him? That fellow? I trust them all as I would trust a coyote with a chicken. But do not fear. If we have twenty men and twenty guns, we will not have to trust any but ourselves. We will take what is ours!"

They rose, and walked back toward the fire. Juan had another question to ask, and he brought it out with some difficulty.

"And if his wife is there?"

Lopez clapped him on the back and chuckled. "You still have that woman on the brain? You are young. If any women are in the house, they are ours, too, just like the silver and the blankets."

CHAPTER
TWELVE

Rebellion broke out suddenly, long after those in power had ceased to believe in danger. A poor man in Taos was jailed for debt. A muttering crowd gathered around the jail, and grew. Indians from the Pueblos joined it, and *peónes* from neighboring ranches, and poor men who owned a little land of their own. They gathered apparently without any purpose, but purpose grew out of their strength. Suddenly they smashed the door of the jail, set the man free, and came pouring out into the plaza, yelling, waving clubs, lifting blades into the air, firing a few old horse pistols and flintlock guns. A pushing, heavy-footed, shouting mob, they began going about the *cantinas*, drinking native wine and brandy, buying at first, then smashing doors and taking what they wanted.

All the time the crowd was growing. Men came riding into the plaza from all the little settlements up and down the valley. All of the fighting men in Taos pueblo came in a body on horseback. At their head rode a big Indian named Tomás Gonzales, a buffalo hunter by trade. Every year he led a troop of Indians to the eastern plains to hunt, and so he led them now, 300 of them, all with the black paint of battle on their faces, all waving the lances with ten-inch blades they used for buffalo hunting, all with bows and full quivers on their backs, a few with long flintlock guns.

Now the mob had a leader. Gonzales climbed onto a platform in the plaza and harangued them. He shouted that long enough all of them had starved and suffered and paid taxes, that the earth belonged to her children, that in the name of God and liberty they would march on Santa Fé and destroy the government. Nearly a thousand heard him. Half of them were Pueblo Indians, and the other half were men of mixed blood who hated their masters.

"All who love God and liberty and are not afraid to die will follow me!" Gonzales shouted. "On to Santa Fé!"

They answered with a yell that broke from every throat at once, and the savage volume of their voices filled them with a conviction of their power.

Word of their coming reached the governor at the palace in Santa Fé the same day. He was sitting in council with four of his colleagues when a man came in to tell him that more than a thousand rebels were camped at Santa Cruz, twenty-five miles from the city, that they were all getting drunk, that they might descend on the capital any time.

Albino Perez, the governor, was a man of pure Spanish blood and of the old Spanish tradition — a man of fifty with a skin of delicate yellow, high, thin features, and a bald head. When he heard of the first threats of rebellion, he had sent to Mexico City an urgent request for troops. 100 dragoons were supposed to be on their way, but no news of their coming had reached him. His personal forces consisted of about twenty-five men, armed with muskets, who composed the palace guard. There was supposed to be a militia that could be summoned through the *alcaldes* in time of need, but this had long since been disbanded because the provincial treasury was always empty. Perez was not a fighting man, but neither was he a coward. He turned to his secretary of state, *Don* Pascual Montoya, who knew the country as he did not.

"What can we do?" he asked quietly.

"We can hire Indians and arm them, and go fight these people," *Don* Pascual replied. "The longer we wait, the stronger they get. If once they reach the town, not a house or a woman is safe. We must go."

"But what Indians can we trust?" asked Perez. They both took pride in speaking quietly, as though this had been only a matter of routine, but both of them knew it was a matter of life and death.

"The Indians of Isleta would be the best," *Don* Pascual said. "They have always been faithful. But they are too far away. We must try in Santo Domingo. I will go there now, while you raise what men you can here in town, and throw a guard across the road."

Under a blazing August sun the forces of the governor rode out of Santa Fé and across the barren reddish hills, dotted with sparse cedar and piñon, that lie between the capital and the cañon of Santa Cruz. At the head of the column rode the governor, his secretary of state, and two younger men who had come with Perez from Mexico City. They all rode fine large horses that shone in the sun. Their saddles were mounted in silver and set upon brightly patterned Navajo blankets. They wore swords, and horse pistols in long holsters hung beside their pommels. They were followed by about half the palace guard — ragged *peónes* with their flapping pants and wide hats, carrying muskets across their saddle bows.

Behind these straggled about 200 Indians from Santo Domingo, all armed with bows and lances, jogging on their small horses with stolid unrevealing faces. Each of them had been given a little money and a few presents, and had been promised a great deal more if they fought faithfully and well. *Don* Pascual himself had dealt with them. They had agreed to everything, promised everything. Yet every time he turned his back, a few of them would be missing. His temper had finally got the best of him. He had one man flogged, and threatened to shoot the next man who left the lines. Then he assigned half the palace guard to bring up the rear with muskets under the command of a man he trusted.

Don Pascual rode with his mouth set in a hard line. He knew that this was a desperate adventure. He knew the rebel force must heavily outnumber his own, and he did not trust the men behind him much more than those he was going to fight. He went without hesitation because there was nothing else to do. The only alternative was a panic flight to the south, and the *don* was not a man to run. Whatever they might have lost in initiative, in resourcefulness, through the long years of ease, the *ricos* had retained uncompromisingly their feudal code of honor.

The heat was terrific. It poured down from a pallid cloudless sky to shimmer like a dance of hostile blades upon the arid contours of a baking land. The *don* had worked hard gathering his forces. He had grown angry, and the blood had gone to his head. Sweat poured down his face and gathered in his eyes, so that the landscape blurred before him, and the heat waves wove a crazy pattern in his sight. The *don* felt no fear and no excitement. What pressed upon his spirit was a sense of doom. He had prayed to God; he had invoked the aid of his favorite saint. He had no doubt the will of God would now be done.

Heat and thirst create a sort of madness that begins when the tongue grows dry and increases until it may become a delirium filled with visions. The *don* thought of the day, thirty years ago, when he had ridden to battle for the first time. He remembered then how fear had gone prickling up and down his spine and had grasped at his vitals like a great hand. He had been filled with fear, but also with hope. Now he knew neither.

It was the heat he couldn't stand. This was the fear of his *siesta*, and suddenly it seemed to him he was lying again in that long cool room where for so many years he had daily taken his ease, blowing rings of blue smoke toward the heavy rafters. Dim and cool the room was, with walls three feet thick. Within those walls it never grew hot, never grew cold. Within those walls was peace and safety. The *don* wished he had never left those walls his grandfather had built, his father had defended. He remembered his first wife, seeing her image with such a sudden and long-lost clarity that it was almost as though the dead had returned. He saw himself, too, a slim young man, and he remembered the joy they had known together in those first years. Her image became bewilderingly confused with that of Adelita, and for the first time he recognized some likeness between them, and he saw rather than thought that it was his own youth he had tried to marry when he took Adelita to wife. He had tried to go back, and he had failed, and that mocking lift of her eyebrows had told him so. "Age and death are foes no man can outride." It was one of the sayings all Mexicans love. "Only the earth lasts forever!" That was another.

They were approaching a place where the road to Santa Cruz crossed a wide shallow arroyo that lay, a strip of white sand strewn with boulders between the hills. To the left, as the road descended, was a high and barren hill. Beyond the arroyo was a long ridge with a scattering of piñon and cedar along its crest, and many large rocks showing in rugged outline against the sky. As the cavalcade rode down into the arroyo, *Don* Pascual concentrated his gaze upon the crest of the ridge beyond him. The light was almost blinding and the dance of the heat waves made the horizon seem alive. He fancied first that the boulders themselves were moving among the bushes, and then that he saw moving figures among the rocks. Suddenly he threw up his right hand and shouted a command that brought the whole troop to a stop in the middle of the arroyo.

Half blinded though he was by sweat and glare, and weakened by the heat, he knew that he had seen the unmistakable glint of sunlight on a gun barrel.

In the midst of that stretch of sand, which slowed their horses and left them far from cover, they were helpless. He whirled his horse and shouted an order for all to ride back toward higher ground. Then the top of the hill came suddenly to life in a roar of fire from half a dozen muskets. No man showed, but only pale red flashes and a gust of blue smoke; one of the palace guards clutched his stomach with both hands, groaned, and pitched forward. The horse of another gave a start, shivered, and fell.

"They are on both sides of us!" the *don* shouted. "Up the arroyo!"

He led the way, and the guard wheeled their horses to follow him. The Indians were milling about like a herd of cattle struck by a storm and were shouting to each other in their own language.

The retreat did not go far. Half a mile up the arroyo a line of horses came riding down from the ridge to form a barrier across it. As they pulled up, the *don* turned and met the eye of Governor Perez. The governor's face wore a look of helpless bewilderment; he was not a man of war.

"What shall we do?" he asked.

"They have us surrounded," *Don* Pascual replied. "There is nothing for it but to get off and fight."

On the crest of the hill behind them he could now see the figures of thirty or forty Indians outlined against the sky, brandishing lances, bows, and guns, and

274

shouting. One of them in front was waving a red scarf, evidently signaling.

Suddenly a great hoarse shout went up from the hired Indians in the arroyo. Almost as a man they wheeled their horses and galloped toward the hill, lashing their scrawny mounts into a plunging run through the heavy sand. Up the hill and over it they went, and disappeared. The Mexicans stared after them for a moment before the full import of the situation came home to them. It was not a charge; it was a desertion. The Santo Domingo Indians had gone to join their fellows from the north.

In the middle of their wide sandy isolation the twenty-odd Mexicans huddled together like a covey of hunted birds. Only *Don* Pascual had any idea what to do. He ordered the men all to dismount and form a circle, standing behind their horses. It was the invariable way of meeting an Indian charge. An occasional musket cracked on the hillside, and arrows whizzed, but the hidden men were too far away to be effective, and they had no need to hurry.

"They are going to kill us all!" said Governor Perez, and his voice expressed not fear, but a great astonishment, as though for the first time he realized that battle is a serious business.

"Of course they are," said *Don* Pascual quietly.

The others cocked their muskets across their saddles and said nothing. Like all Mexicans, they faced death well.

Now they could see men on both sides of the arroyo running from bush to bush and from rock to rock, kneeling to shoot. A man dropped with an arrow in his throat, and a horse fell upon the man behind him.

"Don't shoot!" the *don* shouted. It would be impossible to hit those darting half-hidden figures. Every shot must be saved to meet the inevitable charge.

Suddenly it came. From three directions 500 yelling, shooting horsemen dashed at the little band. Muskets and horse pistols fired at them, but not more than a dozen of the enemy were stopped. The rest came yelling down upon the defenders like a pack of hounds upon cornered game. The little group was crushed and obliterated by sheer weight of numbers. Yelling Indians with uplifted lances fought and jostled to get their blades into the fallen men. Gonzales, the leader, rode through them on a great bay stallion he had stolen from one of the looted ranches. He towered above his men on their ponies. His great bull voice roared for order.

Presently the head of the governor rose above the milling mob. It was impaled on the point of an Indian's lance, the eyes staring, the mouth open, the tongue grotesquely protruding as though in an imbecile defiance. Another Indian suddenly placed the cocked hat of the governor, with its plume, rakishly on one side of the head. A great shout of laughter went up from the whole band.

"God and liberty!" someone yelled, and a thousand voices echoed the words as the rebels turned and rode back toward Santa Cruz with the head of the governor borne before them — a savage symbol of authority repudiated.

The dust of their going disappeared over the hills. In the sandy arroyo lay some twenty bodies, stripped and scalped. The sun went low; the shadows lengthened, softening the face of the land. The peace of desert evening fell upon the quiet dead.

CHAPTER
THIRTEEN

Riding hard, straight up the valley, went twenty men, driving their extra horses before them. These men were bandits who ordinarily would have ridden across the mesas and through the hills, sticking to the high ground and the byways, moving by night like wolves. But this was a time when rebellion held the highways, and authority took flight or went into hiding.

Word had come to Lopez that the governor and most of his colleagues had been killed near Santa Cruz, that the forces of Gonzales were marching on Santa Fé to proclaim a new government in the name of God and liberty, and incidentally to loot the palace, the homes of all government officers and of everyone else who did not give formal submission.

The whole of the lower valley, stronghold of the *ricos*, was in a panic. All of them believed that unless help came quickly from Mexico City, the rebels would march south and loot all the great estates. Lopez and his followers rode past houses that were dark, where barking dogs were the only sign of life. On the road they met no travelers. Lights showed only here and there in humble houses, and in the little roadside *cantinas* where *peónes* and other common folk met to drink and dance. These were more than ever lively. Even after midnight they came upon lighted *cantinas*. Men and women crowded to the doors when they heard the rumble of galloping horses and stared at the armed riders, and sometimes shouted a greeting.

They had started about noon, and they would ride all night. About two o'clock in the morning Lopez called a halt at a roadside saloon near Bernalillo. In this little wine room were gathered fifty *peónes* and servants, to discuss the confused and exciting reports of rebellion that had reached them.

The bandits crowded up to the bar and ordered drinks while everyone else fell back respectfully and watched them. Lopez drank three brandies in rapid succession, tossing off each one in a single gulp. He threw a handful of *pesos* on the bar, and turned to face the room. Everyone looked at him respectfully, expectantly. He was the recognized leader, and he looked his part — a big man with two pistols and a knife at his belt, a splendid red and black sombrero pushed back from his brow, heavy silver spurs on his heels.

"*Amigos*," he said, "do not fear us. You are all poor men. Your cause is ours. We are riding to Santa Fé to destroy tyranny in the name of God and liberty. Never again will a man be tied to the post and lashed in this province. Never again will he be taxed for the benefit of a government that robs him. Never again will any starve who can work. We will take the land away from the rich. We will take power into our own hands. In the name of liberty, with the help of God, we will triumph!"

279

Juan listened to his chief in amazement. Only two days before, Lopez had ridiculed revolution in general and the leaders of this revolution in particular. Moreover, Juan knew that he had waited cannily until news of the battle had reached him, and he was sure that the rebellion was a success, at least for the time being. He was riding like the devil now, in the hope of reaching Santa Fé before the looting was over.

The crowd gave him strong encouragement. They cheered his speech, and the women stared at him and whispered to each other. When he walked up to a pretty girl and chucked her under the chin, she giggled with delight. He roared a good-humored laugh, walked to the door, and paused dramatically with his right hand upraised.

"¡Amigos, a Dios!"

But before he could leave the room, a young man came rushing forward with a knife in his belt and an old musket in his hand.

"Señor, señor," he pleaded breathlessly, "let me go with you! I have a good horse."

Lopez nodded a careless assent, and, before they were mounted, three other recruits had joined them.

After that Lopez ordered a halt at every lighted wayside saloon, and in each one he made his speech, sometimes to thirty or forty. Increasingly his speech became more eloquent, his swagger more grandiose. Always he drank straight brandies, tossing them off with a quick lift of his head. Almost always he added two or three recruits to his company, so that soon he was riding at the head of a small, unorganized army.

280

Juan rode, quiet and alert. In the bars he stood uneasily, eager to be on his way again. He drank nothing. His whole being was tense with a feeling of impending climax. He was ready for battle. He yearned for action. Excitement pounded in his blood. It was Lopez that worried him most. Lopez sober was a cautious fellow, who would generally keep his word because it was good business. He trusted no one, but he could be trusted, within limits. Drunk, he was treacherous and deadly. When he drank, hatred rose to the surface of his being, and trouble was in sight for someone. He killed only when he was drunk, and he drank only when he wanted to kill. Juan knew it well.

They made their last stop at La Bajada, only twenty miles from Santa Fé, and here all lined up for a last drink. They were so many now that the room would hardly hold them, and the barkeeper, pop-eyed with fright, could not serve them. Laughing young men vaulted over the bar, broke in the head of the barrel of wine, passed it out in cups and gourds. Lopez stood in the middle of the group, leaning back against the bar, lifting a gourd of wine high in the air.

"God and liberty!" he shouted his toast. "Death to the *ricos*!"

A great shout went up from all of them, and they lifted their hats and drank.

Lopez turned suddenly upon Juan, who stood at his elbow. Juan was just setting down a gourd of wine untouched.

"Drink!" Lopez ordered him. "What ails you?"

Juan stood staring at him. With a movement so quick and adroit that perhaps no other saw it, Lopez drew a pistol from his belt and shoved it against Juan's stomach. His narrow eyes had a glitter that Juan had seen before — the same deadly look they had worn when he killed the man at Ascension.

"Drink!" Lopez repeated.

Juan laughed, picked up his gourd, drained it, and set it down again. Lopez already had turned away and was shoving his pistol back into his belt.

"¡Vamos!" he shouted, and led the way to the door, followed by his laughing, drunken army.

CHAPTER
FOURTEEN

In Santa Fé the plaza was filled with a drunken crowd of Mexicans and Pueblo Indians, going from bar to bar, drinking and shouting. Every saloon was filled, and in every gambling hall the roulette and monte tables were crowded. The houses of the rich were dark, and not an aristocrat was to be seen in all that gathering. It was as though the population of the little capital had suddenly turned dark and turbulent; the primitive had risen to destroy its masters.

Every man was armed. The red light from doorways flashed on the long blades of lances. Almost every man had a knife at his belt; many carried bows, some long muskets, others shotguns and short heavy rifles of the kind used for buffalo hunting. Taos Pueblos, in the white robes peculiar to their kind, looked ghostly in the dark and showed faces painted black and red when they poured through the doors of saloons and gathered in stolid ranks about gaming tables. Wide-hatted peónes in flapping pants and cotton shirts, with heavy spurs clinking at the heels of moccasins, made up most of the rest of the crowd. Here and there were men better dressed and armed, with pistols in their belts, wearing long leather leggings, and most of these were bandits.

A confused excitement ran through the crowd in a guttural rumble of talk and laughter, in the scrape of restless feet, as it milled around and around, restless with a sense of sudden release, of impending climax. Here and there the rumble of voices exploded suddenly into a shrill laugh, a yell, a curse. Knots of men gathered about brief fights that were generally smothered and broken up by the weight of the crowd. Now and then a musket roared, and a long red flash leaped skyward.

Lopez halted his band before the largest gambling hall in town, a long narrow room lit by hundreds of candles, filled now like a cattle pen with shuffling shouting men. Juan stuck closely behind Lopez as they pushed their way into the place. Why was the man coming here? If ever they were going to the Montoya house, now was the time. Juan was filled with a straining anxiety that seemed to sharpen his senses. He looked not at all at the crowd about him. He watched Lopez only.

He saw the man signal to the older of the Sanchez brothers, who was never far from him, and then whisper a word in the man's ear. Sanchez nodded, and shouldered his way out of the crowd, followed by two other men he touched on the shoulder as he went.

Juan suddenly saw light; Lopez would never ride to the Montoya house with all the rabble he had gathered at his heels. They would get out of control and take the looting into their own hands. Here Lopez intended to lose most of his army of liberty. A chosen band would slip out one by one and go to claim their prey.

Lopez shouldered his way to the bar and ordered brandy. Juan stood closely beside him. His hand rested upon a pistol that he had put inside the band of his pants where it did not show. He studied the face of Lopez as the man stood, staring at his cup. Sweat streamed down Lopez's cheeks and his eyes had a fixed look. He was still steady on his legs, and, when he lifted his drink, his hand did not tremble, but nevertheless he was visibly drunk — drunker than Juan had ever seen him before.

Suddenly Lopez turned and looked at him. It was the same look Juan had seen before — as unmistakably deadly as the lifted head of a rattlesnake.

"For the love of God!" Lopez exclaimed. "Why are you always right beside me? Are you my shadow?"

Juan silently cocked his pistol without showing it. He smiled at Lopez. "These are dangerous times, *patrón*," he said. "Something might happen to you."

Lopez snorted at him, and turned to hammer on the bar for another drink. As soon as his back was turned, Juan wriggled his way to a point near the door where he was concealed by a group about a table. He studied the room. He saw that several men of the band were missing, and he saw several others slip out one by one. Then he, too, went out and made his way to where their horses were tied at a long hitch rack a little way up the street. As he had expected, eight men stood beside their horses, ready to mount. He walked up to his own horse and stood there. No one paid any attention to him. It was too dark to recognize a man at more than a few feet.

285

They all stood in silence for perhaps fifteen minutes. Then Lopez appeared unexpectedly from around a corner. Juan knew he had gone out the back door of the hall so as to give the rest of his followers the slip. Lopez was not too drunk to be cunning. He mounted his horse, and Juan noticed the slight forward lurch with which he settled into his saddle. Without saying anything, he rode up the street at a jog, and the others followed. As soon as he was clear of the plaza, he spurred his horse, and they all went up the narrow street that led toward the mountains in a thundering gallop. This was the street, leading straight to the governor's palace, along which most of the richest families lived. It was quiet now, and every house was dark.

CHAPTER
FIFTEEN

The house where the Montoyas lived stood back from the road in the black shadow of thick-leaved cottonwood trees. It was a solid earthen mass, blankly resistant as a rock or a hill. No light showed, and there was no sound of life. It looked dead. High narrow windows were barred and shuttered, and the heavy double door was of oak and iron.

Silent, soft-footed men gathered before the door. Lopez whispered an order, and four went behind the house and came back with a long pine beam of the kind that were brought from the mountains to be used for rafters and pillars. All took hold, backed away, and charged against the door three times. The third time it crashed and burst inward.

"Look out!" Lopez shouted. They all leaped back on either side of the door — and got what they expected, for there was a long flash and the roar of a musket. Then all rushed in. There was a groping struggle in the dark, and a *thud* of blows. Someone struck fire and lit a torch of fat pine. Its flare showed an old man lying dead beside a musket. He was the doorkeeper. Somewhere in the depths of the house running feet and voices could be faintly heard, and one shrill scream. Then it was quiet again.

They stood in the narrow hallway that pierced the front of the house and opened on the courtyard. Lopez pushed open a door to their left, and they all crowded into a long room where the red light of torches showed mirrors hung on a whitewashed wall, low red couches, a great fireplace banked with evergreen boughs, and in a corner niche the wooden figure of a female saint with hands folded and eyes uprolled, as though demurely, grotesquely she deplored this intrusion.

Candles were lit; the bandits stood silently, a little confused, staring about them at the magnificence they had invaded. They had come to ravage the house of a *rico*, but several of them took off their hats, moved by a long habit of respect in the presence of anything that bespoke wealth and authority. This was the great reception hall of the house. There was another door at the other end of it. Presently behind this Juan heard low voices, women's voices, as though in altercation.

Then the door opened, and Adelita came in. She stood before the doorway. Her black hair framed her chalk-white face, and her eyes, with pupils deep and wide, looked enormous. Her breast rose and fell beneath a loose white bodice. The bandits stared, open-mouthed.

"Who are you, and what do you want?" Her voice was thin with fright, but it did not tremble.

Plainly all the others were taken aback, but not Lopez. He came forward, making a profound bow.

"*Señora*," he said, "we are the agents of a new government that has this day taken the capital in the name of God and liberty. It is our duty to take charge of your house."

He moved nearer to her, and she shrank back against the side of the door.

Lopez laughed. "*Señora*," he said with unction, "do not be afraid. I will take care of you. You will be my charge as long as these troubles last, and no other shall come near you. *Señora*, if you will step into the other room, I would like to speak with you alone!"

He made a gesture with his hat, inviting her to pass, but she only shrank back against the doorway, her eyes roaming the room in desperation.

Juan had stepped quietly forward while Lopez was speaking. He stood behind Lopez, and between him and the others. His hand was upon his hidden pistol. He had been trying for more than a minute to catch her eye, and now at last he succeeded. She was looking over the shoulder of Lopez, straight into Juan's eyes, and he saw her lips part, her eyes widen in an expression of amazement. With his hand low and hidden from the others, he signaled her back through the door.

For a long painful moment she hesitated, then backed through the door, Lopez following. The instant they were both across the sill, Juan leaped after them, closing the door behind him and leaning against it. Lopez whirled, drawing his knife with a swift movement that was almost a reflex. Juan shoved his drawn pistol into the man's stomach. For a desperate moment they stood staring at each other in silence.

289

"Drop it!" Juan said. "And keep quiet!"

A shot now would bring the whole crew. It was only a matter of seconds until one of the Sanchez brothers came anyway. Juan stepped close to Lopez, pressing the pistol against the man's stomach with one hand, while with the other fist he struck upward at his jaw, rising on his toes, putting every ounce of his weight and strength into the blow. Lopez went over backward, like a chopped tree, the loose *thud* of his fall telling that he was senseless. Instantly Juan turned and dropped the long wooden bar of the door. He stooped and snatched the pistol out of Lopez's belt. Then he turned to the girl.

"Quick!" he said. "You know the way . . ."

She did not hesitate this time, but ran before him to the door at the other end of the room. He followed her, stopping only to bar another door behind him.

The house, like all of its type, was simply a long single row of rooms about four sides of a courtyard, each side pierced by a hall, and most of the rooms connected. She led him through several rooms dark as caves, taking his hand to guide him, and out through another hallway. He saw that they were in the high-walled enclosure behind the house.

"We must get to the street!" he said.

There was no way out but the great carriage gate, barred with a heavy oaken timber resting in iron slots. He lifted the timber with difficulty, opened the gate, and they emerged upon a narrow alley. Juan was breathing hard. So far, so good, but now what?

Running to the mouth of the alley, he looked up and down the road. Across it, a band of young fellows with their arms about each other's shoulders were strolling drunkenly and singing. There was a single other figure coming toward him — that of a *peón* woman with her great black cotton shawl hooded over her head on which she carried a large white bundle, balancing it easily.

Juan stuffed his guns into the band of his pants and ran to meet her.

"*Señora, señora,*" he said breathlessly, "excuse me." He dug into his pocket, pulled out a handful of silver *pesos,* took her hand, and put the money into it. Then he lifted the bundle off her head while she stared at him amazed. "*Señora,* I must have your *rebozo,* too," he explained. He snatched it off her head. Then he showed her one of his pistols. "Walk on," he said. "And do not look back."

He ran back to the alley and gave Adelita the shawl and the bundle.

"Put it on!" he ordered. "Carry the bundle on your head and walk behind me!"

He took off his spurs and his hat and threw them away. Then put on his serape over his shoulders the way a farmer did on a cool night.

The common people always walked in single file, men first, then women, and then children if there were any. Walking thus, these two looked like any pair of country people except that Adelita could not balance the bundle without putting her hand to it.

They had not gone 100 yards before three horsemen came charging down the road, but did not even glance at the fugitives. Juan felt a little better, knowing that the pursuit had passed them, but he was afraid to enter the plaza where the light of torches and lanterns would fall upon their faces. He circled it warily until he found a place to hide the girl in the shadow of a wall.

"Don't move until I come back," he said.

"But what if you don't come back . . . ?" she started a protest in a small voice.

"Then you will have to look out for yourself," he said, and turned quickly away. There was no time to argue. He looked back once, and saw that she had stayed hidden.

What he needed now was horses, and he needed them quickly. The plaza was crowded with horses, but also with people. It would be impossible to take one without risk of being seen. He finally returned by back ways to the house and watched it from the shadows across the street. It was blazing with light now, and he could hear men shouting and talking. Most of the horses still were there. He crept toward them under the trees from shadow to shadow. No one was outside. He swung into his own saddle and took the bridle of the horse nearest. He rode away at a walk, for a clatter of hoofs would surely bring pursuit. It took all of his self-control to go slowly, watching over his shoulder, until he was 100 yards away. Then he quickened to a trot, and soon reached the place he had left Adelita.

She needed no instructions now, but climbed onto the other horse and followed him as he led the way out of town by dark and little-frequented roads. As soon as he was clear of the last house, he shouted to her and spurred into a run down the road to a little village that lay a few miles west of the capital. After the long suspense there was infinite relief in this burst of speed.

The village was strung out along the road for several miles. Juan studied each house as they rode past. He was aware only of the immediate need to hide until the first pursuit and search were over. He also needed food. He knew that many must have deserted their houses when the revolutionists came, and that many others had gone to the plaza in Santa Fé. It was a deserted house he sought now.

He rode up to one that showed no light, and rapped on the door. A frightened woman opened it a crack and asked him what he wanted. Juan inquired his way to Santa Fé and rode on. He tried another door and no one answered. He got off his horse, forced the door with his shoulder, struck a light, and found himself in a typical *peón* home, almost bare of furniture, with a corner fireplace, a blanket-covered pallet rolled against the wall, a string of chile hanging from a rafter, a chest for clothing. He brought Adelita inside, hid the horses behind the house, closed the door, and barred the window so that the light of a single candle would not show.

Then he turned to face her. For a long moment they stood staring at each other. Juan could find no words. Until then he had been carried along in a swift rush of action. Now for the first time he felt the full surprise of this incredible moment.

293

At first her own face reflected a bewilderment like his, but she was quick to recover. She drew herself up proudly, composed her features. One hand fluttered about her hair; another smoothed her rumpled dress. She was recreating herself in the image of haughty dignity — the image of her proud kind. As she did so, she seemed to recede from him, to set herself apart; all at once, she was a *rica*, looking down upon him from the heights of her self-assurance.

"You have brought me here, I don't know why," she said. "I thank you at least for getting me out of that house. What do you want?" As she spoke, she pulled a little buckskin bag out of the bosom of her dress, and made as though to open it. "I have a little money here . . . and some jewelry."

What did he want? She was going to pay him, with *pesos* or a ring! He could feel hot anger pouring into his blood, driving him toward action. She, the woman who had sent him to the whipping-post — she would pay him off! She was the *rica* again, patronizing, proud — and he was the beaten slave, the one who had run away and found his power.

He moved toward her, his hands clenching, his breath coming hard. The look of assurance in her eyes gave way before him as she did, step by step, until she leaned against the wall, her breast heaving, her eyes wide.

He seized her, as he had once before, by both arms. She neither spoke nor moved, but stood staring into his eyes. Suddenly he crushed her against him, his lips pouncing upon hers. Had she struggled, had she cried — but she did neither. She hung limply in his embrace.

He released her slowly. He stepped back a pace, like a fighter staggered by an unexpected blow. All the rage was gone out of him, all the violence. His knees trembled, and his muscles went soft. By simple submission she had repelled him more effectively than by any resistance. The touch of her yielding body left him helpless.

Again it was she who first recovered poise. She smoothed her hair and smiled at him faintly, but with that same mocking lift of the brow. "I wondered if you had the courage," she said.

Juan shook his head in bewilderment. "I have the courage," he said, "but you have killed the wish. For a year I have dreamed of revenge. And now . . ."

"And why revenge?" she asked.

"Because you had me beaten . . . you sent me to the post!"

"I?" The surprise in her voice was unmistakable. "I had no power to have anyone beaten . . . no more than you! And I told nothing! You don't think I would have told!" Her voice broke off upon a note of rising indignation. Her eyes blazed.

Juan said nothing. He could not doubt her. It was suddenly clear to him that she had been too proud to talk, just as he had been. All the time he had blamed her — for what?

"After all," he said at last, speaking humbly and with difficulty, "I have nothing against you."

"It is kind of you to say so." There was a sort of weary sarcasm in her voice.

"You know your husband was killed the day before we came?"

She dropped her eyes, and nodded. "He was a good man," she said. "But I never loved him, and I do not pretend to mourn him."

Juan stood looking at her, not knowing what to do or say. There she stood, within his reach and wholly at his mercy, yet as far away as ever. She was still a *rica*, and he was a hunted bandit. His hatred was dead, if it had ever been real. He felt nothing but sympathy now — and a desire without hope.

"Where do you want to go?" he asked. "What can I do with you?"

"What you wish," she said. "You may leave me here if you want to. Someone will find me."

"Yes," he said, "but God knows who. I cannot leave you here."

"And you?" she asked. "Where are you going?"

Juan laughed a little grimly. "I am meat for buzzards if either side catches me now," he said. He saw something like pity in her eyes. Her pity was one thing he did not want; he was filled with a sudden desire to boast, to justify himself, to make her understand that he was now a person in his own right. "I am bound for the south," he said. He shifted his money belt into view. "I have as many *pesos* as I have miles to go. In Sinaloa I have friends waiting. I will take up land and build a house!"

He stood taller, and his eyes shone as he spoke. He believed in his future.

"You had better be on your way," she said.

"I cannot leave you here. Listen . . . I will take you to the Pueblos. I have a friend in San Felipe. You will be safe there. A woman is always safe with the southern Pueblos. Then you can go back."

"Yes," she said wearily, "I can go back! I can go back and sit on the floor, and drink chocolate, and wait. And if I wait long enough, maybe some other man will marry me. And then I can sit somewhere else, and wait . . . for him!"

Juan listened to this speech, open-mouthed with amazement. He had thought of her so long as a person of high and enviable place, surrounded by luxury and privilege, it had never occurred to him that she could despise her destiny.

Before he could say anything, there was a roar, and drum of hoofs outside the door. The sound transformed him suddenly into a man tense and alert. For twenty minutes he had forgotten everything but Adelita. Now he was instantly brought back to the realities of the situation.

He held up a hand to keep her silent, and listened. Four horsemen in a run! They swept past the house, and the drum of hoofs died in the distance. Some of the Lopez gang sent to look for him!

"We must get out of here," he said, "and lose no time."

"But you . . ." she started to protest, when he stopped her.

"Keep quiet," he said. "I will not leave you here, but you must do what I say."

He began rummaging the room, raiding a wooden chest of the kind in which all Mexicans keep clothing. He dug out a pair of stained and greasy buckskin pantaloons, an old serape, a battered straw sombrero. He tossed them to her.

"You must put them on," he said.

She stood staring at the garments, holding them gingerly.

"Hurry!" he commanded. "You cannot ride far in the clothes you wear, and you must look like a man."

She went obediently into the next room and he began to rummage for food. A white cheese made of goat's milk, a handful of dried beef, a few tortillas, a skin of wine — it was not much, but better than nothing.

Adelita reappeared, looking like a slim boy dressed in his father's cast-off clothing. She smiled at him. "Now I know I am safe," she said. "I never looked worse in my life."

The woman had courage, Juan thought. Thank God for that!

"Listen!" he commanded. "You must ride behind me, and you must keep quiet so I can hear. If I hear horses coming, I will leave the road at once, and you must follow. You understand? Then let's go!" He left some money behind for what they had taken.

It was a light night, with half a moon riding low in the sky, and a heavy cloudbank rolling up in the east. They rode at a jog. Juan was living in his ears, and every few minutes he stopped, the better to listen. They had traveled perhaps five miles when he heard the faint distant rumble of hoofs, coming from the south, and what surprised him was the volume of the noise. It sounded at first like the running of a great herd of driven horses.

He wheeled his horse and spurred away among the juniper bushes until he was 200 yards from the road. Adelita was close behind him. In a clump of brush he pulled up, hid the horses, bade her dismount and neither move nor speak until he returned. Then he crept back to a point where he could see the road.

The rumble of hoofs came closer, grew in volume. Then over a rise they came, a cavalcade of horsemen such as he had never seen before. In front rode an enormous fellow on a great pacing mule, wearing a cocked hat with a plume. Another man, not clearly visible, rode on the off side of him, and behind them in a column of fours came no less than 100 others. Juan had never seen any men like them, but he knew by their plumed helmets and the perfect order in which they rode what they must be — Mexican dragoons! The army of the Republic had come to put down the rebellion!

Juan watched them out of sight. Then he crept back through the bushes to where he had hidden the girl.

"It is the soldiers!" he told her. "Your side has won."

"My side?" she said. "I have no side, no more than you. I am only a woman."

"Anyway, you will be safe. They will drive the rebels out of Santa Fé. You can go back there tomorrow."

"And you?" she asked.

"I will be safe when I cross the Río Grande below El Paso," he said. It was true. But how would he ever get there? Every man who had taken part in the rebellion would be a hunted man from now on — every man caught under arms who could not explain himself. He said no more, but rode on, more alert than ever.

Clouds were piling higher. They covered the moon. The night grew darker, still and sultry. If he could get to San Felipe with the girl before daylight, leave her there, and get into the hills to hide until another night! That, he knew, was the one safe course.

It was a question whether they could make it, and what was worse, he had something to struggle with besides distance and weather. He did not want to leave her — at San Felipe or anywhere else. Her one kiss still burned his mouth. And yet what else could he do?

The storm struck them on the windswept top of a mesa. It was a pelting rain at first, and then a wind-driven hailstorm that stopped and turned their horses, drenched, and chilled them. When the worst of it was over, and they rode on again, splashing through puddles, with chattering teeth, he knew that the storm had decided the issue as far as getting to San Felipe was concerned. They would have to hunt shelter and hide until another night. To go forward now would be for daylight to catch them on the road.

His one great advantage was that he knew every foot of this ground. He knew that five miles north of the road at the foot of the mesa was a deserted ranch with two buildings that still had roofs intact. It could be

300

reached now only by a deserted trail. There he could hide the horses as well as themselves. They could build a fire, eat, and get warm. When daylight came, he could climb up the mesa and watch until another night.

This was his second night without sleep. Excitement had sustained him until now. The chilling downpour had made him aware of a great weariness. All at once he knew that he must find shelter, rest — quickly! He felt like a hunted animal ready to go to earth.

When they left the highway, they rode side-by-side. Presently their eyes met. Two bedraggled and hollow-eyed creatures, they looked at each other and smiled. She put out an icy hand and touched his own. Her fingers trembled; her teeth chattered — but she smiled.

"I am sorry, *amigo*," she said. "You chose a heavy burden."

He smiled back at her, shaking his head. He could find nothing to say, but he was grateful for her words. Friends, now they were in misery — two human wretches, drenched and frozen, worn out, hunting shelter and a moment of rest.

With the horses hidden behind walls, he pushed open the door of a little adobe hut fast going to ruin. More than once he had camped there. The roof leaked, but the rain was nearly over now, and there was a corner fireplace. It was better than camping in the open, because the walls hid the flame, and smoke does not show at night. He kindled a fire laboriously, with stiff fingers, gathered wood, and piled it on the flame to

301

dry. Adelita helped him as best she could, scratching her hands on the sticks.

The leaping, warming flames were inexpressibly welcome. They stood steaming before the fire, feeling the blood creep tinglingly back into their frozen hands. Juan uncorked his skin of wine, and they drank deeply, and wine and fire filled them with new life. He opened his precious package of food and spread it on the floor.

"Wait!" she commanded. "Keep your back turned. I cannot eat in these rags."

He saw that she had sheltered the bundle of her own clothing beneath her serape.

"Now you may turn!"

She was a lady again, slightly rumpled, but wholly dignified. She rolled up the sleeves of her bodice and turned it in at the neck. She smiled at him.

"Now I am dressed for dinner," she announced with a laugh.

Juan grinned back at her. He worshipped her courage. "You make life hard for me," he said.

She looked at him curiously but said nothing. She cut the cheese and served him with a touch of formality. "*Señor*, allow me."

But neither of them ate much. A great and terrible weariness was falling upon him like a heavy hand, and he could see it in her eyes, too. Moreover dawn was fading the sky.

Reluctantly he killed the flame. He spread saddle blankets on the earthen floor. He motioned toward them.

"You must eat," he said. "And I must watch."

"But you are tired."

"Better be tired than dead." He laughed shortly and went out, closing the door behind him.

He climbed to a point from which he could see almost to the highway. It was a safe place — if only he could keep his eyes open. But, as the sun came up and warmed him, this became more and more a struggle. It became finally impossible. Again and again he dozed off, and shook himself awake by a desperate effort.

Finally he knew there was but one thing to do. He must make her watch while he slept, at least for a few hours.

He went to the hut and shook her awake with some difficulty. But presently she pulled herself together.

"Listen," he said. "You must watch for a while. Come with me."

He led her to the point he had chosen, made her sit down behind a rock.

"If anything moves between here and the road, you must come and wake me at once," he said. "And when the sun is straight overhead, when there is no shadow of the rock, then you must wake me anyway. You understand?"

She nodded.

He stood looking at her a moment. "I put my life in your hands," he said.

"You saved mine," she replied. "I will not fail you."

He went down to the hut, stumbling a little in sheer weariness, flung himself down upon the floor, and was asleep almost instantly.

CHAPTER
SIXTEEN

Her voice seemed to come at first from a great distance.

"Juan, Juan!" she was crying. "Get up, you lazy *peón*! The soldiers are here! We are going home!"

When he looked up, she was standing over him, nudging him with her foot. It was half a minute before he fully recovered his senses. Then he saw men standing in the door — helmeted men with carbines in their hands. He scrambled to his feet and walked out into the glare of the sunlight, blinking, shaking his head. Adelita followed him.

There were three of the men — an officer and two privates of the dragoons.

The officer seized him by the shoulder.

"Who are you?" he demanded. "How do you come to be here, under arms and with this woman?"

Adelita gave him no chance to reply. She stood, still and haughty, the image of high-born self-assurance. "I have told you who he is!" she said sharply. "He is my slave. My husband bought him for three hundred *pesos* many years ago in Taos. Now he is worth a thousand. You have no more right to him than you have to my horse. Shoot him if you want to. But you will have to pay what he is worth!"

The officer was polite, apologetic. He turned to her with a bow. "*Señora*," he said, "your identity requires no proof. I can see that you are a lady. But this man . . . *señora*, I do not like to question your word, but my orders are to shoot all men found under arms. This man is heavily armed, and he has all the look of a bandit."

She stamped her foot on the ground. Her face blazed indignation. "I have told you that I made him take me away from my home in Santa Fé when the rebels came. Do you think I would let him come unarmed? Certainly he is armed. I armed him. I am going back to Santa Fé with him now."

The young officer was plainly puzzled. "If I could go with you . . ." he said, "but I must keep on down the valley."

Adelita suddenly changed her tone; she smiled upon the young officer charmingly. "I am not asking you to go with me, *Señor Capitán*," she said. "Your company would be a great privilege, but you have more important things to do. I only ask you to trust me. I will take this man back to Santa Fé. And I hope you will not come merely to see that I have not lied."

The officer smiled. It would, after all, be a serious mistake to shoot a valuable piece of property. "*Señora*," he said, "I ask only that you show me some proof which I can repeat to my superiors. Is there, perhaps, some mark upon the man that you know?"

She thought a moment.

305

"Certainly," she said. "I once had him beaten, and he bears the stripes."

She turned to Juan.

"Kneel down!" she ordered.

Juan knelt.

"Pull up his shirt and look!" she commanded.

One of the men pulled Juan's shirt up over his head, showing the long welted scars that striped his back from neck to waist.

"Is that not the mark of a slave?" she asked.

The officer hesitated a moment. Doubt was written all over his face, as well it might be. He knew only that he had found a heavily armed refugee hiding with a young woman who wore the clothing and jewelry of a *rica*. It was a hard enough situation to understand on any terms. But he could not turn back with them now, and he could not bring himself to shoot the man before the woman's eyes. In spite of himself, he longed to please her. He laughed, a little ruefully. He bowed to Adelita.

"*Señora*," he said, "I will hope to see you in Santa Fé. On your way there, ride carefully. Not all soldiers are as easily moved by beauty as I am."

He bowed again. Then he shouted an order to his men, and they all mounted and clattered down the trail in a gallop.

Neither Juan nor Adelita moved until the soldiers were out of sight. Then they turned to each other in a natural impulse. All the haughty self-assurance and all the bravado were gone from her face now. She held out her hands to him in the sudden weakness of reaction. She would almost have fallen if he had not caught her.

"If they had shot you, I would never have looked at my own face again," she said. "They came so suddenly, there was no time to warn you . . ."

Juan said nothing. Danger past was danger forgotten to him. He was wholly absorbed now in the mountains, the overwhelming fact that she had come to his arms of her own wish, that for a moment at least he possessed her.

At last with an effort he held her away from him, looking gravely into her eyes. "I owe you everything," he said. "But for you, I would never have run away. You have made me what I am. What can I do for you? Where do you want to go?"

"Can you still ask?" she demanded. "I want to go with you . . . wherever you go. I will be your woman. I will help you build your home. I want to be useful for something! I want to work with my hands!"

For a long moment Juan stared at her, incredulous, struggling with confusion. He had thought of her so long as a being of another kind, from another world — that she belonged to him was a fact he could hardly grasp.

"But I have been a bandit," he began. "I am a hunted man. And you . . ."

"I am a woman," she said. "And to a woman, when she loves, a man is nothing but a man. My mother married a bandit. The blood of a bandit is in me, and the love of a bandit, too."

Juan drew her to him again. His surprise was gone. This, after all, was the vision come true.

"I saw it long ago," he said. "But I never dared believe it until now."